Wild
BEAUTY

A SOUL SISTER NOVEL

#1 *NEW YORK TIMES* BESTSELLING AUTHOR
AUDREY
CARLAN

Cover Design: Jena Brignola

Copy Editor: Jeanne De Vita

ISBN: 978-1-943340-18-7

To all the women out there who never felt beautiful…
You are perfectly beautiful exactly as you are.
Scars and all.

Wild
CHILD

A SOUL SISTER NOVEL

Chapter
ONE

"CHIN UP, TITS OUT, BACK STRAIGHT, HEAD HELD high. I've got this." I coached myself and inhaled a hard and fast breath while staring at my image in the entryway mirror of my childhood home.

Kerrighan House.

A home for orphaned girls. Well, it used to be. Now it's just home. The place each of us "sisters" visited on a regular basis just like any normal siblings would to see their parents. In our case, it was *parent*, singular. But the love Mama Kerri gave to each and every one of her girls was a thousand times that of any family I'd ever seen or stayed with before arriving here almost two decades ago. I was eight then, a frightened and scared little girl. At twenty-six now, I was back in my old bedroom and once again frightened and scared out of my mind.

"He's dead," I told my image while staring in the mirror. "He can't get you." I watched my reflection and forced myself to unlock my jaw, soften my appearance, and gaze into the mirror as though it were a camera. This was the same way I prepared for my photo shoots. As a model, I had to be a master at masking my feelings. And I used to be the best at it. But now, when I look in the mirror, I not only see the mass of scars running up and down the insides of my forearms, but also the fear I have yet to shake even after three months.

Parents I didn't know and would never meet blessed me with medium brown hair with incredible natural auburn highlights that I grew to the middle of my back. Emerald green eyes with a hint of a blue sheen stared back at me. Plump lips on a heart-shaped face that women and men around the world adored. I ran my hands over my large breasts and down the sides of my waist to hips that were once very rounded. The hourglass shape I normally rocked was looking a little thin. I'd lost weight after the ordeal, but then I put some back on. My clientele preferred me to model their clothing, bathing suits, and especially lingerie when my body was between a size fourteen and sixteen. After three months of physical healing and mental hell, my size fourteens were a little loose. But I knew my body looked smokin' hot, soft, and sensual at that size and larger. That didn't mean I hated on women who were smaller than me. Every single one of my seven foster sisters weighed less than me, and all of them looked amazing in their own skin. Which is how I used to feel, until a portion of my skin was blistered and burned beyond recognition.

"Addy! Baby girl, you ready or what?" my foster sister and best friend Blessing asked while clomping down the stairs in her sky-high stilettos.

I glanced at my sad self in the mirror one last time hoping I could fulfill this new contract. It was going to set me up for a huge payday, not that I needed it. Still, I liked knowing I had a ridiculous amount of money saved in the event that me or one of my sisters needed to be bailed out. I'd lived my adolescent years prior to Kerrighan House uncertain where my next meal would come from, worrying whether or not I'd have to fight other hungry kids in one of the many foster homes I stayed. Until the day I walked into the open, loving arms of Mama Kerri and my new sisters. Once I was settled at Kerrighan House, I promised myself I'd become something amazing one day. Make enough money to take care of myself and everyone I loved. Which meant basically Mama Kerri, the world's greatest foster mother of all time, and my seven foster sisters: Blessing, Sonia, Simone, Liliana, Genesis, Charlie, and the recently deceased Tabitha.

Tabby.

My eyes started to tear, and my heart pounded a loud bass drum beat against my chest as flashes of Tabby teasing me, of taking my picture, of her laughing sprinted across my mind.

"Girl, I said are you ready to hit it or what? These are huge clients of mine and now yours. They'd understand if it were too soon, but Boo, they'd have to hire another model. Now you know I prefer when *you* rock my clothing and lingerie, but this client has the power to get my designs into the regular box stores. We're talking Macy's, Nordstrom, Dillard's and more. Right now, everything I sell is boutique and upscale, but I want to rake in the real cash. You know what I'm talkin' about."

I closed my eyes and swallowed as I nodded. "I do, Blessing. I understand and I'm ready. I swear I am. It's just scary this first time out."

Blessing wrapped a long arm around my shoulders and stared at the two of us in the mirror. Blessing was an inch shorter than me, but in heels, she towered over my five-foot, eleven-inch form. Her corkscrew ebony curls were bouncing all around her head in a perfectly stylized 'fro. Her black skin shone like silky smooth river rocks and felt just as soft. She smelled of her customary coconut oil mixed liberally with a light, breezy perfume that reminded me of Spring on the stony shores of Cannes, France. A place we'd visited many times together on different photoshoots.

"I'll be right there. Every second, every minute. You'll never be alone, okay?" Her reflection spoke and her on-yx-colored eyes seared straight into mine with a seriousness that couldn't be denied. My girl was in "Big Sister Mode" and had been since Simone and I had survived a madman. Blessing on a good day was protective of the family she chose in all of us and Mama Kerri. After our lives were threatened and we lost Tabby, that protection gene of hers became extreme. Knock down, drag out, she'd cut a bitch if they so much as looked at one of us cross. Unfortunately, this did not help the situation with the paparazzi.

Once word got around that Senator Sonia Wright's bio-logical sister Simone was involved in the Backseat Strangler case, and that two of her foster sisters were also involved, the press went insane. I had been kidnapped, but Tabitha ended up dying. When my identity was released—Addison Michaels-Kerrighan, international plus-sized model—and the world found out I was famous in my own corner of the market, things got intense. The paparazzi followed all of us incessantly. They camped outside Kerrighan House wait-ing for one of us to exit and go about our daily routines. By now, Blessing and I were the only ones still staying with Mama Kerri. The rest of our sisters had gone back to their homes and schedules, only coming back here to meet up for family dinner each week as usual.

I clenched my teeth and grabbed my giant sunglasses from the table underneath the mirror where I'd left my purse and plopped them on my nose. Blessing grabbed hers, a fashionable circular pair with gold trim that went perfectly with her stunning blue jumper and gold belt cinched around her tiny waist. Her booty, however, was high, rounded, and so hard you could bounce a quarter off it. Blessing worked out almost as much as Sonia did, but mostly to offset her insatiable appetite. Probably one of the things that we bonded over when I arrived and was put in the same room as her all those years ago.

"Lunch after?" I put my purse over my shoulder and my other hand on the doorknob.

Her lips pursed together in a small grin. "For sho,' Boo. Now let's give the vultures a good shot, eh? Good to show 'em we're all just fine. Maybe they'll move their smarmy asses back to whatever hole they crawled out of and leave us all alone."

"One could only hope." I chuckled and opened the door.

Instantly we were hit with what felt like a thousand camera flashes and a roaring blast of questions.

"Ms. Michaels, how does it feel to survive the Backseat Stranger?"

"What does the Senator have to say about all of this?"

"Is there anything you can tell us about Wayne Gilbert Black?"

Blessing gripped my elbow tight and led me to the black Escalade and driver she'd hired to shuttle us to and from the job.

"What did he do to you?"

"Are you going back to work after such a trying experience?"

"Were you tortured?"

I was tugged from behind by an unknown hand and I cried out in sheer terror. Stars blinked in my peripheral vision as a cold sweat hit my temples and at my nape.

Blessing spun around and shoved the reporter back so hard he tripped on his cameraman and fell backward into a fellow paparazzi member who caught him. "Don't you lay a finger on my sister!" She hollered at the top of her lungs. "All of you should be ashamed of yourselves. Following me and my family around. One of the members of our family died! Many women and a couple men lost their lives to that bastard. Leave us alone. Let us have some peace! We have enough to deal with." She looped her arm around my shoulders and the driver pushed his way through the growing crowd and helped usher us into the car.

"Shit. Next time I'm hiring bodyguards," she huffed and fluffed her 'fro. "You okay?"

I trembled for a moment but got my bearings the farther away we made it down the road and away from the crowd and their intrusive line of questioning. "Yeah, I'll be all right."

Blessing took my hand and interlaced our fingers, then set both of them on her thigh. "I'm going to take care of you, Addy. No one is gonna hurt my sister on my watch. That you can bank on."

I smiled and chuckled, then squeezed her fingers. "My Big Badass Sister has my back."

"That's right. And I always will."

I leaned against her side and laid my head on her shoulder. "What would I do without you?"

"The good news is, we aren't ever gonna find out,"

Blessing touted as though it were fact. And to her, it was. Though I knew better.

Evil always found a way to taint the good in the world. That evil had already claimed the life of our foster sister Tabby. Anything could happen to any one of us and there was nothing we could do about it.

◡

Click. The camera flashed and I was back *there*.

In that chair.

That dark, freezing cold basement, with rats and other vermin scurrying around my feet.

My chest was tied with thick, uncompromising ropes. My arms zip-tied, forearms facing up so he could continue with his torture against the inner flesh of my arms.

I glanced down at the blistered, ravaged tissue of my inner arms with a detached, vacant assessment. Seeing the torn, bleeding, black wounds on my arms in the only way I could—as if they weren't mine. The scent of burnt flesh seared my nostrils. I desperately held back my need to vomit as my mouth watered around the cloth gag. It was tied so tight it dug into the edges of my mouth, abrading the sensitive tissue every time I attempted to free myself.

Another camera flash.

"Addison..." A somewhat familiar voice reverberated in the cavernous space around me. I blinked rapidly as my mind swirled while I tried to focus on that tone. It was kind. Compassionate. Connected to someone I loved.

Blessing.

Click.

I shuddered at the sound and shook where I stood, skyrocketing back into that dreaded chair.

The masked attacker was coming back.

He would continue hurting me.

He was going to kill me just like all those other women.

My only hope was they'd find him before they got to my sister Simone. If she were spared, my soul would be free. I could die knowing she was safe.

I had no idea when I got off that plane and met the driver in front of the airport holding a sign with my name on it that I was willingly walking straight into my own personal Hell. He looked the part. Wore all black. Had a Town Car. Knew my name, when I was to arrive. Everything.

Smart girls knew better.

And I was a smart girl. Mama Kerri made sure all of her foster daughters got the appropriate education and graduated high school with good grades. I had a dream and worked toward making that dream a reality. She told us there was no mountain too high when it came to our lives and career goals. I believed her. Took everything she said as gospel and worked my ass off...literally.

I was one of the most coveted plus-size models in the industry. I had millions in the bank. But there was no amount of money in the world that could save me from the Backseat Strangler.

"Addison, honey, you're scaring me!" Blessing's voice broke me out of a cold sweat and catapulted me back to the present. I shook like a leaf where I stood under the unnaturally hot lights of the backdrop for the photoshoot.

"Where am I?" I trembled in her arms.

Blessing put her hands to the sides of my neck. They were cool and steady. I shivered in her arms. She placed her face directly in front of mine, her dark eyes fixated on me.

I looked into those familiar, loving eyes like they were my talisman. The only connection I had to my safe place.

"Addy, you are in the middle of a photoshoot," she said calmly.

I shook my head. "He's here..." I choked out on a guttural whisper.

She shook her head, her black curls bouncing along with her. "Boo, he's not. He's dead. You're in the middle of a shoot in downtown Chicago. Behind me are your clients and the photographer."

I looked over her shoulder at the myriad of bodies standing around and staring at us. I clenched my jaw realizing I'd had another *moment*. That's what we were calling them. "Moments." Which was essentially a really kind way of describing my mini-freak-outs. I lost all time, space, or any sense of where I actually was and found myself stuck back in that basement with a serial killer. The place where both Simone and I watched our sister Tabitha sacrifice herself in order to save us.

Tears filled my eyes and started to fall.

"Okay, that's a wrap. Bring me her robe." Blessing snapped her fingers at the young fashion design student that she had mentoring under her.

The girl brought my robe and Blessing helped me put it on over the delicate pink bra and panty set I wore.

I wrapped my frozen form and allowed the soft chenille fabric to remind me there were soft and beautiful things I could count on to bring me back to the here and now. Something sizzled in the air, an electricity I could feel that forced me to look up.

Click.

The photographer on the job took a random, candid shot. He was positioned at the lens, his face hidden behind his equipment. I hadn't been concerned with who was behind the camera, only that this was my first job back after *the incident*. Now I needed to see the individual or I might go back to when "he" was taking pictures and filming me.

All I was able to see was the man's long, sandy brownish-blond hair falling around his shoulders. He moved his face and his brown-eyed gaze met mine.

It was as if in that second he saw right through my eyes to the empty, broken, frightened woman beneath the perfect hair and makeup.

Click.

I twitched as gooseflesh rose on my skin, but as long as I looked into those earthy, tranquil brown eyes, I felt grounded. No longer floating aimlessly across an endless expanse of deep, pitch-black waters with no hope for shore. In his eyes, I found my footing. I curled my toes against the cool floor, cementing where I was in that moment.

This man, the photographer with his soulful eyes, trimmed beard, and mustache, held me centered to the here and now with a single look. No longer was I wading back into the dark memory of that night when my entire life changed.

I removed the robe, stared into his gaze, and handed the robe to Blessing. "I'm okay. I'm going to finish."

"You sure? You don't have to. The clients understand what you've gone through. They've agreed to Photoshop the scars marring your arms, but I know them well. They'll understand if you're not ready," she assured me.

I shook my head, my gaze set on the photographer.

I lifted my chin toward him. "I've never seen you before."

One side of his lips twitched up into a small yet sexy smile. "I'm new to fashion photography. And if you're okay to continue, I'd love to finish." His gaze darted to the lens. "We've gotten some great shots. Most of them after you took a breather. You're a wild beauty. The camera loves you."

I smiled. "That's what they all say when a half-naked woman is standing in front of them."

He chuckled and the rich baritone sound warmed my body from the inside out.

"I'm Addison Michaels-Kerrighan. And you are?"

"Killian Fitzpatrick."

Interesting name for an intriguing man.

"You ready to continue or do you want a break?" he asked, no hint of judgement in his tone.

I pursed my lips. "As long as you don't hide behind the camera," I stated shakily, then added a soft, "Please and thank you. Apparently, faceless men behind cameras are a new trigger for one of my *moments*." As soon as I'd shared that, I balked at my own stupidity. I had no idea why I'd given up something so personal to someone I didn't know, besides the fact that he had honest, kind eyes, great hair, and a sexy smile.

"I'm here for you, whatever you need."

Surprisingly, I laughed. "Again, that's what they all say," I teased, taking a deep, cleansing breath and letting out all the fear and ugliness that had crept up. I shook my arms and legs as though I were flinging off water, but mostly was just trying to toss aside the negative tragedy that plagued my every waking minute. "Just get a good shot."

"With you, Addison, I'm not sure there are any bad shots. Though I think with a little time and focus, we could find magic together." His voice had a warm, comforting tone, laced with a hint of innuendo.

My cheeks heated and I quirked my head and smirked.

Click.

He took another candid shot, glanced at the viewing screen on his camera, and smiled. "Incredible," he whispered.

For the next half hour, I focused on nothing but the man behind the lens. Flirting without really trying to flirt, but it was almost impossible not to with such a mysterious, hunky guy staring me down with his chocolatey gaze and perfect-looking, kissable lips.

Just as I bent over into a seductive blowing-a-kiss pose, there was a commotion by the entrance to the large open space. I glanced over to see a flurry of uniformed officers along with my sister Simone's boyfriend, Jonah Fontaine, flashing his FBI badge and storming over to where I was.

He pulled me into his arms and locked them around me so tight, his face going straight into my hair. "Jesus, I'm so glad you're okay," he breathed, fear and now relief coating his tone.

I patted his back and looked over my shoulder at Blessing. Ryan Russell, Jonah's partner in the FBI, was whispering to her. Her eyes widened to an unnaturally large size and she nodded.

"Excuse me. What's going on here?" Killian approached us while Jonah continued holding me.

He pulled back, put his hands to my shoulders, and then his gaze scanned my barely dressed body. "Shit, Addy.

I'm sorry." Jonah's voice was rough, deep and sounded embarrassed.

Blessing found that moment to dash over to us with my robe in hand. "Here." She thrust the item at me.

Killian took the robe. "Allow me." He opened it, and I put my arms through it quickly and tied it at the waist.

"Thanks," I murmured, but he hadn't moved away. In fact, he stepped closer and put his hands onto my shoulders from behind in a rather affectionate gesture that was so far from acceptable I would normally have shrugged him off and nailed him for touching me. Something inside me however appreciated the warmth imprinting from his palms into my shoulders, soothing me in an uncertain situation. Instead of addressing his handsy approach, I focused my attention on Jonah.

"Is Simone okay? Mama Kerri?" I hurriedly asked.

"What's going on? Why are the FBI and police at our photoshoot?" Killian interrupted, nothing but concern in his tone.

Jonah frowned and took in the possessive hold Killian had on my shoulders. "Who's this guy?"

That's when Killian moved around me and held out his hand. "Killian Fitzpatrick, but my friends call me 'Fitz.' I'm the photographer."

Once more Jonah narrowed his gaze, as though trying to assess the hunky photographer's motives. Regardless, he shook his head then circled the conversation back to me. "We need to put you into custody. Get the family back together. There's been, uh, a development in the Backseat Strangler case, and I'm sorry to say, honey, it's not good."

I gasped and stepped back. My entire body went on

autopilot, shaking uncontrollably. Killian watched me like a hawk with that assessing photographer's eye and likely knew the very instant fear had taken over my ability to speak, or even function. I started to shake and my limbs turned to Jell-O. I was about to fall to my knees when Killian wrapped his arm around me and brought his face close to my own.

"You're safe. Whatever happened, right now, you're safe. Just breathe, yeah?" He stared into my eyes and I focused on watching the color in his pretty brown eyes darken while he audibly breathed. Naturally I aligned my breathing to match his until the woozy, loose-limbed feeling dissipated and the shakes stopped altogether. "Better?" he asked.

I nodded as Blessing came over to us, her gaze astute as she pulled me into her arms. "You okay, baby girl?"

I glanced at Killian, wishing I was still in his hold but still feeling safe surrounded by my sister. "What do you mean there's been a development?" I asked Jonah.

"A woman was murdered. Not only did she resemble you, but she also had one of your magazine pictures crumpled up and clenched in her hand. There were burns up and down her inner forearms much like yours and she'd been strangled."

"What? No!" Tears filled my eyes. "What does this mean? He's dead. I watched him die with my own eyes by Tabby's hand. He bled out in that basement. He can't be alive!" I choked out through my tears.

Jonah reached out and ran a comforting hand down my bicep. "I know, Addy, but until we know more, we can't take any risks. That's why I was so relieved when we found you. Both of you had your phones off. I had to call your agency to find out where you were. Simone is beside herself, honey.

We need to take you home. Talk all this through and make a plan."

I closed my eyes remembering the last time we were all brought together at Kerrighan House. We were told about Simone narrowly escaping the Backseat Strangler and how a body had been found dead in her apartment. Things got so much worse after that.

I nodded numbly. "I need to change. Blessing, can you, uh, talk to the clients. This is only the first of twelve shoots we were supposed to do for your new lingerie line. I'm so sorry."

Blessing took a breath and shook her head. "Don't you worry. I'll handle them," she said and then left to do just that.

"I can be available anytime, anywhere. I'm freelance, and I even have my own setup at home," Killian offered as Jonah turned around and spoke to Ryan. Killian continued, "If you have the product, we can shoot anywhere depending on if you're up to it."

The weight on my shoulders felt too heavy to bear. I had no idea what I was about to be facing or what to do.

He pulled out a card. "My cell phone number is on the back. Call me. We can discuss making new plans... Or you can just call me to talk."

I reached for the card, but he held on to it. "Talk?" I asked.

His lips lifted into a small smile. "Talk, text. Get to know one another by phone, until I can ask you out properly."

"Wh-what? Ask me out? Like on a date?" I asked as though the request was so beyond foreign it was spoken in a different language.

My response had him grinning. "Yeah, Addison, a date. When you're up to it and things cool down. For now though, sometimes it helps to talk out an intense situation with someone who's not involved. Sounds like you've been through a lot and are about to go through more. I know how that feels. Drowning in the thoughts you're too afraid to share with your loved ones."

I nodded, feeling every word of what he said. Putting my fears and anxieties on my sisters and Mama Kerri had to stop. They'd been through enough.

"Call me," he reiterated.

"Um…"

"Addison?"

I licked my lips and blinked, not sure what to say or do. So many things were coming at me all at once.

"Just reach out. We can talk about everything or nothing, but I'd like to hear from you. I'll worry if you don't."

"You'll worry about having my foot shoved so far up your ass you won't be able to eat. Ever." Jonah growled, catching our conversation and clearly not liking what he was hearing. He tugged me to his side and away from Killian. "Come on, Addy. Let's get you home."

"Okay. And Killian, I'll call." I fingered his business card.

"I'll be waiting. Be safe."

I barely had it in me to smile sadly.

Safety was an illusion. I didn't think I'd ever feel safe again.

Chapter
TWO

IGHT BELOVED WOMEN WERE ALL STARING AT ME, EQUAL expressions of worry plastered across their loving faces. Simone was glued to my side, meaning her thigh and my thigh were touching from hip to knee. She held one of my hands in both of hers. Mama Kerri was on my other side, holding my other hand. Sonia per usual was pacing, her type-A personality and supreme intellect trying to put two and two together while Jonah and Ryan stood across the room. Liliana, Charlie, and Genesis sat quietly on the opposite side of the huge U-shaped couch. Blessing sat dead center, legs crossed, a sexy stiletto-covered foot kicking the air in barely controlled fury as she leaned back against the couch, arms crossed over her chest.

"You told us that the Backseat Strangler was gone. History. Dead to rights. Now you're telling us there's a potential copycat or worse, a second killer?" Sonia stopped mid-pace, spun around, and glared at Jonah and Ryan.

Ryan held his hands up in a placating gesture. "Senator Wright, I understand this an upsetting development, but the FBI is on top of this. Jonah and I and the entire team are hunting down every possible lead in order to figure out if this is connected or not."

"Just to be clear, you don't know for sure whether it's a copycat or a second killer?"

Jonah sighed. "Sonia, it's not as simple as that. It looks like it could be either."

"Are you even sure it's connected? Maybe this is a sicko that is obsessed with Addy's image in a magazine. She's gorgeous. Lots of men want her." She gestured at me and huffed. "Look at her. Right now, she's freaked out, scared out of her mind with puffy eyes from crying, and she still looks like she could do a shoot for Victoria's Secret and sell a warehouse full of product in the process."

"Love you too, SoSo," I said, my own way of thanking her for the compliment. Especially since the woman was an elegant beauty herself. All poise and purpose with that white blonde hair and red lipstick.

"No one here is taking any ideas off the table, Senator," Ryan pushed thoughtfully and rather respectfully, which would go a long way with Sonia. "We're just trying to make sure we cover all the bases. But the biggest worry is that this particular victim was burned with cigarettes on her inner arms prior to being strangled. That detail was never made public. The press was informed that Addison had been kidnapped and hurt in the process but nothing more. Also, the victim is white, late twenties, brown hair, green eyes, a fuller figure, and had one of Addison's images placed in her hand and left for us to find."

"*Dios mio.*" Liliana gasped and made the sign of the cross, then closed her eyes. Her short, curly brown hair was down hanging around her face, just touching her shoulders while her lips moved in what I knew to be a silent prayer for the lost soul. Liliana, my Latina sister, had a strong sense of faith in the Almighty. The most religious woman in our family, she went to church every Sunday and sometimes

Bible study on Wednesdays as well, whereas I considered myself more of a spiritual person like the rest of us.

"Why Addy?" Blessing asked.

Ryan's gaze moved to Blessing and softened. "One theory is that she got away. And that made the killer angry. Another is that there was a killing duo. One being the dominant and the other the submissive. The dominant died and so now the other is seeking revenge. Or perhaps he feels the job isn't quite done. Which also means Simone isn't safe either. Frankly, none of you are. Then of course there is the matter of a copycat. However, like I said, the public didn't know about the burns to Addison's arms, leading us to believe whoever murdered this woman knew that intimate detail, which makes it more plausible that there was more than one person committing the initial crimes."

Jonah pushed off the wall and came over to me where he kneeled down bringing him to eye level. He put a hand to my knee. "Okay, sweetheart, this is the hard part and a portion of why we brought you all together."

I frowned and swallowed against my suddenly dry throat. "How so?" I croaked.

"You were with the killer for almost an entire day. Did you ever see two men at the same time?"

I shook my head. "No, I..." I thought back to being there. In that dark basement of that rat-infested, disgusting building. I couldn't help the flinch that stole across my face.

Mama Kerri wrapped her arm around my back and turned my chin toward hers lightly. "Don't go all the way back there, baby. See yourself as though you are outside of your body. Think about the room. What did it look like?"

she asked softly, her blue-green gaze kind and familiar, her hold warm and comforting.

"Um..." I licked my lips and tried to imagine looking at myself from an outsider's perspective. "It was dark. Gray. Cold. Every so often I'd feel a rat rush past my feet and legs where they were tied to the chair."

Charlie made a whimpering sound as her eyes filled with tears. Liliana took her hand and held it.

Mama's eyes filled with tears too, but she didn't let them fall. Her strength like a magic balm over my wounded soul. "What else do you remember?" she asked through a thick voice.

"Water or pipes leaking."

"I remember that too. I hear it all the time in my dreams." Simone squeezed my hand. "There were big pipes and giant water tanks and a concrete floor."

"What did you smell, chicklet?" Mama asked.

I frowned and thought back. Instantly the memory of the scent seared through my nostrils and I coughed. She rubbed my back as I took deep breaths reminding myself I was here in my safe place, with people who loved me.

"Like mold or a damp, dank, closed-off space. There was no fresh air at all," I answered.

"Okay, that's good. Now think about the man."

I shook my head adamantly. "I don't want to," I whispered as panic rose through my system, and more tears filled my eyes and fell down my cheeks.

Jonah's dark gaze was tortured as he assessed me. "Ry, I don't think we should continue..."

These men were counting on me. The safety of my family was in my hands. Any detail might help them. "No, no,

I'm okay. I have to face this and if it could help catch whoever hurt this woman and will keep my family safe, I'll do whatever it takes."

"You sure?" Jonah rubbed my knee back and forth.

"Yeah, but I don't know if there's anything that can help you. The man that tortured me was definitely Wayne Gilbert Black. I'd know his hands anywhere. I watched repeatedly as he pressed the cigarette into my flesh over and over again. There was no second man. Not that I saw. But maybe there were cameras? He did film me with his phone."

Jonah nodded. "Yeah, we've watched the footage. You were so brave." He tightened his hold on my knee. "We're gonna get this guy and I'm sorry to say all of you are going to have to hunker down again. We just can't take any risks."

"The press is going to have a field day with this." Sonia groaned and pulled out her cell phone. "Quinn? Yeah, we need to talk. I'm thinking we're going to need that apartment we used three months ago. There's another madman on the loose," she said and walked out of the room and toward the kitchen.

I slumped against Mama Kerri. "Why me?"

She shook her head and rubbed my back. "I don't know, baby, but we'll figure it out. Jonah and Ryan are excellent investigators. They will leave no stone unturned. Right, gentlemen?"

"Absolutely." Jonah reached out a hand to Simone who took it and stood up. "We think it's best if you all bunk up again until we know more."

"Can we stay here?" I asked.

"I have an excellent alarm and have never had any problems. And you and Simone live just down the way. I imagine you could be here in a minute or two with a simple phone call, right? Plus, there's always the press, avidly watching the house." Mama's voice was wise and controlled.

Ryan reached a hand to the back of his neck. "I don't know. We could ensure patrol does drive-bys of the house every couple hours to ensure a police presence in the neighborhood. I think most of you will be okay here. Sonia has her own team guarding her and the building added twice as much security after the last guard was taken down. It would be better if you could stay somewhere more secure, but the most important people to watch right now are Addison and Simone since they were directly connected to the Backseat Stranger."

Genesis stood up and slapped her hands down the sides of her legs. "Well, I'm going to get Rory from Aunt Delores at the flower shop, go back to my house, and once again pack up a weeks' worth of clothing."

"I'd prefer you not go alone," Jonah stated. "If you guys need to leave for any reason, like work and such, it would be best if you do so in pairs and check in with one another regularly."

"I'll go with Gen, pack up some clothing," Liliana said.

"Charlie and I can do the same as our places are close to one another and I've been here with Addy the past three months anyway," Blessing announced. "No skin off my nose to stay longer. I'll call the client and inform them that the shoot is off until further notice."

That bit of news caught my attention, and I shook my head. "No way. I'm not quitting the job. It's my first one back. And if I let these bastards control my life for another three months, I'll never come back. As it is, I'm twenty-six going on twenty-seven. I don't have many more years in my prime, and this is your big chance to get your plus-size lingerie into the major stores. I'm not going to hide under a rock any longer. I need to live my life."

Simone nodded as she crossed her arms over her chest and rubbed her biceps. "I get it. I understand exactly where you're coming from. If we quit, the bad guy wins. We just need to be safe about it."

"Baby, I don't know if she should put herself out there…" Jonah warned.

I stood up and put my thumbs in the back pockets of my jeans. My finger encountered the card I'd slipped inside earlier. I pulled it out and read the inscription.

Killian Fitzpatrick, Photographer and Photojournalist.

I held out the card. "That photographer from today said he wanted to complete the job. He also stated he was freelance and not only could go where I needed, but he has a studio of his own. Maybe we can work out a deal to take the photos we need privately?"

Blessing snapped her fingers and pointed at me. "That's not a bad idea. And you felt comfortable with him."

More than comfortable, actually, which was a strange surprise. Not to mention the little bit about him wanting to date me. My cheeks heated and Blessing's lips twitched.

"You like him," she accused.

I frowned and shrugged. "He was nice."

"Nice," she snorted.

"Yeah."

"And hot in that white, artsy, probably wears a man bun with all that long-ass hair type of way." She grinned a radiant, bright-white smile.

"Blessing... Mouth, darling," Mama warned. She did not like her girls to curse. Thought it was common and unladylike.

"Sorry, Mama." Blessing apologized immediately and then turned back to me. Her dark eyes assessing and filled with mischief. "Okay, okay. Let me work my magic with the client. Explain that we have an unexpected snag, and will need to take the shoot offsite, but that we'll get them all the pictures they need of each item to make my designs practically walk themselves out of the store on their own."

I smiled wide, the first real one I'd had in months. It felt a little achy and awkward but still good. Like putting on an old, comfy pair of shoes that might not always be in fashion but were still well-loved and fit perfectly.

"Do you want me to call the photographer or should I expect you to?" she asked with a smirk on her pretty face and full, glossy lips.

"I will." I jumped on the request like I would have jumped on an offer of a plate full of street tacos. Because *tacos*. There was always room for a taco. I'd never be convinced otherwise. Besides, Killian asked me to call him. Practically begged. Well, begged might be pushing it, but he did say he'd be worried if he didn't hear from me, and now I had an excellent reason to contact him.

I fingered the card and put it back in my pocket. Then Mama went off into the kitchen to cook which was something she always did when she was worried. One by one each of my sisters except Simone hugged me and gave me words of encouragement before taking their leave. I in turn apologized for the trouble which they all took in stride. You could knock over a Kerrighan sister, but you couldn't ever keep her down.

Man, my family was the *best*.

"Addy, baby, I've got fresh baked cookies and tea brewing," Mama called from the kitchen. Sweets and tea, her answer to every ailment.

Simone chuckled then turned to Jonah. "I'm going to hang out with Addy and Mama Kerri. Do you think your dad and Luca will mind if I don't make it back to work for the rest of the day?"

He dipped his head and took her mouth in a sweet and fast kiss. "Not at all. I'll call them on the way back to the office. Stay here. Don't leave for any reason. I'm gonna get Amber and bring her by before I head back out."

"Honey, we don't need our dog here." Simone tipped her head to the side.

He threaded his hand at the back of her nape. "Simone, that dog would fight to the death to protect her mama. I want that added layer of protection for my girl and her family, yeah? Just let me have that. It will make me feel better when I'm out chasing down a monster."

She rolled her eyes but then smiled and pecked him on the lips. "Okay, babe. You can have that."

"Love you," he whispered and kissed her once more. I looked away and stared out the window, because every time they were close I felt like I was intruding on a private moment even if it was innocent. One day I hoped to have that for myself. A man who adored and worried about me. For now, I was thrilled that at least one of my sisters had it.

"Bye, Addy," Jonah called out.

"Bye and thank you!" I said, waving.

Jonah smiled at me and then glanced at Simone and winked.

Both of us sighed simultaneously, then looked at one another with big smiles and burst out laughing. Simone put her arm around my waist. "Come on. Mama's got cookies, and I missed lunch."

"Me too."

"My girls haven't eaten lunch?" Mama hollered. "I'll make you some sandwiches first! Fuel before sweets," she amended as we entered the kitchen and sat at the picnic-style table we'd grown up with.

"Now, tell me about this photographer?" Simone wiggled her eyebrows and grinned.

"Go for Fitz," the warm honied voice answered when I called.

"Hello, Mr. Fitzpatrick?" I asked just to clarify.

"Yeah, you've got him."

"Hi, um, this is Addison Michaels-Kerrighan…you were the photographer on my shoot this morning."

"Addison, hey, I'm glad you called. Everything go okay with you being absconded by the FBI?" His tone held humor, so I knew he was joking.

"I wasn't absconded by the FBI. My somewhat brother-in-law got a little over-protective about a situation that I'm once again involved in."

"That suit was your brother-in-law?"

"Technically, not officially, but it looks like it's going that route. He and my sister Simone shacked up a couple months ago and she's now the office manager at his father and brother's construction company."

"Tight family unit," he surmised.

"On both sides, yes."

"And the murdered woman? How are you involved?" he asked conversationally.

I sucked in a deep breath and let it out.

"You don't have to tell me if you don't want to," he stated softly.

I closed my eyes. "It's not that it's too personal it's just...scary. A situation I find myself in that I never thought I would. And I'm barely healed from the last frightening experience."

"I gotta admit, I looked you up on the Internet after our session this morning. You were kidnapped by the Backseat Strangler."

"Yeah. My sister Simone was in the wrong place at the wrong time. The guy crawled in the back of her car. The FBI pulled her over, which is how she met her boyfriend Jonah—the suit, as you said. The killer shot them both but thankfully none of them were wounded beyond repair. Then he went on a bit of a spree."

"Were you close with the other victims?"

Tabby's lifeless gaze staring up at nothing in that hell-hole flashed across my mind. "Look, it's really kind of you to want to talk about it, but I don't really want to get into it further. And it's not the reason I called."

"Okay. I can appreciate that. Though I hope you're talking to someone about it all. Saying things out loud takes away some of the power they have to hurt you emotionally and mentally. And I know a survivor when I see one. I've been in your shoes, so to speak."

"What happened to you?" I asked instantly.

He chuckled. "Now that conversation is for another time. Maybe over a bottle of wine and a nice meal."

"Are you always this forward?" I fired off without thinking.

"When I'm talking to a beautiful woman I'd like to know more about, yeah, I am. Though it's been quite a while since I've met anyone that flips my switch."

"Smooth, real smooth." I laughed. "You photograph models and you're smokin' hot. I'm sure a lot of pretty faces flip that switch," I teased.

"You'd be surprised. And I told you that photographing models was a newer venture."

"What did you used to do before fashion photography?"

"I was a war photojournalist," he said rather tightly.

"Oh, wow. I didn't expect that."

"Not many people do. It's a specific type of position and the good ones have special training. First, I served in the Army. Brought my camera. Took photos and shared what we saw and a lot of what we did. It blew up from there. After my four years of service as a soldier, I did ten years as a photojournalist."

"And now?"

"Now I take pictures of things that are beautiful. Things that bring me joy, not pain."

"I see. Noble work. All of it."

"Thank you. You said you called for a specific reason?"

"Oh yeah. You stated earlier that you'd be happy to continue the photoshoot on a freelance basis and that you had a studio?"

"I do, yes. And I'd definitely be interested in photographing you again. The camera loves you."

I bit into my bottom lip as butterflies took flight in my stomach. "Well, in an effort to give you full disclosure, we'd need to do the full shoot, whatever is intended, outside of the normal process."

"You mean because of the homicide that your brother-in-law mentioned?"

"Honestly, I don't really know. All I know right now is that the Backseat Strangler may or may not be a duo or a copycat killer and that person is on the loose. He killed a woman that looks very much like me and had a picture of me torn from a magazine in her hand when the cops found her."

"Jesus, Addison. I'm sorry. You must be out of your mind with fear."

"I'm not exactly jumping up and down and doing the limbo that's for sure." I chuckled dryly but it felt off and disingenuous.

"Anything you need, I'm happy to help."

"Well, that's part of it. We'd have to keep the project incredibly hush-hush with very few people around to aid us, if any at all. I simply can't put anyone's safety at risk. As it is, if you take on this project, you need to understand that you too will be under a microscope, and also may be in danger."

"First of all, I'm a trained soldier and survived fourteen years of active wartime situations. Four in the Army, the other ten capturing it. I've spent more of my life in danger than out of it. I also have a very secure home, alarm system included, and a mean as hell Rottweiler. Taking the pictures old school is my preference. If we're allowed carte blanch with the photography, I can promise you they'll be unlike anything you've taken before."

"I'm not sure what the initial vision and scope was for the project, but a lot of that is out the window and the client really wanted me in the product—which is great, because the designer does too. The entire line is lingerie with some robes, teddies, and the like. High scale, expensive. We have to make the pieces look incredible. They were designed by my sister Blessing who you met today, and she really needs this contract to take her business to the next level."

"Your sister? Blessing Jones, the fashion designer?"

"Yeah?"

"She's your sister?"

"Yes." I frowned. "Why?"

"Baby, she's black and you're white."

My heart melted when he called me "Baby." Then his words sunk in and I cracked up laughing and kept going until my belly hurt. It's not something I thought about, but it would probably be a little strange to an outsider.

"We're foster sisters."

"Now that makes a whole helluva lot more sense."

I giggled. "I bet it does."

"When do we start?"

"I'm ready when you are. Blessing is confirming the change with the clients and I have no doubt she'll be able to talk them into it. So, it's really up to when you're available to take me on."

"Oh, Addison, I can definitely take you on..." He laughed, and my cheeks heated, while the redness kept flowing down my neck and to the top of my chest where my nipples took notice and hardened beneath my clothes.

"Killian," I whispered his name, realizing it sounded rather husky, hinting at something more when more between us should not even be on the table right now. My life was an absolute mess, and no one deserved to get dragged into it. Especially a war veteran who made it clear he had his own demons to contend with.

"Just messing around. I promise I will be the pillar of professionalism...while on the job. Outside of work, all bets are off."

I groaned and he laughed once more.

"Let me know when you have the go-ahead. I'll make sure the studio is set up and we have what we need. I'll e-mail your sister to get information on the scope of the full project. She gave me her card before the two of you left today. The client didn't provide me anything when I arrived earlier other than you standing in front of the first backdrop, which I found rather uninspiring, to tell you the truth. I think we can do far better than what they had available and blow their minds."

"Thank you, Killian, for being willing to do this. I know the circumstances are unusual..."

"Fitz. Call me Fitz."

"Okay, call me Addy."

"Addy. I like it. Suits you," he murmured, and the sound of my name coming from that warm honeyed tone sent a shiver of excitement skating through my veins.

"I'll text you when I know more. Thank you, Fitz."

"You're welcome, Addy. See you soon."

"Yes, I believe you will."

Chapter
THREE

LIVING IN A HOUSE WITH NINE WOMEN GROWING UP HAD seemed nothing but normal. Now as adult women, even though there are only eight of us with Tabby gone, we have added Rory, Genesis's three-year-old daughter, Jonah, Simone's man, Amber, their dog, and Ryan, Jonah's partner who slept on the couch. Apparently, an enormous house filled to the brim with women didn't deter the one man in our lives from calling in reinforcements by having Ryan stay. The upstairs was abuzz with activity, and I was glad I was an early riser because I caught a shower first and had first pick of the fresh baked cookies Mama Kerri left on the counter wrapped in tinfoil.

Blessing dashed down the stairs and stopped at the bottom where I stood sipping my tea and shoving a second cookie into my mouth. The woman moved as though she was in sneakers when she clearly had on four-inch heels. I wasn't sure if I'd seen her in flats in the last few years. My sister from another mister was top to toe a fashionista. I couldn't fault her for that because not only did she look fantastic all the time, but she also gave all of us free clothes she designed, and it was her job to look good. So good, I could see FBI hot guy Ryan Russell's mouth drop open and his eyes heat while he scanned her form from where he was folding a blanket and setting it on the couch he'd just slept on.

"Hey." She nodded, putting a rather large gold hoop into her ear. I took a minute to appreciate all that was Blessing Jones-Kerrighan. She wore a see-through black shirt that gathered at the neck but was completely backless and sleeveless. Under it she had on a black bandeau top that covered her average sized tatas that left nothing to the imagination but absolutely highlighted her glorious dark skin. The sheer shirt was tucked into a pair of cream-colored, slinky dress slacks that curved magically over her tight booty and came down in a taper at her ankles. There she rocked a pair of stunning red heels that boasted a sexy ankle strap. Her nails were painted fire engine red, the same as her glorious pout. Her hair was up in a pineapple-type shape but artfully pinned that way, so her curls were on point.

"Daaaaaauuuuummmmm, girl. You got a hot date?" I teased when she turned around and grabbed her bag.

"Yeah, with you and your photographer. Then once we get you settled, I'm off to meet clients in the city."

"You're not planning to go alone, are you?" Ryan interrupted. He stood a few feet from us and placed his long arms up above his head as he took hold of the wood that framed the entryway from the living room to the kitchen area. The sleep shirt he wore stretched along his muscular frame proving he took care of his body much like his partner Jonah did. The simple loose black pajama pants he wore gifted us a hint of what the man might be packing down under and it did not look small. Yowza!

I watched with glee as Blessing's dark gaze took in all that was Ryan Russell from his golden, layered hair on top that was cropped short at the sides, his scruffy jaw, and down that long, somewhat lean but definitely muscular form all the way to his bare feet.

"Tall glass of milk," she murmured. "Too bad you're in law enforcement." She sighed as if genuinely disappointed in that factoid, while he frowned.

"Excuse me?" He tilted his head and ran his hand down his broad chest to his stomach where he rubbed his abdominals, then rested his hand at his hip.

The man was good-looking to be sure. No, he was *seriously* good-looking, but nowhere near as glorious as Killian Fitzpatrick. Not to mention his eyes were glued to my sister like she was eggs and bacon, and he was ready for his morning meal.

"Nothing." She let out a cute, flirty sigh as the doorbell rang. "There's our muscle now." She ran her gaze up and down Ryan's form once more. "Hmmm," she sighed again a little dreamily and rather teasingly if the way that Ryan's heated gaze was staring at her ass as she approached the door was any indication. This development definitely had my interest.

"Identification, please." She held out her hand.

The three giant bodybuilder-type men were at the door. They wore cargo pants and black matching polos with a stitched red insignia and black, lace-up combat boots. Each beefy man dug into his pocket, got out his wallet, and handed her his ID. She read them and backed up. "Wait here a minute, please." She smiled, then closed and locked the door, leaving the three strangers outside to be hounded by the paparazzi that were forever waiting for a glimpse of me, Simone, or Sonia.

Blessing turned around and brought the IDs over to Ryan. "Are these real?"

Ryan grabbed the three identification cards and evaluated them front and back. "They look legit, but I'd need a barcode scanner or my work computer to be certain. Did you hire security without running it through the FBI?"

She shrugged and snatched back the IDs. "Yeah. I count on *no man* to take care of me and my own." Blessing scanned the IDs. "Meh, if they look legit and have the same names the security company I hired last night gave me over the phone, I think we're safe. I mean it's not like the psycho killer knew we'd hire this particular company. And besides, if the company is outside of the FBI and hired straightaway like I did, how would anyone be able to infiltrate them?"

Ryan grunted. "That is not how this works, Blessing. Jonah's going to lose his mind. Our fucking chief is going to lose his mind. The fact that we're even involved would usually be a no-go, but since we're not technically *related* to Addison, we were able to stay on the case. You may have just compromised that."

"What's done is done," she murmured still looking at the IDs.

"Security?" I perked up.

"Yep, a bodyguard for you and one for me. Jonah has Simone, Sonia has a team, and Gen, Charlie, and Liliana will have the third man driving them around and making sure they get to and from work safely. That same man will turn around and pick them all up to take them back home after work. Mama Kerri will be here or with Aunt Delores at the flower shop. Anyhoo, are you ready? I've got your favorite hair and makeup guy meeting us at the photographer's address. When he gets you all beautified to your standards, we'll relieve him of his duty. Your bodyguard will stay the day with you, but I told him he'd likely be outside the door since you'd be working and I figured you wouldn't want some hulking dude watching you take pictures in lingerie. The other man will stay with me since I have meetings all over the city this week."

"Did you by chance think to mention it to me last night?" I moved further into the kitchen, rinsed out my cup of tea, and placed it in the sink. I wasn't exactly fond of others scheduling my life for me.

Blessing put a hand to her hip. "Sista, don't even use that tone with me. A dead girl who looks like you is being mourned by her family today. That will not be me." She pointed up the stairs. "That will not be our mama or our other sisters. We've grieved enough. You know how it is, Boo." She shook her head. "I take care of what's mine, and whether you like it or not…You. Are. My. Family. No sick motherfucker gettin' his filthy hands on my sister again. No way. Nut uh. Not happening." She fluffed her hair. "You hear me? You feel me? Do I need to explain further?"

I pressed my lips together. Classic Blessing. She was worried about our safety, so she did something about it. Even if it meant pissing me off in the process, she'd do what she felt she needed to do and ask forgiveness later. Since her heart was in the right place, and a bodyguard was a damn good idea, I let it go.

"You looooooooove me." I shimmied my shoulders and grinned playfully.

She groaned. "Girl…"

"You can't live without meeeeeee," I flaunted, and spun

in a circle dancing until I danced my way to her and bumped her hip with my own. "Admit it, and I won't complain that you did all of this without my knowledge." I rubbed my temple to her shoulder.

Blessing sighed heavily, pursed her lips, then rolled her eyes. "Fine. I love you."

"And you can't live without me," I pressed, just to get her goat.

She growled. "I can't live without you." She shook her head and bumped me back to the side. "Now get yo' shit and let's go meet artsy hot guy so you can drool all over him and take some pictures and make my designs look pretty."

I reached for my big slouchy bag that had my standard model essentials of two pairs of high heels—one black, one nude—lip-gloss, panties in both black and nude, as well as a strapless bra, boob tape, lotion, and other various items I didn't leave home without when I was heading to a job. I currently had on a worn pair of jeans and a crop top with a men's long-sleeve dress shirt I'd tied in a knot at my waist. The sleeves hid my scars, but I also thought it looked cute. I slid my feet into a pair of brown leather flip-flops. "Okay, ready."

"Are you seriously going to wear those?" Her upper lip rose into a snarl of disgust. "You know I despise a flip-flop. They are not shoes. They are annoyances that make tons of noise when you walk and can ruin any outfit...unless you are on the beach in a bathing suit. Even then I wouldn't be caught dead in a pair but that's the only time they are acceptable."

I looked up to the ceiling and grouched. "Lord, give me strength to survive this day without smacking my sister."

"Oh, you gonna get smacked all right," she said, and then promptly slapped my ass.

"Jesus, women are whack," Ryan mumbled, and then entered the kitchen. "Is that coffee I smell?"

I jumped away from her and laughed at the surprise prick of pain then scrunched my nose and glared at Blessing. "You know I'm going to get you back." I chuckled and rubbed my bum as though it was sore when it really wasn't.

"Whatever will get your ass into gear. And be my guest. Revenge is best served cold; I'll be waiting to retaliate, and you know I won't stop until victory is declared."

"Yep, definitely whack." Ryan shook his head and shuffled to the coffee pot.

"Cups are in the cabinet below the coffee pot," I lied and covered my smile with my hand.

Blessing's eyebrows rose, and she tipped her head to the side to watch the show.

As expected, Ryan leaned over, giving us a sexy as sin view of one stellar rear end.

Blessing mouthed, "Damn," and fanned her face with her hand.

I barely contained my laughter but enjoyed the view.

Ryan opened the cabinet and found pots and pans. "No cups..." He glanced over at us checking out his fine booty and stood up with a grin.

"Oops." I shrugged. "I meant the cabinet on top. Sorry."

"Didn't your mama ever teach you not to lie," he quipped.

"Yes, she most certainly did." The woman herself came down the stairs in a fluffy robe, her multicolored glassed on the tip of her nose, and her strawberry blonde hair a wild lion's mane around her beloved face. "My girls being good?" She cocked an eyebrow.

I nodded. "Yes, Mama."

"Always," Blessing lied.

"Mmm hmm. Didn't I also teach my girls not to be late for work? And I noticed three shadows standing at the door through the glass as I was coming down the stairs. There a reason for that?"

"Shit!" Blessing dashed to the door.

"Mouth, darling." She sighed and then came to me, cupped my face, and kissed my cheek. "How's my baby this morning?"

I pressed my cheek against her hand, burrowing into the most precious touch in the world to me. "I'm good, Mama. Ready to get back to work. Hoping the day doesn't bring more bad news."

"Well, we're going to be hopeful and focus on the good we have. One another, a warm home, clothes on our backs, food in our bellies, and a whole lotta love, right?"

I nodded and she patted my cheek. "Go be beautiful for the camera, chicklet." She opened her arms and I went into them like a duck to water. "Don't let anything tear you down, my precious girl. You are loved. You are beauty. You are a gift. Remember that." She squeezed me tight and I inhaled her wildflower scent and let it soothe me straight down to my bones.

"I love you, Mama."

"And I love my girl. Let Blessing off the hook about her overprotectiveness, okay? She doesn't know any other way to protect her family. And she's lost a lot."

I nodded against her hair and breathed through the tears that wanted to surface. Today I'd be strong, I'd be beautiful, and I'd get the job done. Not only for Blessing but for myself. I needed to make strides in my recovery and getting back to work was just one hurdle toward that goal.

"Mama loves you." She kissed my temple and backed up. "Did you eat something?"

I grinned. "Yeah, I had cookies and tea."

"Please eat a good lunch," she requested, shuffling over to where Ryan was leaned against the cabinets, one arm crossed over his chest and the other mimicking that pose but holding a cup of Joe.

"Good morning, Agent Russell. Can I make you some breakfast?"

I waved at Ryan. "Bye, Mama," I said as I headed toward the front door where a huge Hispanic man stood sentry. He wasn't overly tall, maybe close to six feet or just under. Though the dude was built. A wall of muscle from top to toe. He had thick, luxurious black hair that was parted at the side and swept back at the top. His face was angular, cut with harsh lines that made him seem dangerous but also sleek, like a wild panther.

"Oh, hello." I smiled.

"Ma'am." He moved to open the door for me.

"You're taking care of my sisters?" I pressed my hand to stop him from opening it.

"Yes, ma'am. Charlotte, Liliana, Genesis, and one small child named Aurora."

I grinned. "Don't let Charlie hear you call her Charlotte." I mock shivered.

He smiled a bright white beautiful smile against his

brown sugar-colored skin. He was clean-shaven and his cologne was a heady, pleasurable mix of musk and man.

"I'm Addy."

"Omar Alvarado." He reached a hand out.

I shook it and took in his kind, warm brown eyes, square jaw, and hulking form. Liliana was going to crush on this man hard. He was exactly her type. Our sprite loved a big guy, and she preferred dating Hispanic men.

"You married?"

His eyebrows pulled together as he frowned. "No, why?"

I shrugged and winked. "No reason. Take care of my sisters."

"I'll protect them with my life," he stated with purpose.

"I'm counting on that."

I was about to open the door when I heard the shuffling of little feet dashing down the stairs.

"Wait, wait!" I heard Liliana holler.

She came barreling down the rest of the stairs, across the entry, and through the living space in a flirty little cotton dress that moved with her before she crashed into me.

I took her into my arms and snuggled her petite frame close. She wore a sweet-smelling perfume mixed liberally with something lemony. She always smelled good enough to eat. I glanced at Omar whose entire body went stock still, but his gaze was absolutely not. It ran up and down my sister's little body and he bit into his bottom lip. Everyone had a tell when they were interested in a person romantically. As a model, I picked up on these things. Especially a man hitting on a woman. People always thought models were loose and down to party. I was not but that didn't mean I didn't get my fair share of being hit on...regularly. Omar was into my sister Liliana. I'd bet my bank account on it.

She pulled back. "I didn't want you to leave without saying goodbye."

I cupped her beloved cheek and took in her beauty. Curly hair just hitting her shoulders. A beautiful espresso color that was a natural gift from the Big Guy. Super high rounded cheekbones, flawless, golden bronzed skin, perfectly arched eyebrows I'd kill for, and plump, cherub-like lips. The woman didn't even need makeup, she was so genuinely gorgeous.

Omar grunted next to us.

"Oh." I lifted my chin to Omar standing next to us. "This is Omar, your bodyguard. He'll be taking you to and from work today along with Charlie and Gen."

She frowned. "Bodyguards... *¿Qué? Por qué?*"

"Blessing's doing."

She rolled her eyes. "That girl." Then she finally took in her bodyguard and her eyes widened and a pretty red hue tinged her cheeks. Liliana lifted her hand and pushed a lock of her hair behind her ear, then looked down at the ground and then back up. "Um, *hola*. I'm Liliana."

He smiled and I watched as she visibly swallowed then let out whatever breath she was holding.

I almost cracked up but I had to get to work. "Well, I'm going to leave you two to your introductions. See you later?"

Liliana nodded. "*Sí*. Um, *te quiero*. Be careful and check in. I'll be worried if you don't."

I pulled her into my arms once more then kissed her cheek. "I love you too, Sprite. Have a good day with your hunk."

Her eyes got big again and she put her hand to her chest. "He's not my hunk..." she defended instantly. A little too quickly if someone asked me.

"I could be," Omar murmured.

"What?" Her gaze slashed to him and narrowed.

"Bye!" I called out, and then I opened the door and entered Hell. As expected, when I exited the house, the cameras started flashing. Blessing was waiting as were the two other bodyguards. One of them took my elbow and led me through the shouting crowd to the black Escalade.

I glanced behind me and saw the other guard doing the same for my sister.

They got us safely into the back of the vehicle as they took the front.

I surveyed the rather large crowd in front of Kerrighan House.

"This is insane. When is this going to stop?"

Blessing sighed. "I don't know." She took my hand and held it with hers just like she did yesterday. Sister solidarity. We may fight, we may bicker, but more than that, we loved one another fiercely. Holding her hand, I felt the tension start to lift.

"Today's going to be a good day. I just know it," I touted desperately, trying to believe it myself.

"Now that's the Addy I want to hear. Positive and driven." She patted my hand for emphasis. "Let's make today our bitch."

"You got it, sister!" I chuckled. "Now tell me what all that flirting was with Ryan. He's exactly your type and you cannot deny it."

"Because he's white?" she challenged.

"Because he's hot and doesn't take any of your lip. And yeah, he's white. When was the last time you dated a brother?"

She fluffed her hair and rubbed her glossy red lips together. "Can't say that I recall."

"Mmm hmm. That's because you stopped dating them back in high school. It's not my first day being your sister or your best friend, woman. So why did you blow him off? It was obvious he was interested."

Blessing made a show of digging through her purse. "He's law enforcement."

"FBI. A little different than a cop. And what is it you have against cops anyway?"

Her face went expressionless. "A black woman with a daddy who's in a gang and whose mother was murdered in gang retaliation does not need to be hopping into a bed with a man of the law. It just won't work. We're from two different planets."

"It's not like you see your father, right?"

She looked away and out the window avoiding my question.

"Blessing, you don't see Tyrell, do you?"

She shrugged. "We're in touch."

"Bless…" My heart started to pound in my chest, and I reached for her thigh. "Tell me you're not seeing your father. You know that's not smart."

"He's my only living connection to my mother." She lifted her chin in a regal attempt to throw me off.

I opened my mouth to object, but she lifted a finger as though she were pointing to the sky, but I knew it was a warning. She was about to get wicked with her tongue and say a bunch of crap she'd regret if I didn't curtail this discussion.

"Don't you even start with me, Addy. I do not have the time or the mental headspace to go down this rabbit hole with you. Let's just let sleeping dogs lie, shall we? My business with my father is my business. Not yours. And I don't want you tattling to Mama Kerri about this either."

"There's a reason why you were raised outside of that life, Blessing."

"And I don't need to be reminded of that fact seeing as it was me at ten years old that found my dead mother with her throat slit after having been beaten black and blue and raped."

I closed my eyes and shivered.

"Now it's on to bigger and better things. Remember?" she commanded.

"But…"

"Leave it, Addy. I mean it. I am in no mood to discuss this further. My personal business is mine to share or not, and I am not talking about my father or his dealings or my relationship to him."

"So, you admit to having a relationship with him?" I covered my pounding heart with my hand.

She groaned under her breath. "Enough," she warned, and I knew I wasn't going to get any more out of her.

"Fine. But I reserve the right to bring up this conversation at another time, preferably over a great meal and a bottle or two of wine."

Blessing nodded curtly. "Deal." Then she pulled out a file from the briefcase she had at her feet. "Here are the full designs for the project." She opened the file, and a myriad of delicate-looking lingerie pieces were laid out in a series of pictures.

I traced the lace edges of one design. "These are breathtaking, Blessing."

"Some of my best work. Beautiful lingerie for my curvy girls, not that it wouldn't look stellar on any size. Look at the scallop along that panty line." She pointed to an eggplant purple set. "What woman wouldn't want her booty looking like it's edged with flower petals?"

"Stunning. And this color will photograph well against my skin tone."

"Mmm hmm. My thoughts exactly. Have that long glorious hair trailing down your bare back, showing that scalloped edge on that fine ass of yours. Girl...I'm gonna be selling like hotcakes."

I grinned wide, loving that she believed my body would be the magic bullet to sell her designs.

"I'll do my best."

She bumped my shoulder. "You'll be perfect, Addy. I have no doubts."

"Show me the rest, and while you do, I'll tell you about the encounter between Omar the hulking bodyguard and Liliana."

Her coal-black eyebrows rose up toward her hairline. "Damn, sounds like I missed something juicy."

I grinned wide. "You did. She could barely speak when she saw him. And he was no better. Looked at her like a dying man walking through the desert in search of a drink and she was a fat glass of water."

"Oh hell." She rubbed her hands together, settling into my gossip. "Tell me more."

Chapter
FOUR

"**A**LL RIGHT, LADIES. IT'S OBVIOUS THE TWO OF YOU ARE used to doing your own thing, but my company was hired to protect you and that's what we're going to do," the driver of our car stated in an authoritative tone, his gaze still on the road ahead.

I felt Blessing jerk and sit up straighter. "Since I hired you, I sure as hell hope you're going to do the job I'm paying you to do." Blessing gave attitude as the dark-haired driver made his way into a strangely obscure underground parking area attached to a ten-story brick and mortar building. It was massive and off the beaten path with a view of Lake Michigan on one side, the city on the other. If I was a betting woman, which I was not—my money was hard-earned and I liked it safely in my bank account—I'd say it was an old factory from back in the day that had been refurbished into lofts.

The cars however in the underground garage were all top of the line. Audi. BMW. Porsche. Tesla and Mercedes to name a few that we'd passed by before the driver pulled directly in front of the underground elevator, using the single handicap-accessible spot. Not cool.

He turned around and faced us both while his counterpart seemed to scan the area vigilantly. His light eyes were blazing with frustration.

47

"Look, you hired me, but it should have been a contract with the FBI. I don't know why or how you escaped out from under their radar, but it's possible this may be the only day we guard you. I looked up your history and saw the news. You, little miss," he pointed at me accusingly, "are in some deep shit. I promise no blowback with my services and that everyone—client and guard—goes home at the end of the day. Hear me?"

I nodded numbly but thought he had a really handsome face with that sandy brown hair and light eyes, not to mention a sexy growl of a voice. And yet he was still scary mad and I personally wouldn't want to anger him further.

He pointed at Blessing. "You didn't say shit about having a serial killer after you. You just hired my company to watch over a bunch of women. Not even so much as giving me the lowdown about the paparazzi we'd see this morning, nor the fact that you're connected to the fuckin' Senator of Illinois." His voice rose and I strained my head back to get a little more space in the car, but found none. He kept going in that pissed as hell tone. "The lack of information stops here. As we head up to Mr. Fitzpatrick's loft, I want all the details. Then I'll determine if it's safe enough to leave one man here or if I should call for reinforcements. Already I have only one guy on three separate women. If I'd known this was more serious, I would have had one per person."

"They weren't exactly involved..." Blessing chuffed.

He shook his head and groaned under his breath. "Doesn't matter. No blowback. If someone wants to get to you," he pointed an index finger at me with a snarl to match, "he or she could easily pick off one of the lesser-protected women in your life. That's what I call blow-back, and I'm not having it. Not on my watch."

"Um, excuse me, Mr..." I tried.

He narrowed his gaze at Blessing. "You didn't even tell the mark our names?"

Blessing shrugged a shoulder, unimpressed, then looked down at her red nails, possibly checking if there were any chips or rough spots. Blessing didn't take any shit from any-one. Especially someone she hired. But in this circumstance, the guy was right, and she owed him an apology.

"Sylvester Holt, owner of Holt Security."

"Mr. Holt. I appreciate your concern and understand it completely. I'm absolutely terrified of what happened to that poor woman and have already been kidnapped and tor-tured myself."

Mr. Holt's angered gaze softened. "Nothing's going to happen to you on my watch. That I can promise. And I've already checked out your guy."

"My guy?"

"The photographer. He's solid. Ex-Army. Spent a decade in war-torn countries and lived to tell about it, and brought back proof the world could see through his photographs. Fan of his work. It's stellar." He offered up the compliment as if it were a throwaway, but it made me desperate to check out Killian's prior work. If I hadn't had to worry about an innocent dead woman who looked like me, I would have al-ready done so.

"Well, that's lovely. You can tell him that yourself." I smiled.

He ignored my response and continued with his de-mands. "Look, Ms. Michaels-Kerrighan, it doesn't change that you are in some real danger and it's my job now to ensure that you're safe. So, you both need to listen to me and my team. We will keep you safe. You don't exit cars alone, walk alone into buildings, or open doors willy-nilly to a house that's bombarded by the press. We take you in, we check the place out, you stay locked in tight under my watch. My guy Lance here will take care of Ms. Jones-Kerrighan. My guy Omar will take care of the other three for today. I have no doubts about my guys' ability to protect all of you. I just want to make it clear that when I tell you to do something, you're going to do it, and not go off half-cocked. Got it?"

I nodded avidly not wanting to piss Mr. Holt off even more. He was definitely a hot guy but also a little unhinged and frightening, if you asked me.

"Do you have the card for the FBI agent assigned to your case?" he asked.

I shook my head. "No, I'm not sure whose been assigned officially, but our sister Simone is living with Jonah Fontaine, and his partner Ryan Russell also stayed over the house last night to keep watch."

"Fontaine and Russel, I know them. Solid agents. If I'd known he was inside the house I would have gotten my information straight from the source."

Blessing looked out the window and pretended to be invisible.

I bumped her shoulder. "See what happens when you go off half-cocked," I whisper-yelled loud enough for both men to hear.

Blessing glared in response. "I did what I had to do and obviously I got the best, so what's your problem?"

I sighed then turned to the driver. "I'm sorry you were ill-informed, Mr. Holt, but we are late for the shoot which means Blessing is going to be late to her meetings if we don't get in gear. Can we talk on the way up?"

He clenched his jaw and folded out of the car abruptly. Lance did the same on my side of the car and opened my door, his eyes not on me but scanning an empty garage filled with fancy cars. It must have cost a mint to live in this building. Mr. Holt did the same for Blessing and together we walked to the elevator.

On the way up, we gave the guys as much information as we knew, which, again, wasn't a lot. All of this just happened. I however was trying to be smart while pretending everything was going to be okay. Hopefully this situation with the girl was a one-off and it would end with the FBI or the local cops doing their thing, and we'd find out it was all just a big coincidence.

Blinders firmly on, I stood back while Mr. Holt knocked on one of two doors in the small hallway of the top floor. Lucky number 10. Looked like each tenant had half a floor, which would have been pretty massive square footage-wise.

Killian opened the door with a smile plastered to his handsome face, then jerked his head back, the smile shutting down instantly. He took in the two big men who clearly had a lot of testosterone and must have worked out like demons, with surprise. Then his eyebrows rose while taking in Blessing and finally landing those pretty brown eyes on me.

I gave a little finger wave but kept quiet.

Mr. Holt stuck out his hand. "Sylvester Holt of Holt Security. I'm going to be assessing your home. Can we chat a moment?"

Killian smirked and winked at me before responding with a wave of his hand for all of us to enter. "Sure, come on in. My dog's currently locked up in the laundry room off there." He pointed to a door where I could hear a dog barking like wild. "Rottweiler. Doesn't take kindly to strangers. I'll introduce him to Addison and team individually if it's all the same to you."

"I'll need to see in that room."

"Of course. I can take you around and when you're ready I'll introduce you. My dog will not attack unless I command it, or he feels that I'm being threatened."

Mr. Holt nodded curtly. "Lance, you're on point." He commanded and the large white dude lifted his chin and crossed his arms, standing right next to us preparing to hold vigil while Mr. Holt did the look about.

My makeup/hairdresser exited from another door which I assumed led to a bathroom since it was one of only two doors in the place, and I waved at him wildly while smiling. "Hi Cameron!" Cameron was dressed in black from head to toe. A tight black T-shirt that fit like a glove adorned his thin frame. Black skinny jeans and black and white Vans completed his bland look. His face, however, was covered in brightly colored makeup. Multi-colored pink, blue, and purple hues shaded his blue eyes. Rouge and contouring makeup had been expertly applied to his face to accentuate the femininity of his fairylike features. He had long, pitch-black eyelashes so flattering you couldn't tell whether they were real or fake. His hair was a startling bright royal blue, cut close to the sides and spiky on top. That was new. Then again, it was always something different. Last time I'd laid eyes on him his hair was bright pink.

Cameron preferred to go wild with hair and makeup which highlighted his craft, versus dressing fashionably forward.

He sauntered over to me and I hugged him before he let me go then pulled Blessing into his arms. I let them catch up on things while I took in the loft. The space was huge. Two walls were completely made out of brick from floor to ceiling. A staircase spiraled up in the corner toward what looked like a super cool indoor/outdoor-like green space where I could see lush plants that had another wrought iron staircase leading to what I assumed was the roof. A little further from that was an open room with glass walls that held workout equipment.

Below in the primary space, there was a long, L-shaped teal couch that sat against one of the brick walls. It could easily sit ten to twelve people comfortably. Tall wooden columns dotted the space, likely holding up the roof. The floors were entirely covered in a medium brown-toned wood. A weird multi-tiered table sat in front of the teal couch with a vase on one tier, a stack of magazines on another. The kitchen was dead center of the room and could be seen from anywhere as it butted up against one of the non-brick walls. There were barstools surrounding the entire thing. No dining table to speak of, not that it mattered because there were four barstools on each of the three sides of the U-shaped kitchen counters. The back wall of the kitchen boasted a double sub-zero stainless steel fridge, a six-burner stove, and scads of cabinets. The sink and more counter space were part of the big, U-shaped setup so it doubled as both eating space and workspace. It felt more like a comfy bar or diner than a kitchen in someone's home.

To the right of the kitchen was a wall of windows. Another seating area in a light brown suede style that looked perfect for lounging on and watching a TV, one of which I didn't see. I'm not sure what the open space was for actually. Past all that there was another staircase that led to an open room. From where I stood, I could see there were doors at the top of that staircase that slid open and closed like shoji screens. That was where I believed I could see a king-sized bed against one wall. I'd need to climb the stairs in order to see the rest.

Under the bedroom section were where there were two other doors completely closed off. I could hear barking from one of them, and the other was the one Cameron exited from, which I'd already ascertained was the bathroom.

In the last corner I saw a huge white photo backdrop and lights with a series of what I knew to be props huddled all around it. Different seats, stools, blocks, two clothing racks that were already filled with bagged items, and a ton of unopened boxes. That must be where we were going to work. I also noted a space heater, giant lights all the professionals used, and some other pulley systems that hung from the open ceiling.

"This place is tits!" Cameron spun around, and I focused on him and his outburst. "I can't believe we're in the home of Pulitzer Prize-winning photographer Killian Fitzpatrick! Isn't it just so extra?" he gushed.

Pulitzer Prize-winning... Say what?

I frowned and looked at Blessing. Her eyes were as big as mine, conveying she hadn't known that tidbit of information either. What the heck was he doing taking fashion photos?

Now I take pictures of things that are beautiful. Things that bring me joy, not pain.

His words ran through my mind. He'd spent a decade photographing war. That had to be tough, but perhaps there was more to it than that.

I spun around when I heard Mr. Holt's and Killian's footsteps coming from where I believed the bedroom was.

"All clear. I'll be doing recon around the building, checking in with my team, and coming in and out. Will that be a problem?" he asked.

"Actually, it will," Killian noted. "I can't work with disruptions. Once Addy and I get in the zone, I'd rather not be bothered. She'll be perfectly protected here with me, my dog, and this." He pulled out a handgun he had tucked in the back of his jeans, then tucked it back at the small of his waist. "She'll be wearing lingerie and I don't want her to feel uncomfortable."

He sure didn't know me. I was the least modest woman of all my sisters. Even Simone, and she let it all hang out. Me, I made my money based on my body and what it looked like clothed and unclothed. If people didn't like it, they could cease looking at it. I didn't go flaunting it out in my everyday personal life, but I wasn't insecure in the least. A man or a woman for that matter liked my curves or they didn't. Why should I try to fit in some box to make others happy? And clearly as proven by my success and the waiting list I still had from designers across the globe, there was a place in the fashion industry for a woman of my size. But I appreciated his concern for me.

I took in the man as he stood with arms crossed over one another staring Mr. Holt down. A scary thing I wouldn't have recommended. Sylvester Holt looked like a defensive lineman. He had control of that massive frame and used it easily to intimidate. And yet, Killian was no slouch. He was definitely a force to be reckoned with. His size may have been more athletic than huge and beefy like my new security guy, but no less strong.

Killian wore an incredible pair of form-fitting jeans that hugged his body to perfection. His thick, muscular thighs strained against the denim deliciously, as did his rear end. I sucked in my bottom lip, appreciating the tight white T-shirt that left nothing to my imagination. The man was blessed with lean, tightly packed muscles that my fingers tingled with the desire to touch.

I swallowed down my nervous response to the gun and his need to ensure my comfort.

Mr. Holt stared at Killian for a long time. Then he must have seen what he wanted to see because he nodded. "I'll do the rounds every thirty minutes and make the hallway outside my door home base." He looked over at me. "Ms. Michaels-Kerrigan, I'd like to get your cell phone number. I've got yours, Mr. Fitzpatrick, and will text if I feel the need to pop in so you can get a hold of your dog. However, if I feel anything or have a bad feeling, I'm sitting inside." He pointed to the teal couch that was the farthest away from the photographing setup. "I'll sit over there if I need to be out of the way."

Killian nodded. "That works."

"All right." He came over to me, we exchanged numbers, and he gave me a few more tips about my safety.

For the first time since Wayne Gilbert Black died, I actually felt safe and comfortable.

"Thank you." I reached out my hand and Mr. Holt took it.

"My pleasure. I'll be right outside or very close at all times. You need me, call, text, or just scream and I'll be there." His eyes rose toward where Killian was standing. "Though I'm thinking Mr. Fitzpatrick has you covered. Still, I'm here."

I nodded. "Got it."

I hugged Blessing and the three of them exited the loft. Killian followed right behind and locked the door.

"I'm going to finish setting up in the bathroom. It's huge. Totally big enough to do my magic on you. Not that you need it, you freak of nature." Cameron huffed, then turned toward Killian. "Woman waltzes in with no makeup and poorly brushed hair with zero product and looks like a goddess." He shook his head. "It isn't fair. You ever see a more beautiful face than that?" Cameron hooked a thumb at me, and I could feel my cheeks heat with embarrassment.

Killian stared straight into my eyes when he spoke. "No, I haven't. She's a one-of-a-kind beauty."

"Don't I know it." Cameron prattled on as he made his way toward the bathroom.

I stared at Killian, feeling a little out of sorts standing alone in a room with him for the first time. "Hey," I said shyly.

Killian came over to me and stopped a couple feet away. "You doin' okay?"

I nodded and pushed a lock of hair behind my ear suddenly feeling shy. "Everything is a little awkward but I'm rolling with it. Thank you for sharing your space and willingly shooting in your home. This can't be fun for you."

He smiled softly. "Why wouldn't having something unearthly beautiful to photograph in my home not be fun for me?"

I bit down on my bottom lip and looked at the floor, trying to hide how much his compliment lifted my confidence.

"I'm still scared."

"Of the guy who hurt that girl?" He clarified.

I shook my head. "No...actually, yeah, that too. It's just... This is my first shoot back after the other thing and now it's blowing up again. I just want to apologize in advance if I randomly I stare off into space or have one of my *moments*."

He stepped so close I could almost feel the heat of his larger frame cocooning mine, reminding me that there was someone perfectly capable of protecting me. Him.

"Last time when you paused during the shoot, you went somewhere. What happened then?" he asked.

"I...uh, went back to that horrible place where I was kept. The guy, he took pictures and video of me. Sometimes the sound of the flash or a picture being taken can send me back there."

He lifted up a finger. "I've got an idea. What if we drown out the sound?"

I tilted my head. "How so?"

"Music, of course. What do you like?"

I shrugged. "Most everything, but I'm really into Lana Del Rey right now."

"She's awesome. Why don't you go get your hair and makeup done while I set up and get some music on? I need to choose the first outfit and props to see what we're working with."

Without any preamble, I closed the space between us and wrapped my arms around his neck. I lifted up onto my toes so I could whisper against his ear while hugging him. "Thank you. For making me feel safe. For giving me a private space. For understanding my issues..."

He wrapped his arms around my body, bringing me flush against his hard frame. I relaxed into his return hug.

"When I say it's my pleasure, I really mean it, Addy. There's something about you. About your beauty. About your body. About your entire package that calls to me, unlike anything I've ever experienced before. I *have* to capture your beauty on film. It feels...*important* somehow."

I trembled in his hold, not because I was afraid, but because the things he said turned my insides to mush and my body to nothing but liquid desire.

I wanted him.

Badly.

"We're going to break all the rules about models and photographers getting mixed up with one another, aren't we?" I whispered against his thick, manly neck where I scented a light cologne mixed with a heady, earthy musk that had to be all Killian.

"I sure as hell hope so." He ran his hand up my back and cupped my cheek, his thumb tracing my bottom lip in a feather-light caress. His gaze seared straight through to the heart of me.

I thought he might kiss me. Wished for it even. I wanted him to lean forward and just do it, even if this was only the second time we'd seen one another. Even if this was a job and it was unprofessional. All those excuses ran out the window when this man had his hands on me. The simple touch of his palm to my cheek and his thumb to my lip made butterflies take flight in my stomach and my blood heat.

Which is also when we heard a crashing sound. He jerked back and spun around, his hands going up into the air. "*Nein!*" he roared suddenly.

I looked around him and saw an enormous, stunning, black and tan Rottweiler barreling my way. I got down on my haunches and opened my arms. "Hi, baby!" I cried out with excitement. I *loved* dogs.

"*Nein, bleib!*" No. Stay. Killian commanded the dog in German, but the dog saw me crouch and he was on a path for maximum contact.

"Come here, sweet baby!" I countered and the dog plowed into me, taking me down to my booty. His face was level with mine and he licked and gave me kisses as I hugged, petted, and fluffed his luxurious coat. Unlike other Rottweilers I'd seen before, this one had a tail which I found fascinating. "Oh, you're a pretty boy, aren't you?" I cooed and kissed at his monster-sized head. He licked me all over, then ducked his massive dome and head-butted my chest.

"Brutus! *Hier. Fuss!*" Come. Heel. Killian spoke in rapid-fire German once again.

Brutus whined but went over to his dad's leg and sat right by his feet panting, his tail still wagging.

I got up off the floor and wiped at my clothing and pushed my hair out of my face. "You have an awesome dog!" I gushed happily. "Does he fetch? My sister's dog Amber loves to play fetch and tug of war." I shrugged. "I'm the best auntie because I could play with a dog all day long and be happy as a clam."

Killian just stared at me silently, his brow furrowed, almost pained.

"What?"

"You just stared down the face of a killing machine and turned him into a playful puppy in a matter of seconds," he said flatly.

I tilted my head and frowned, then pointed at that dog. "He's sweet as pie."

Killian shook his head. "No. He isn't. You should have seen how long it took to introduce your friend Cameron and I'm still a little nervous to have him out of the laundry room until that guy leaves."

"No way. Really?"

He petted the top of his dog's head. "More surprises with you."

"How so?"

"Sweetheart, my dog is dangerous. He's a trained protector. He will bite first and protect me to the death. And you crouched down and opened your arms like a lamb left to a pack of hungry wolves. You seriously have zero self-protective instincts. We're going to have to work on this, baby. This is not good news."

I pouted. "I can't help it if dogs love me. I'm like the dog whisperer guy. I have never met a dog that didn't like me. It's a gift."

He shook his head. "We'll see about that. Brutus, *hier.*" He snapped *come* in German, then led the dog toward the laundry room. Every couple feet he slowed, glancing back at me sadly, tail between his legs. Poor baby. I felt his sadness.

"Can't he hang out with us?" I pushed. "He's sad now. That makes me sad." I gave him my best pitiful look.

Killian ran his hands through his glorious hair in what I gathered was a heaping dose of frustration. Man, I wanted to run my hands through that hair, preferably while kissing him.

"After your friend finishes, then maybe," he compromised.

Still, I pouted. I really wanted to hang out with the dog.

"That 'maybe' is going to turn into a no…" he warned.

"Ugh, fine. Spoilsport. Bye, baby boy! See you soon, honey." I cooed at the sweet dog.

Brutus wagged his tail and I grinned. "See? He loves me."

"I'm beginning to see a trend," he said softly.

"What's that supposed to mean?" I fired back.

He just laughed and led his dog back to his stupid laundry room cage for the time being. "We've got work to do." He pointed to the bathroom door where I figured Cameron was eavesdropping and had already seen and heard the entire conversation.

"Fine, but during breaktime I get to play with Brutus!" I stated flippantly, flip-flopping my way toward my beauty team of one. Blessing was right. These shoes did make a lot of noise, especially on hardwood floors.

"We'll see about that," he stated in a way that made it sound like I wouldn't be getting my way.

"Yes, we will!" I yelled again, not one to easily bow out of a challenge.

Chapter
FIVE

"**S**TOP FRETTING! YOU LOOK FAN-TABULOUS!" CAMERON ran his fingers which were covered with pomade through the curls he'd put in my hair to make them look more natural. I had a ridiculous mane of hair and I was grateful for it, but if you wanted it to look a certain way, it took a load of product and a lot of finagling. Which is why I left it down, in a ponytail, or a messy bun most of the time.

He fluffed both sides and shoved two portions in front to fall over my shoulders and caress the sides of my cheeks. Killian had hung the first item he chose to photograph on the door handle earlier for me to grab. It was an emerald green teddy and matching panty number that made my eyes pop. What I loved most about this piece Blessing designed was that it would look incredible on every woman. Most of her designs were like that. Victoria's Secret would weep at the beauty she created, and I secretly hoped they'd see these designs blasted across the globe and choose to hire my sister to design an upcoming line.

I tugged on the center lacing between the cups in order to plump and lift what the good Lord had already been kind enough to give me. I had a killer rack that looked good in bathing suits and lingerie of all types. Big boobs will travel.

The part that made this teddy special was that if someone was less endowed, they could tighten the lacy strings on the mini-corset style stitching at the cleavage, and it would pull their breasts up and together, giving them the illusion of a more bountiful bosom. Genius, if you asked me. I wondered if I should suggest Blessing hire a smaller model to come in and photograph in the same outfits so that the buyers and the big box stores could truly see that these designs worked for all women and all body types. I kept that idea in the back of my mind to share later. I was sure she'd thought of the same, but it never hurt to consider a good idea twice.

I ran my hands down the bust and over my ribcage where the satiny fabric tucked in with some stellar hidden ruching and flared out at the hip in a flirty manner. This accentuated the waist and hips without making the wearer feel boxy. Women liked to feel voluptuous and curvy regardless of however many curves they sported, and this was another trick to the design. The edges were all framed in a matching emerald green lace that gave the piece a timeless and maybe even old-fashioned forties-glamor feel.

"You look perfect, Addy. Go knock the hot photographer dead. Make him drop his camera and fight a stiffy. Hell, I'm fighting a stiffy looking at you and I'm happily married to a man." He waved his face with a dramatic flare that was all Cameron.

I giggled and grabbed the robe that went with the teddy and put it on, tying it at the waist. This one went down to mid-ankle. Another cool feature of Blessing's designs was she had a robe in every color from the line so if someone wanted to cover up or give a little show to their mate or walk around tending to their children with the sexy lingerie underneath, they could.

Together the two of us walked out.

"I've left clips and other gadgets so you can change your hair to an updo or bun rather quickly. I wish I could stay the day, but Blessing updated me last night. I'm really sorry you're having to deal with this…especially so soon after what happened." He grabbed both of my hands once we made it to the front door. "I'm here for you, Addy. Day or night. You know that. Right?"

I smiled wide and hugged him. "Thank you, Cameron. Your love and friendship mean the world to me. Say hi to that hunky hubby of yours and let's plan dinner sometime next month when all this is hopefully just a bad memory."

His gaze left mine and moved toward the area where I could see Killian was setting up huge white boxes in the center of the floor that he'd also draped in white paper.

"Maybe it could be a double date." Cameron waggled his eyebrows overtly.

I rolled my eyes, sighed, turned him around to face the door, and pushed him closer to it. I unlocked and opened the door with a flourish.

"You good?" Mr. Holt asked, hand up to his ear where he held a cell phone.

"Yep, just seeing my friend out. Bye, Cameron, and thanks again."

"Not a hardship to make you even more beautiful." He air-kissed both my cheeks and then waved.

"Lock it," my bodyguard commanded so I nodded and did as he said.

I spun around. "Cameron's gone. Can we let Brutus

out?" I asked, immediately making my way to where Killian now stood behind his camera and tripod. There was a table next to that where his shiny black gun sat. I stared at the gun, my body turning cold, and I wrapped my hands around myself in a protective barrier.

"Maybe later..." he said, and then I didn't hear anything.

All I saw was that gun.

Only it was a different gun. Lifted up, the muzzle flashing twice. My sister Tabitha's body jerking in midair as she came down on the attacker with her blade.

I jolted with each remembered shot and backed up, my vision not seeing anything in front of me but a dark, dank room and my sister's lifeless body on the floor bleeding out, her eyes still open, seeing nothing.

I shook so hard my teeth chattered and my skin felt like icicles were needling every centimeter of my flesh.

"Addy. Come back to me." A rushed voice spoke close to me.

I shook my head as I felt someone's hands close around my biceps.

"No!" I choked out. "Please, no!" I could feel my entire body shutting down, blackness taking over my vision.

Then I was surrounded by warmth. It oozed into my icy skin and replaced the sensation with golden waves of heat. I burrowed closer to the feeling.

"That's it, Addy. Come back. You're safe. You're right here." I heard a voice I recognized but wasn't super familiar with.

I blinked several times and saw a pinprick of light. Bright white light. Then it got wider and wider. The voice in my ear soft and soothing...serene. Like stepping into a natural hot spring for the first time. The earthy scent surrounded me as the white light widened and I saw hints of blue sky peeking through.

"That's it, baby. Come back. I'm right here. I've got you, Addy. I won't let go."

"Don't let go." I clutched onto the warmth as though my life depended on it, pressing my chest flat against it, wrapping my arms tighter around it. Keeping it close. Filling me up with all that was good and right.

The darkness crept from my view and I saw the brick wall with the big window leading to an amazing view of the lake and sky beyond. My back was being rubbed up and down as I came to myself one breath at a time. With each swipe of his powerful caress, my vision cleared, and I realized I was in Killian's arms. He held me so tight to his body, there wasn't room to slip a piece of paper between us. He continued to run his hands up and down the length of my spine.

"Breathe. I've got you. You're safe," he reminded me.

I did as told and then the tears hit, filling my eyes as I slowly eased away. "I'm...I'm sorry. I don't know what happened. I just saw the gun on the table and..." I licked my lips and let my hair fall against my face as I stared at my bare feet. Embarrassment pressed hard against my chest like a battering ram, the earlier warmth I'd siphoned off of Killian turning to a blazing inferno of mortification and shame in its wake.

He put his hands on my biceps once again and dipped his head. "Addy, look at me."

I shook my head sullenly, wanting to run and hide. To

call Mr. Holt and have him whisk me away to the safety of my bed at Kerrighan house. I hadn't even been back to my apartment since I was tortured and kidnapped by a madman and I thought I was ready to work? With a man like this? A Pulitzer Prize-winning photographer? What the hell was I thinking? I trembled where I stood. I *wasn't* thinking. Just like when I walked willingly into the car of a madman.

"Addy, snap out of it!" Killian jerked me back into his arms in a tight hug.

This time I didn't wrap my arms around him and hold on like he was a long-lost prince charming. I wasn't worthy of such compassion. My life was so messed up and this man... He had it all. He didn't need my kind of crap.

"I'm sorry, Killian. I'm going to go..." I pulled forcefully out of his arms and started to head to the bathroom to change back into my street clothes.

"No, you're not. We're going to hash this out, then we're going to take some amazing pictures."

"I don't think it's a good idea. Maybe I'm not ready..."

"You were balls to the wall ready until you saw my gun. Then you lost it. My fault. I should have been more sensitive to your history. I promise that will not happen again. I'll be more mindful."

"You shouldn't have to change anything about yourself for me. You shouldn't even need a gun. You shouldn't have to open your home and do all this in your private space. Everything is so upside down." The tears threatened once more and this time I had no hope of them not falling.

He reached for my hand and walked me over to the teal velvet couch. He sat down and tugged on my hand until I was sitting next to him. He turned so he was facing me.

"Addy, I want to be here taking these photos. And not just because you're gorgeous and I want to date you."

I could feel my cheeks heat again for another reason. This time not attached to shame.

He took both of my hands inside both of his. "I see in you what I see when I look in the mirror."

"How so?" I frowned, uncertain where he was going with this admission.

"Fear. Shame. Courage. Insecurity. But most of all, I see the desire to get better. To find yourself amongst all the tragedy. That's all any of us want to do, especially after a traumatic experience. Sometimes when I close my eyes, all I see are my brothers in arms being blown up. Children shot dead in villages that had been turned to rubbish. Women raped and mutilated beyond repair. It's all there waiting like a villain in the back of my mind and I'm helpless to it."

I shifted my body more toward him, pulling a leg up and under my bum. "That's awful."

"It is. And what you went through was awful too. You and I are not so different, Addy."

"H-how do you get past it? How do you make it go away?" My voice shook and he rubbed my hands with his.

"One day at a time. Talk it through with friends, family, a therapist. All of these I've done, and it helped. Still, at night, the fear and trauma can pull me from a dead sleep and make me believe I'm back there, running for my life, fighting to survive, still capturing the events on camera. I've only been out of it for a year and a half, Addy. You've only just come out of your experience in the last few months and you've been tossed right back into your own personal Hell. Give yourself a little grace. You are not made of stone."

He ran his hands up to my inner forearms and the worst of the puckered scars. He traced them as I tried to pull back. I didn't let anyone touch them. He didn't relent but held tighter. "These wounds hurt and will forever be a part of you. The scars are now part of the story that is Addison Michaels-Kerrighan. And sweetheart...every inch of you is pure beauty."

Tears tracked down my face. "And your scars...are they part of you too?"

He inhaled so deeply his nostrils flared and his brown eyes turned a darker shade of espresso. Then he stood tall, lifted the hem of his T-shirt, and pulled it up and over his head. A magnificent torso seared across my vision. Pecs that were squared off, a smattering of light brownish-blond hair that ran along the center in just the right amount that made a girl itch to run her fingers through it. I followed that line of hair as it went down not a four pack, but a solid, defined six-pack. Abdominals like speed bumps I'd love to run my tongue in between playfully. His jeans were fitted but slung low on his hips, giving my eyes a feast of those two indents between a man's waist and his pelvis that made a girl like me go bonkers with lust. Before I could get enough eye candy he slowly turned around. At first, I thought he was gifting me a better view of his fine ass, until I saw the carnage that was the skin of his back.

White puckered lines ran up and down his muscular form alongside smaller, more rounded and jagged scars, some of them still pink and healing. They must have been deep like mine. I gasped and stood abruptly, hovering my hands over the destroyed flesh.

"Fitz..." I whispered as I touched a single finger to a

scar at the top of his shoulder and followed the gnarled, bumpy flesh all the way down to his tailbone. He shivered and clenched his hands into fists. I could visibly see his chest rise and fall with the effort it took to stand there vulnerable to my gaze and touch. Without thinking, I pressed my body to his back, both of my hands curling around two mighty shoulders, and I rested my forehead to the center of his spine between his shoulder blades. "Who did this to you?" I whispered, my voice barely recognizable.

"IED loaded with shrapnel." His head fell forward, but he didn't move away so I didn't either. "I was photographing my old unit when someone behind me stepped on it. The roar of the bomb going off was so loud I couldn't hear for a full two days after that. I woke as a fire on my back was being put out. There were body parts of men I served with lying all around me. I'll never forget opening my eyes and seeing a severed hand with the tan line of a wedding ring still visible, only two feet in front of my eyes."

I let the tears fall as he shared his horrifying experience.

"And that wasn't all, Addy. There's more. So much more, but the experience scarred me physically and emotionally for life. I'll never forget that day. How the sun hit the sky just perfectly. The sounds of people I cared about, loved like brothers, laughing only minutes before their lives were snuffed out. My camera survived. I have pictures of some of my friends only moments before they took their last breaths. That is part of my story. Part of my legacy. Part of who I am." He spun around and pulled me into his arms. "What happened to you, it's only part of your story. The rest is still unwritten. You have the power and the ability to move on. To live. That's what I tell myself every time I feel sorry for myself over what happened. Over what I lost. I get to *live* when they didn't. It's my job now to make sure I don't waste the life I've been given."

I lifted my hands up and cupped Killian's cheeks, his beard and mustache combo soft against the palms of my hands. "Thank you. For sharing your story. For showing me this part of you."

He closed his eyes as though he were letting my touch sink into him. He blinked and put his hands to my wrists where I still cupped his cheeks. "Don't give up, Addy. Push through. You've lived through hell. Now's the time to live the life you want."

"What if I don't know what I want anymore?" I admitted a truth I hadn't been willing to even entertain myself. Leave it to this man to dig straight into the heart and truth of me.

He smiled softly. "Then allow yourself the ability to find out. But don't stop living in the process. If you do, those bad guys, the people that hurt you, they win."

I nodded as he lifted my hand from his cheek and placed a warm kiss to the center of my palm. "I want to photograph you."

"Okay… But can we let Brutus out now? He's been locked up forever and I hate that my being here has messed up his ability to roam free in his home."

Killian closed his eyes and let out a long chuckle. "Woman after my own heart."

"More like woman after doggie snuggles." I teased to lighten the heavy that we'd just shared. It was beautiful and I'd never forsake it or share it with others, but he was right. We both needed to move forward.

"Go fix up your face. Your makeup is smeared and I doubt you want that in your photos. I'll get Brutus out and settled."

"Deal." I clapped and bounced on my feet a couple times before dashing to the bathroom to fix what I most certainly messed up with my moment and crying jag.

◯

"Open the robe and let it fall off a shoulder, and then lean back over the block, one hand on the edge," Killian instructed.

We'd gotten past the heavy moment and I'd fixed my hair and makeup and given Brutus some pets. Tossed his toy across the room a few times, allowed his good mood to change my previously sour one. It had worked like a charm.

"Like this?" I rested both of my elbows on the higher block, my butt on the lower one, and kicked one leg out.

The camera snapped quietly as Lenny Kravitz sang "American Woman" through the surround sound. I swung my foot playfully and smiled as though I were having a blast when in reality the position was super uncomfortable and one I wouldn't be able to hold much longer.

"Relax… This isn't working." He sighed.

I frowned. Occasionally a photographer would claim a setup wasn't working and change it up. Those days meant much longer sessions in much more difficult positions, and I was already exhausted from the lack of sleep last night and the emotional outpouring we had about an hour ago.

Killian brought the camera over to me and showed me the still frames. They were beautiful, but the more I stared the more blah I felt about them too.

"I mean, they'll probably be great for a catalogue or a website purchase but something's missing." He tied his hair back away from his face in one of those artsy man buns I adored. The man was so naturally sexy. He worked barefoot, and climbed up and down a ladder, crawled on the floor, sat in a chair, basically everything that could give him the angles he wanted. I loved working with professional photographers who did that. They weren't afraid to get dirty. They were solely focused on getting an incredible shot and that tended to make me more money. Win-win.

He sighed again and glared at the camera. "They're too damn cold. I feel like the jewel tones in the teddy, the sheen on your skin…all of it is beautiful and warm, but the white background and the barren square blocks are doing nothing for me." He pursed his lips and turned around and stared at the suede brown couch that was up against the brick wall across the other side of the room. "Feeling adventurous?"

I grinned. "Always."

"Let's try my couch."

"Are you sure you want your home in pictures that could end up on billboards?" I reminded him of what was at stake.

"I want the perfect shot. One that will not only accentuate your beauty and down-to-earth appeal, but the lusciousness and warmth of the apparel. I know we were told to use the backgrounds that could be manipulated but I'm thinking we do both. Give them the online standard catalogue image and then something artful and more consistent with your fashion spreads in magazines."

I made my way to the kitchen in the center where I'd left my drink and sucked down a few gulps of a bottled water before heading over the couch. "And what do you know of my fashion spreads?"

He grinned and manually rolled one of his giant lights on wheels over to the couch. He plugged it in and fired it up. The couch instantly had a spotlight on it that I had to admit, was pretty mesmerizing.

"I told you I looked you up. When I research something, I'm thorough. Please sit in the circle so I can gauge the lighting." He pointed at the spotlight on the couch.

I sat down in the center as he fiddled with things. "Already I'm liking this better. Your skin looks luminescent and that green against the light brown of the couch does wonders for the contrast and tones on that fabric."

I watched as he went back and got his handheld camera. Killian preferred to hold the camera in his hand when he shot. A lot of photographers chose to use a tripod of sorts when they shot because it reduced the possibility of movement blurring the image.

"Can you do a few poses?" He ducked his head behind the lens.

Feeling bold, I undid the robe and artfully laid it over one side of the couch. If it was caught in the picture, the buyer would see there was a robe to purchase too. I turned to the side making sure my torso was on full display giving a good view of the tatas, but also lifted my hip up. The camera clicked. I pulled at the side slit of the teddy until it opened all the way up to my hip where the panties could be seen.

"Perfect. Pull up a little more on the nightie and we'll be able to see the edge of the panties as well as that ass I'd like to take a bite out of."

My mouth dropped open in shock and he snapped like wild.

"Christ," he swore, and I smiled as he adjusted his jeans at the crotch. If I wasn't mistaken, there was definitely heat rising alongside something else. My heart pounded and I changed position, getting on both knees on the fluffy surface and facing him dead-on. I lifted my hands into my hair, let my mouth fall open in a sultry inhale move I'd been taught by a few pros when I first started, closed my eyes, and twisted my arms in a way that my scars would not show.

The camera spang to life.

I waited a moment, opened my eyes, and tugged on the lace between my breasts, letting the two sides of the teddy's thin shoulder straps fall delicately along my outer arms as though I was getting ready to remove it.

More clicks.

I got into the music and the more moody and far more comfortable location to the point where I ended up lying down on the couch, my hair spread all over the seat cushion while Killian stood above me, straddling my form. I'd pulled the teddy up to bare my stomach with one hand so you could see the entirety of the lace and satin panties. There I hooked one edge of the side at the hip with my thumb and tugged it down just enough to make it look like I was getting ready to remove them. Hoping the image would portray a woman rocking amazing lingerie who was ready to be made love to.

"Fuckin' hell. I should be paying *you* to take these photos. Fuck me running. This is so much better than taking pictures of the battles overseas." He snapped a few more then looked at the screen intently.

"That would be really hard to do, don't you think?" I winked at the camera playfully when in reality I was absolutely winking at Killian.

"What would?" he asked.

I grinned and he snapped a photo.

"Fucking while running. I mean, you'd have to carry me, though I imagine the bouncing would be pretty spectacular." I cocked an eyebrow.

His entire body went still. "Are you trying to make this hard on me?" He narrowed his gaze.

"Hard?" I snickered and bit down on my bottom lip as I blatantly stared at what I knew was a pretty hard package behind that denim. His eyes heated and I couldn't help but squirm under the direct punch of desire pounding off him in waves.

He was turning me on.

This shoot was making me hot and bothered.

I was connecting with this man on a visceral and emotional level and I hadn't even tasted his kiss yet. It was mind-boggling, the chemistry and heat between us.

"Addy, I'm holding on by a thread here. I'm doing my best to be professional when everything in me wants to lay right on top of you and work that insane body of yours until you're hoarse from screaming my name in nothing but sheer pleasure. Then I want to do it over and over again."

I licked my lips as his blunt words rolled through me making my nipples harden and arousal flood my system. He followed the movement of my tongue with his steely gaze. "That is quite the predicament," I barely whispered.

He stepped off the couch and shook his arms and shoulders and tipped his neck from side to side as if relieving tension. He was mumbling something under his breath that I could just barely hear. It sounded like, "Get it together, Fitz. Do not put your hands or mouth on her."

"Who asked you not to put your hands or mouth on me?" I lifted my chin in affront and put my hands to my hips.

He closed his eyes and dropped his head shaking it steadily. "Addy, you know I want you. I've made that perfectly clear. What you haven't said is whether or not you want me too. You've tossed a few teasing innuendos but I need to hear those exact words…"

Before he continued, I said what he wanted to hear.

"I want you too."

He lifted a hand as though he were going to ward me off. "What?" He frowned.

I smiled. "I want you too. But I'm not the kind of girl that bangs a guy she barely knows."

"Does she kiss a guy she barely knows?" His teeth sunk into his plump bottom lip.

I ginned, lifted my hand, and crooked a finger for him to come to me.

"Oh yeah. I'm absolutely that kind of girl."

Chapter
SIX

THE MAN MOVED AS THOUGH HE WERE GLIDING. HIS FRAME powerful and flickering with energy, filling the air around us in a magnetism I couldn't deny. Didn't want to.

He made it to me. Stood with only an inch between our bodies.

I tried not to squirm. Tried not to be the first one to reach out and take hold.

One of his sandy blond eyebrows rose up his forehead. "I'm here. Kiss me."

A dare.

I licked my lips and his nostrils flared.

Ever so slowly I cupped his furry jaw and traced his top and bottom lip with my thumb in a similar gesture to the one he did with me earlier. He put his hands to my hips, bracketing them and easing me toward him until our bodies were pressed together. I could feel the heat of his breath against my face.

I dipped forward, letting just my lips graze his. He opened his mouth slightly. I flicked out my tongue and it touched the very tip of his. I pulled back at the tiny sizzle of arousal that slid through my form. With my other hand I tunneled my fingers through his glorious hair and cupped the back of his nape. The hair around his mouth tickled my lips and I went to press deeper. Our lips just touched when Brutus barked wildly and barreled our way. He jumped and crashed into us with his mighty paws, both of us tumbling down onto the couch.

"*Nien*, Brutus! What is the matter with you? You have lost your mind, boy!" Killian scolded.

Brutus jumped over our legs and up onto the other side of the couch where I sat panting. He pressed his wiggling body against my side and licked my chin, then the side of my cheek. Laughter rumbled up my chest and I fell into belly-shaking guffaws as Brutus continued to bark excitedly and give me kisses. My neck, my shoulder. Whatever the sweet baby boy could reach.

"Guess we have someone else who plans to claim you." Killian ruffled his dog's head and accepted the lick to his hand. "Your timing could have been better, buddy," he admonished.

A hard knock pounded on the door and the dog instantly went from sweet puppy to vicious killer in two point five seconds. He leapt off the couch and raced to the door barking like mad. He jumped against the wooden surface in a ferocious manner that actually stole the laughter from my lungs and made my hair rise. Brutus snarled and barked as though he would destroy whatever was on the other side that dared knock on his door.

"*Sitz*," Killian commanded, and the dog abruptly sat near the door, growling.

Wow. Apparently, Brutus liking me was a serious fluke. Killian was right. Perhaps I needed to be a bit more careful.

Killian made it across the loft pulling his phone out of

his pocket. He walked to a spot further from the door and pointed. *"Hier, sitz."* He used the same forceful tone and the dog moved to exactly where he pointed and then sat, his body facing the door, ever alert.

"Yeah, I'm coming," he said into the phone then pushed the thing into his back pocket again before opening the door.

Mr. Holt stood with his gun out and at his side. "I heard the dog barking, wanted to check in." He gazed at the dog sitting still as a statue then his gaze lifted and came to me. "You good?"

I nodded and grabbed the robe I'd left on the couch earlier and shoved it on.

"I know you're working and Ms. Jones-Kerrighan did not specify the hours, but it's coming up on six p.m. Omar and Lance have already taken the ladies to Kerrighan House and are now waiting downstairs to take you home."

"Oh, wow. Time really flies. I'll just be a minute!" I called out and dashed to the bathroom, quickly dressing in my jeans, shirt, and flip-flops once more.

I carried the lingerie out and went to the clothing racks and rehung the items. Really, they needed to be washed, especially after things got a little heated during our session, but these would end up being mine to keep. Another thing about having an insanely talented fashion designer sister was I got to keep the clothes I modeled for her. Not usually the case with the other designers I did shoots for.

"I'm ready, I'm ready." I flip-flopped my way to the guys and skipped them all together and went over to Brutus and crouched down, putting my arms around his solid form. His tail started to flap against the wood floors. "Okay, you be a good baby for your daddy." I kissed his snout a few times and petted his head. "I'll see you soon. Maybe I can bring you a treat?" I lifted my gaze to Killian who had his arms crossed over his beautiful chest and was shaking his head with a wicked grin plastered across his handsome face.

"He's not allowed to eat people food unless it's meat or veggies. Healthy stuff."

"Ah, does he get to have dog treats?" I asked.

His lips twitched. "Yeah, if they're organic."

"You give your dog organic food? Mama Kerri is going to love you." I grinned.

"If that's your mother, I look forward to meeting her," he commented brazenly, insinuating that he'd be all for a meeting with the parents even though we'd just met ourselves.

A niggle of fear mixed with excitement alongside antic-ipation blasted through me. Meeting the parents was a big deal. I'd know since there'd never been a man I found wor-thy enough to meet the woman who raised me. My sisters at bars and events, sure. Not Mama Kerri. For some reason me and the rest of my foster sisters treated Kerrighan House and our foster mother as our sacred haven. Only boyfriends, or girlfriends in Charlie's case, were invited over after a good period of dating had been completed. We weren't going to bring guys that we simply dated in and out of each other's lives. Which is why Jonah's pretty much the only man seen regularly around our family. Except of course Ryan has been tagging along quite a lot, but I attributed that to him being so closely connected to Jonah.

"Um...I don't know about that," I murmured and stood.

"Can we have a minute alone?" Killian asked my bodyguard.

One side of Mr. Holt's lip curled up and he lifted his chin then shut the door. Before I could respond, Killian reached for my wrist and pulled me toward him. He wrapped his arms around me and held me in his arms, loosely. He didn't go for my mouth or resume what had started not long ago in front of the couch, which I kind of wish he'd do, but no longer felt bold enough to suggest. The moment had been broken and I felt weird and out of sorts, wanting to leave and get my head together to go over everything that happened.

"We on for tomorrow? We have eleven more outfits to shoot and I have some ideas," he said running his hands up and down my back in a soothing move that made me melt against him naturally. I pushed my hands into his hair and let my fingers run through the silky strands several times getting to know the feel, weight, and thickness of his beautiful locks.

He crossed his hands and rested his wrists against my lower back above my bum.

I eased my head away so I could see his face. We both stood there staring into one another's eyes. My greenish blue to his light brown.

"I had a good time today and honestly that's a miracle. A testament to how comfortable you made me feel, especially under the circumstances. Thank you." I wanted him to know what today meant for me without being too gushy and girly.

He smiled and it made his entire face light up.

"Me too. Same time tomorrow?"

I nodded. "Well, probably. We're going to have to check in with the FBI. Cameron's schedule, and all of that. I'll know more when I catch up with Blessing tonight back at Kerrighan House."

"You're staying there?"

"All of us are."

He frowned. "All of your sisters, your mother, and…"

"Probably Jonah who you met and his partner Ryan. And Rory, my niece. And Amber of course." I grinned looking forward to playing fetch in the backyard with the goofy golden retriever. *I should get a dog,* I thought for the thousandth time, but dogs and travel weren't conducive to one another. I couldn't get a dog and then pawn him or her off on one of my sisters or a dog-sitter or even a boarder when I needed to travel for work.

"Full house." He set his hands to my hips. "How many sisters do you have again?" he asked.

"There's Sonia the Senator of Illinois as you probably found out when you looked me up."

He nodded.

"Her blood-related younger sister Simone. You've met Blessing. Then of course there's Liliana, Genesis who has a child named Rory. Then Charlotte who goes by Charlie and won't answer to Charlotte unless Mama Kerri is chastising her. And then you uh…know about Tabitha who passed away."

He lifted his hand and cupped the back of my head bringing me into a full body hug. "I'm sorry, baby. Didn't mean to bring up your loss again. I just want to know you better."

"And what about you?" I teased.

"For the most part, I'm an open book."

I eased away and tugged my purse further up on my shoulder. "Somehow I doubt that."

He shrugged and grinned. "Try me."

"Maybe I will. I'll bet there are some secrets to uncover."

His eyes heated once more and then he rubbed his hands together. "You've got my information and I've got yours. Text or call me tonight with the plan for tomorrow. I'll be here whether it's early or late. Just give me a heads up."

I stepped forward again and let my hands lie flat against his chest, resting on his mighty pecs. On instinct, I lifted up on my toes and kissed his cheek just above the beard before letting go abruptly and walking backward to the door. "Today was fun." I put my hand to the knob.

"Yes, it was. See you tomorrow, Addy."

"Bye, Fitz." I used his nick name, feeling more comfortable doing so now that we'd hugged, touched tongues, and spent a pretty great day together, considering. I waved and opened the door, and was greeted by Mr. Holt who was already holding the elevator door open.

Within minutes I was in the back of the Escalade and tearing down the streets of Chicago headed toward Oak Park where Kerrighan House was located.

The very second I entered Kerrighan House I was bumrushed by a sultry blonde bombshell. Simone's body slammed me against the wooden door as her arms wrapped around me so tight, I could barely breathe. She shook in my arms and I gripped onto her, suddenly scared something had happened.

"Si, honey, what's the matter?" I cooed into her ear softly.

"I-I...I just needed to see you. You took so freakin' long

to come home and I got scared, and then I thought…" her body positively vibrated against me, her fear a palpable thing.

I held her close for a long couple minutes looking at the big U-shape sectional and noticing Jonah with his head in his hands, elbows to his knees, their dog right next to his side keeping vigil. He lifted his head, and his dark brown eyes came to mine, concern coating his chiseled features, his square jaw firm and unrelenting.

"Everything okay?" I asked fearful that perhaps there was more happening in the case.

Jonah stood and made it to where Simone was literally clinging to me. "Let her go, baby. She's fine." He put one hand to her back, the other to her hand. "Addy got home safely from work as expected," he reminded her while using his fingers to pry her death-grip off my shoulder. She pulled back and her blue eyes were ravaged with worry as they soaked in every inch of my face.

"You're okay?" she asked.

I cupped her cheek. "Today was a good day. I had a blast taking pictures and it was all wonderful. No problems." I felt it wise not to bring up my trigger moment seeing the gun or the horrifying story Killian shared with me.

"No problems," she repeated. "You're okay."

"Yep, perfect as a peach but hungry as a hippo!" I teased making reference to the game we all used to spend hours playing until it drove Mama Kerri bonkers with the noise of the slapping plastic hippo mouths as they clamped to eat the white balls.

"Soup's on!" Mama called from the direction of the kitchen.

I inhaled the smell of Mexican food and my mouth watered.

I smiled wide. "Is the Sprite cooking with Mama?" I didn't hide the hope in my tone. Liliana was an amazing cook. She'd taken it upon herself to learn how to make Mexican food, something her and her biological mother did before she died and the Sprite showed up here at nine years old. Her meals were restaurant quality, and I could not wait to fill my belly!

Simone blinked a few times as though trying to clear her mind of the worry and fear and switch gears. She smiled back and nodded excitedly. "Oh yeah. Apparently, she pissed off her bodyguard, so she's angry-cooking."

I hooked Simone around the shoulders and bumped Jonah playfully until he chuckled, the concern of Simone's response to my being later than normal disappearing with every second that passed.

"We should poke the Sprite more often. Every time she's mad we eat so well." The smells of chilies and rice filtered through the air. I rubbed at my growling belly realizing the only thing I'd eaten were the two cookies that morning.

Together Simone and I went to the kitchen where I found what I'd hoped. Liliana at the stove fluffing a huge batch of Spanish rice. Three glass nine-by-twelve-inch trays of what I knew were enchiladas smoldered on the counter-top covered in foil. Mama Kerri was at the counter mixing a family-sized salad.

"Those tomatoes from the garden?" I asked conversationally, letting Simone go and heading to Mama Kerri.

She studiously tossed the greens and veggies in the large wooden bowl. I leaned over and kissed her cheek.

"Just picked these beauties this afternoon along with a fresh yellow squash," she boasted.

Mami Kerri was like a whimsical garden savant. The backyard looked like something out of a movie. Lush green trees, a sun garden, a greenhouse, and more. Three times she'd turned down both Blessing and I pushing her to submit pictures of her work to home and garden magazines. Claimed her bragging rights were her family eating healthy greens she'd grown herself and reminding us that her backyard would be a perfect place to get married. Something she'd started suggesting recently to Simone and Jonah whenever they were in attendance together at a family dinner or gathering.

Apparently, Jonah was all for tying the knot, but Simone was still skittish and wanted to live together for a year in their home first. Smart move if you asked me. Since Jonah just wanted Simone happy, he relented. Much to Mama Kerri's dismay. The woman wanted more grandchildren and reminded us she wasn't getting any younger, but we were most certainly getting older and should start settling down. None of that prevented us sisters from entering into a secret pool about when Simone and Jonah would get engaged. I'd been forced to contribute because betting wasn't my thing, and I'd chosen their one-year anniversary.

"This looks so yum, Mama," I cooed and patted her back before moving behind Liliana to look over her shoulder.

"Whoa, refried beans too? Who do I have to thank for pissing you off?" I wrapped my arm around Liliana's waist, and she leaned back letting me give her a hug before she groaned.

"That stupid *gran idiota*," she hissed.

"Big idiot eh? Sounds like fighting words." I leaned against the counter and waited for Liliana to explode.

She stirred the beans rather viciously and I bit my tongue to hold back my laughter.

"So, he told me to stay put. What? *No soy un perro.* I don't think so, big man!" she barked.

"I only caught a little bit of that, Lil. Something about treating you like a dog?" I gathered.

She held up a wooden spoon toward my face as though it were a weapon. Her coffee-colored eyes were blazing white-hot fire and her curls were bouncing all around her cheeks with her jerky movements. She was beautiful normally, but angry...watch out. Her high cheekbones boasted a rosy tinge, and her lips were a bruised dark burgundy, probably from biting on them so often in her fury.

"He left me in the car when he went to pick up Charlie at the Center," she spat.

The Center referred to the charitable youth center that Charlie ran which worked to help wayward kids, especially those dealing with their sexuality, gender issues, abusive or nonexistent parents, runaways, and more. Charlie often worked with Genesis who was a social worker managing a huge caseload. Both of them had degrees in child development.

"Okay, so why is that a problem?" I treaded lightly not wanting to make her angrier, not that I thought that was possible.

"She gave him the slip." Charlie snorted as she entered from the backyard where they'd probably been playing with Amber and Rory. I watched as she set an empty beer bottle on the counter and headed to the fridge.

Mmm…beer and enchiladas sounded heavenly. My stomached growled loudly.

"I did not give him the slip! *¡Mierda!*" Now the word *shit* I knew. Everyone in this house knew all the Spanish curse words courtesy of growing up with our girl.

"Cursing in Spanish is not acceptable either, Liliana." Mama Kerri turned her head and looked at the Sprite over her glasses.

"*Lo siento.*" She mumbled *sorry* before setting the spoon in the holder and lifting the pot and setting it on a cooling rack next to the enchiladas. "I remembered I needed a new mascara and Mama had mentioned needing some Epsom salts, so I left the car to visit the Walgreen's across the street. I knew it would only take a few minutes. Honestly, I thought I could make it back before he did with Charlie. You know how she's always dragging her feet."

I pressed my lips together really hard. I knew the laughter was going to roll out of me any second.

"Don't put your bad behavior on me, sister! Besides, I do not drag my feet! I run the entire center, Lil. It takes time to close down a building and make sure everyone is out for the day and night." She flicked the lid off her fresh beer and held it aloft pointing the neck of the beer at Liliana. "Don't pull me into your crap because you got a talkin' to by a hot guy and you're embarrassed."

"A talkin' to?" I asked, now super-interested in what went down.

Liliana glared at Charlie and then turned to me, hands on hips, attitude at a hundred degrees Fahrenheit. "*El idiota arrogante* yelled at me the entire way home. Telling *me,*" she pointed at her chest with dramatic flair, "how I made bad decisions and could have been hurt or hurt *mi hermana.* I did no such thing. I went to the store. For five minutes!"

"Well, not saying that you were wrong or anything, but he was hired to keep you safe. You leaving the car probably freaked him out pretty bad, no?"

She narrowed her pretty eyes. "Are you on his side?"

I shook my head and lifted my hand in a placating gesture in front of me in order to ease her ire before she took away my ability to eat her awesome food. She could be scrappy like that. "Nope, not even close. I'm just saying it takes time getting used to having a bodyguard and the guys Blessing hired are serious about their jobs. Just this morning Blessing and I got our own talking to. So, you aren't the only one."

She tipped her head to the side. "You were yelled at too?"

I nodded. "Yep."

"Hmmph. Blessing should give a call to those jerks' bosses. I mean, she's the client, not them."

I did not think it was a good time to tell her my guard was the boss. It would do no good.

"Jerk isn't a curse word, but it isn't pretty, chicklet," Mama warned getting out a stack of plates and setting them on the counter where the rest of the food was laid out.

This was also when Jonah entered the conversation. "Actually, right now I'm going to take the position of ensuring all of your safety." Simone cuddled up against her man's side, arms around his waist and back so her head could rest on his chest where he stood.

"We're going to have to get on the same page. Each and every one of you needs to be protected. Thankfully, I was able to smooth over the security issue with our chief but only because Blessing happened to hire a team that not only has one of the highest success rates in the biz, but they are also on retainer with the FBI. The bureau will be taking over the contract and all of you will start following our rules. What happened to that girl was horrible and after what went down with Wayne Gilbert Black, we're not taking any chances with any of your safety. Are we all on board or do we need to hash this out further?"

I shrugged. "I'll do what I'm told. As long as I can continue working, I won't go mad. I'm happy to have a bodyguard. Mr. Holt, though scary and rough around the edges, was very respectful of giving me space to work."

Jonah nodded.

"After dinner I'll sit with each of you and get all of your schedules for the week so we can assign the security team accordingly."

Genesis, Blessing, and Rory entered through the back door along with a bouncing Amber who had a bright green tennis ball in her mouth.

"Auntie Addy!" Rory squealed and raced her little feet across the floor until she slammed into my legs. She hugged me and looked up at me while I put my hand to her bouncy dark curls. "Can I play dwess up wit you?" Her incredible amber eyes were huge and filled with joy. I soaked up every ounce of her love, beauty, and innocence.

"After dinner we can totally play dress up. But I want to be the princess!" I demanded haughtily.

She nodded. "I'll be Queen."

"I heard that." Blessing complimented Rory, a note of pride in her words. "Never be the princess when you can be Queen, sugar," she boasted.

I rolled my eyes, dipped my head, and kissed Rory's

forehead, then lifted her up and put the almost four-year-old on my hip. She immediately started to play with my long hair, running her fingers through it in a way that was uniquely her. Rory played with all of our hair and maybe it was because her mama was always teasing her own curls or maybe it was her way to connect personally with an individual. I thought maybe it meant she'd be a hairdresser one day. I could use free haircuts for sure.

Gen plopped onto the bench seat and I sat down next to her with Rory in my lap, content to play with my hair and watch everyone move around the kitchen readying to eat.

"You look tired, Gen." I noted the purple smudges under her eyes.

She yawned, covering her mouth. "Yeah, it's hard to sleep in a bed with a four-year-old that kicks like she's having night terrors but is actually sleeping merrily."

"I'm sorry you have to stay here again. It's all my fault."

Gen twisted to face me. "Addy, none of this is anyone's fault, least of all you. No one has the right to taunt or hurt others the way this person is. I'm more worried about you with this being so soon after the other thing," she said softly, her words chosen only for me to hear.

I sighed and Rory climbed off my lap and pranced over to where Blessing was stealing tomatoes from the salad. She held her hand up and Blessing stole one and handed it to our niece who acted as though she'd stolen a cookie.

"I'm good, really." Before I could say another word, Mama Kerri put two steaming hot plates full of enchiladas, beans, and rice before us.

Both of us looked at our plates, picked up a fork, and dug in without further conversation. Food before drama.

Always. We'd come back to it later as we did with everything else in our lives.

Mama set plates down all over the table and each of my family members took a spot. Rory crawled up into her highchair which no longer needed the tray. Mama pushed it to the table and Liliana came up behind her with an already cut up enchilada, beans, and a small bowl of rice with a spoon. Rory filled her spoon with beans and shoved the entire lot into her mouth humming happily.

The only one missing was Sonia who worked late most nights and Tabitha who'd never sit at the table again. My heart squeezed at the thought of Tabby but instead of delving back into that grief, I looked around the table. Mama Kerri at the front, Jonah at the end—the resident male of the family at this current time. Simone next to his side, Charlie next to her, and then Blessing. Me sitting next to Gen and Rory, and Liliana on my other side. Ryan would likely pop in later. I smiled and took in everyone's happy faces and felt blessed. This was the family I'd show the man in my life.

Was that man Killian Fitzpatrick? I guessed only time would tell. I was hopeful though. The chemistry between us was promising. I watched as Rory picked up a bite of chicken and tossed it to Amber who smartly sat next to the highchair to get all the scraps.

"Rory," Genesis warned. "I saw that. No more for Amber."

"Doggie hungry, Mama," she claimed.

"Doggie has a food bowl and can eat any time she wants. That food is for your belly to nourish you so you can be big and tall."

"And a queen," Rory stated serious as a heart attack.

Blessing chuckled. "My girl," she touted loud and proud.

Genesis took a full breath and let it out slowly. "And a Queen."

"Damn straight," Blessing added and plopped a bite of gooey enchilada into her mouth.

"Blessing, seriously?" Mama Kerri chastised her again. "The mouth on my girls." She shook her head. "The world is going to think I've raised a bunch of hoodlums, not successful, intelligent women with wide and vast vocabularies."

"Sorry, Mama." Blessing grinned and then made big eyes at me until I laughed.

"I love my family!" I blurted loudly for the entire table, the gushy feeling in my stomach growing and spreading up my chest to the point where I could no longer contain it.

I heard the door slam in the other room and Jonah stood abruptly, hand to the gun at his hip. Sonia walked in wearing a navy power suit and a smile that slipped off her face as she took in everyone eating. "What, you couldn't wait? I'm like ten minutes late."

"SoSo, you're forty-five minutes late and most of the time you're more than that," Simone clarified.

"What'd I miss?" she asked tossing her briefcase on the counter near the phone and grabbing the plate Mama had already made for her that was covered in tin foil. "Thanks, Mama," she said pulling back the tin foil and tossing it into the recycling.

"Addison loves us," Charlie supplied helpfully.

Sonia smiled and took in my face. Her eyes were the color of the clearest blue sky. "I love you too, sister."

Now that was all I needed. My family. Good food. Laughter. And love.

Oh, and maybe a hunky photographer.

Chapter
SEVEN

THE COVERS SLIPPING BACK AND THE CHILL AIR PIERCING MY skin woke me from an exhausted sleep. I opened my eyes to Simone putting a knee to my childhood full-sized bed and sliding down beside me. I pushed back until my booty hit the wall so she'd have enough room.

She turned to her side and tucked both of her hands in prayer position under her cheek as I covered her up with the comforter.

"Couldn't sleep?" I whispered even though Blessing sleeping in her own bed across the room wouldn't wake. That woman slept the sleep of the dead. You had to scream her name or physically shake her, which is why she had the loudest, most annoying phone alarm in the universe.

Simone shook her head. "Bad dream."

I inhaled slowly and wrapped my arm around her waist keeping our faces close together. "Tell me about it."

She shook her head. "You don't want to know."

"Si, you haven't needed to get in bed with me in an entire month. You've been triggered by that girl being murdered. It's okay to talk about it, because I worry about you too." I reached out and pushed her golden blonde locks off her cheek so I could see her entire face.

Simone licked her lips, and her voice shook when she

spoke. "I was walking through the park at night. I tripped on something and fell. And I came face-to-face with your dead body. Your eyes were open and there were blue rings around your neck."

"Sister, that is not going to happen to me." I ran my fingers through her hair and kept doing it, wanting her to feel my presence as much as hear my words.

"It was so real, Addy. Like Tabby. One moment I was walking along and then, boom, you were dead. I can't survive losing another sister. I think I'd actually go insane." I could hear the pain and desperation blanketing her words.

"How are your therapy sessions going?" I asked, making sure my tone wasn't judgmental. I hadn't brought myself to seek therapy, instead I'd spent the last three months hiding at Mama Kerri's and pretending everything was fine. Using my need to heal as the reason for my time away from work as well as the excuse for not seeing a therapist. Something Mama Kerri urged me to do regularly.

"Fine, I guess. Though I left work early today and went at Jonah's urging. The therapist thinks that seeing you and my family happy and doing well will help, but mostly she feels like it's time alone that will ultimately fix the problem."

"Makes sense."

"You said you had a good day doing the shoot. Blessing told me you had one of your moments when you were with the clients before Jonah and Ryan showed up yesterday. Is it better in private at the photographer's home?"

"Actually, yeah, but if I'm being honest, I had a moment there too."

Her voice rose a little in surprise. "You did?"

"I'm not made of stone." I used the analogy Killian had shared with me earlier.

She smiled. "You always seem like you're just fine. So strong. I feel like a loser compared to you. I wasn't hurt the way you were, and I still have to crawl into bed with you to make sure you're breathing and alive. Check in on you all the time. It's stupid but I can't help it."

I petted her hair some more. "I like that you worry about me. Check on me. Makes me feel more normal when everything still feels so out of whack."

"It really does. And it's like, just when things were starting to feel as though they were going well, and we're trying to move on, we're thrown right back into it all again."

"I know. But you trust Jonah, right?"

"With my life."

"And he loves you more than anything in the world. And he knows your family is all you care about. He's going to do everything in his power to keep me and everyone else safe. You have to have faith he will do as he's been trained."

"Yeah, you're right." She yawned. "Tell me about the photographer. Blessing says he's totally into you and your type. Anything happen today?" I smiled wide and her eyes got bigger and she nudged me. "Tell me! Brat!"

I reached for her hand and held it with my own. "He's ridiculously gorgeous. I'm talking off the charts, the most beautiful man I've ever laid eyes on."

"Whoa, that's huge since you take pictures with models."

I nodded. "He has thick, long hair that falls past his shoulders. It's a light brown-blond tone. He's got a beard and mustache combo thing that gives him that gruff, manly edge."

"Oh, you've always dug guys with facial hair."

"Totally," I breathed. "He's taller than me which is awesome."

"Because you're an Amazon at five foot eleven."

"True."

"What else?" She giggled.

"His body is cut. Like, full six-pack."

"Jonah has a washboard stomach, and I'm telling you, girl, the amount of time I spend running my fingers along it…" She sighed dreamily.

I snorted.

"Wait, how did you see his stomach? Hmmm?" she asked as light bulbs obviously flared in her brain.

"Like I said, I had one of my moments. He helped me through it and then shared some of his own horror stories. He used to be a soldier but more than that, he was a photo-journalist capturing battles and traveling with the Army as they fought overseas. He saw a lot of people die, many who were friends."

"Oh my God, that's awful." Simone squeezed my hand.

"It is. He got hurt. IED. He survived but he has a lot of scars, all over his back. I think he showed me because he didn't want me to feel alone or ugly because of my scars, ya know?"

"Wow. I mean I hate to say that's amazing because it was probably terrifying what he went through, and the losses he sustained immeasurable, but the fact that you have that in common, it's a pretty powerful and an unusual connection. Is there any chemistry there? I mean, romantically?" she asked, hope coating her tone.

I grinned. "Definitely. He's already told me he wants to

date me but of course now that's a bit hard when I'm trying to keep a low profile and have a bodyguard watching me at all times."

She shrugged. "Still, it can be done, as you know from my experience."

"True." I chuckled. "And we did have some sexy photo sessions. At one point I felt…" I shook my head. "No, it's stupid."

She prodded me and lowered her voice to an even deeper whisper. "Tell me. I'm dying to know now."

I took a deep, fortifying breath. "Okay. But I swear if you tell anyone else about this part, I'm going to tell Jonah about that time you pissed your pants screaming at a rock concert and I had to go buy you an XXL men's T-shirt at the stand and give you my belt so you could wear it as a dress."

Her entire body jerked, and she narrowed her gaze. "You wouldn't dare…" she hissed.

"I so would if you share what I'm about to tell you." I lifted my hand and held out my pinky.

"Fine, but this better be good." She hooked her pinky with mine and we kept them locked while I told her my truth.

"Okay, at one point the photos weren't working for him. So he moved us to his comfy couch. We got into it and I started feeling, you know, sexy."

"As you should because you're freakin' hot."

"Thank you. But when I say I got into it, I got really into it. At one point he was straddling my form and taking pictures of me from above. I got so turned on I know my panties were damp."

"Oh shit! What did you do? Did you sleep with him? Tell

me you slept with him!" She let out the question in a gush of air.

I scrunched up my nose. "No, I didn't sleep with him, but I did start kind of showing off and acting overtly sexy like I was…" I groaned. "Like I was making love to him through the camera. Showing myself off and teasing him."

"Holy hell." She fanned herself. "That gives me ideas for private time with Jonah. Then what happened?"

"Well, after he adjusted his very large erection…"

"Oh shit," she snickered.

"Yeah, *very* large," I repeated because it was worth repeating. It was that big. "I told him that I didn't have sex with strangers."

"Boooooooo. If there was ever a time to let loose and live a little Addy, this was it."

I shook my head. Simone was forever the risk-taker. Always ready to live fast and hard in all the ways that could be taken. I knew that me and the rest of the women in my family were beyond thrilled she'd found herself a structured, rooted man who could keep her wild side in check.

I groaned. "Don't start with me about living big. I'll have you know I did kiss him…kinda."

She frowned. "What do you mean kinda? You either kissed him or you didn't."

"Well, we were about to, and our lips were barely touching and then we touched tongues for a split second before his dog jumped us, knocking us onto the couch, and then my bodyguard freaked out and banged on the door at which the dog lost his mind at the possibility of needing to protect us."

Simone put her hand over her mouth and laughed so hard she shook the entire bed.

I sighed loudly. "Can you go back to your own bed now?"

"That's what I'm here to do." I heard Jonah rumble from the doorway of my shared room with Blessing. He wore a pair of plaid pajama bottoms and nothing else. His nicely cut chest on full display. Dang, Simone was not wrong. Her man had a killer body.

"Simone, we agreed you'd wake me up and we'd talk about why you felt you needed to see your sister, and here you are, back in her bed. Another man would get a complex when his woman prefers the company of her sister in bed with her over him," he said in a teasing tone.

I nudged Simone and she sat up. "Sorry, babe. I had a bad dream. Needed to see her." Her entire form slumped with the admission.

He cupped her around the nape and lifted her chin with his thumb until she looked into his eyes. "You better now?" His voice sweet and filled with compassion.

"Yeah." She turned to me. "Thanks for the talk, and the laughter."

"Remember what I said…"

She grinned. "I hope tomorrow brings more good things with your hunky photographer."

I smiled and put the covers up to my chin. "Me too."

"Hunky photographer?" Jonah murmured.

Simone wrapped her arm around Jonah's waist. "I'll tell you about it later."

Smiling, I closed my eyes and was out in minutes, dreaming about said hunky photographer.

The morning brought absolute chaos. Blessing forgot to set her alarm, so we were both awakened by Mama Kerri telling us that our bodyguards were not so patiently waiting in the kitchen drinking coffee. Since I had Cameron to beautify me and I showered last night, I let Blessing have the bathroom and the last of the hot water for herself.

I tossed on a pretty navy dress that had tiny little flowers on it and one-inch-thick shoulder straps. It had an awesome corset-style bodice that was woven into the fabric, so my boobs were lifted and looking voluptuous as all get out. I added a thin white cardigan to hide the scars and slipped my feet into a pair of bright white Keds-style shoes that were actually Kate Spade. I'd accidentally walked off a fashion shoot wearing the shoes and had called my agent, who in turn notified the client, but they told me to keep them. Rich people didn't stay rich by being spenders. They stayed rich by holding onto their money and investing smartly. To me, this meant I got a free pair of cute tennis shoes and a fat paycheck for the job.

With quick feet I dashed down the stairs and was not only met by Mr. Holt, Lance, Jonah, and Ryan, but also a frowning Mama Kerri who was busily making tea and putting out cookies.

Tea and cookies meant bad news.

"What's going on?" I asked shoving my wild hair out of my face.

Jonah's jaw was tight, and his face set at grim. "Come here, Addy. We need to have a talk."

"I need to get to work…" I wanted to shove whatever the hell it was as far away as possible and put my head firmly in the sand where no one could hurt me.

"Baby girl." Mama wrapped her arm around my shoulders and led me to the kitchen table where we'd had an amazing family dinner filled with love and laughter just last night. I wanted instantly to go back to that. She then retreated and got me a cup of tea and a plate of cookies.

I closed my eyes knowing whatever was coming was going to be very bad.

"When was the last time you've been to your apartment?" Jonah asked sitting next to me.

My apartment. "Um, I don't know... Maybe a couple months? After the situation, I went back to get most of my clothing and essentials, but I've not been there since."

"You haven't been back to your place in months? What about your mail?"

"I had it forward here. Why?"

Jonah looked at Ryan and then reached out and took my hand. Mama Kerri cuddled against my back and my heart started to pound an erratic beat.

"I'm so sorry to tell you this, Addy. Last night neighbors complained to the super that the floor of your building stunk to high heaven. They narrowed it down to your apartment. The super went in to check it out. No one had seen you in a while and they suspected that you weren't there. They uh... Sweetheart, they found another murdered woman."

I jerked back but Mama held on. "What?!" I gasped.

Jonah held my hand between both of his. "She's been there a while, Addy. At least a month according to the coroner's initial findings last night. Her purse was there so we know her identity and she looks very similar to you. Not only that, but we also found clothes lying next to her body that had been torn. The body was dressed in something that we believe was yours."

"Wh-what?" I couldn't even comprehend what they were saying.

"She'd been strangled just like the others and burnt with cigarettes up and down her inner forearms just like you. Based on the estimated time of the murder, we believe she was killed and left for you to find. Since you didn't go back to your apartment, the killer didn't catch your attention. Then he killed Hillary Johnson, the woman in the park, making a more public attempt to get your notice."

I closed my eyes as my body shook. "I-I don't know what to say."

Mama Kerri tucked me to her side. "You don't have to say anything, baby girl." She wrapped her arms around me, and I held on. Instead of tears, I went completely numb. Shock being the prevailing feeling setting in.

Jonah ran his hand up and down my arm from shoulder to elbow. "Do you know a woman by the name of Alison Wills? She was a receptionist at a law firm downtown. Maybe you crossed paths with her in the city or for work?"

I shook my head, the name not ringing a bell at all.

"Okay, I know this is hard to hear and you need some time to process but, sweetheart, we're going to need to take you to your apartment."

I jolted in my mother's arms and shook my head. "Nut uh. Not going back there." I was firmly in the Simone camp. She didn't step foot in her apartment after her friend Katrina was found murdered in her home and I was taking a fat page out of her playbook.

"Addy, we need to know what might have been taken,

if anything. The body won't be there. I can make sure the scary stuff is covered up, but you're the only one who would know if something important was missing. Often serial killers take trophies, like the family photo that Wayne Gilbert Black took from Simone's house. That led us to understand that he was going after you Kerrighan sisters. It's an important part of the investigation."

I shook my head and pushed away then I stood up abruptly. "Is that all?"

Jonah frowned and Mama worried her fingers.

"For now, yeah, honey. That's all we know."

"I need to get to work," I stated flatly not allowing even a speck of emotion to enter my person. I was not prepared mentally or physically to deal with this new tragedy and all I could think about was getting the heck away from these guys and this case and going back to Killian's where I felt safe and protected from all this nastiness.

"Chicklet, do you really think you should go to work today?" Mama Kerri asked softly in that knowing maternal tone that sunk deep into the heart of my fear.

"Blessing is counting on me," I said with zero emotion.

"Blessing will understand," Mama offered.

"No, I need to go." I looked at Mr. Holt. "Am I with you today?"

He nodded curtly.

"Can we go now?" I asked.

"Yeah, Ms. Michaels-Kerrighan. We can go now. I parked in the back alley so we can avoid the paparazzi."

"Wonderful," I said as though it was anything but. "I'm ready now."

"But you haven't eaten or anything…" Mama fussed.

I held out my hand. "I just…need to go."

"Addy…" Jonah sighed. "When can we take you back to your apartment?"

I winced at his request. "I don't know. I need to think. Give me a little time."

"You've got it." He put his hands in his pockets and looked at me with those sad, dark eyes. "And you know, we're all here for you. Simone, me. Ryan. Your family. You're not alone in this."

He was wrong. I absolutely was alone in this. It was *my* apartment that was violated. *My* clothing that the killer put his victim in. *My* torture that he'd reenacted on two innocent women so far.

It was my fault those women were dead.

I was the problem.

I needed to get out of there.

Get away from it all.

"Can we go now?" I asked a second time.

Mr. Holt nodded and I followed him out the back door.

We drove in complete silence into the heart of Chicago, the city abuzz this early in the morning. Mr. Holt didn't say a word, leaving me to my peace. He parked in the same empty accessible spot as before closest to the elevator in Killian's building.

He led me out of the elevator, and I stood there woodenly as he knocked on the door.

Killian opened the door wearing another pair of jeans and a black T-shirt this time that set off his lighter hair brilliantly. His welcoming smile died the second he took in my face.

He reached for my hand and pulled me inside.

Brutus was barking like mad in the laundry room and I could tell that Cameron hadn't actually showed yet because the bathroom door was open and the light off.

"I'm going to do my rounds," Mr. Holt stated, and I watched as Killian nodded, then turned to me. "What's the matter?"

I blinked and just stared at his face. Not capable of saying much of anything. The numbness was soaking into my body, heart, and soul. There was nothing left of me to give. Not even my words.

He stared into my face for long minutes. His jaw firmed and his eyes flashed with annoyance. "Stay here," he commanded and then stormed away in the direction that my guard headed.

I didn't stay where he told me to. I moved over to one of the big windows facing Lake Michigan. There I stood, holding my cardigan wrapped tightly to my chest and watching the waves crash against the shore and the white boats dotting the surface in the distance.

"Jesus. You're fucking shaking like a leaf," Killian said coming up behind me and placing a chenille blanket over my shoulders. "You're not working today and you're not going home. I'm keeping you here with me. You need some fucking space from the shitshow."

Again, I didn't speak. Even when he turned me to face him tucking the blanket more securely around my body.

"I'm going to call Blessing and have her cancel Cameron and tell your family where you're at. Mr. Holt updated me on what happened. You're not going anywhere, especially that fuckin' apartment."

My lips trembled as I stared into the prettiest, most kind

eyes I'd ever seen. This man was worried about me. Angry on my behalf. His sole concern was me and my well-being. Nothing else mattered. And he took charge. Taking care of me the only way he knew how, by doing it himself.

That was when I broke.

Shattered.

Burst into tears.

He pulled me into his arms and let me cry. I did so for a long time. Not saying a word, just crying until I couldn't cry anymore. When my tears turned to snuffles against his powerful frame and warm chest, he eased me back so he could look at me.

"I'm going to make you a hot toddy. Whiskey, tea, and honey. All of that sound okay?"

I nodded.

"Okay." He led me over to the comfy brown couch and got me settled. I cuddled into the corner, tucking the blanket around me tighter. He reached for a remote and pressed a couple buttons. A whirring sound entered the space and a white projection screen like at the movies popped down from a hanging box in the ceiling I hadn't noticed before. Movement behind caught my attention, and I turned to see the window turning darker inch by inch. It was as if there were blinds or some type of dark screen inside the window casings that shut out the bright white daylight.

The room darkened, and I sighed.

He knelt down near me and handed me a TV remove. "This is the same as normal ones, it just looks intimidating. There's the power button, the guide button to pick a show, and of course you've got your volume up and down, channel up and down, and the numbers to use if you know what channel you want to watch. I've got Netflix, Hulu, and all the normal stuff. Pick your poison while I make you a drink."

"Okay," I croaked, finally using my voice.

He cupped my cheek. "Is there anything else that I can get you that would make you more comfortable? Anything in the world, Addy. You want it, I'll get it."

"Brutus," I whispered.

He smiled and nodded. "Of course. I'm offering her the world on a string and she wants my dog. Lucky guy," he teased and walked barefooted across the long open expanse toward the laundry room door, his phone already to his ear.

Brutus popped out of the door wagging his tail at his daddy. He pointed to me and the dog looked my way. I waved.

"*Pass auf,* Brutus." He spoke in German, but I didn't know the words he'd said. Something like the word guard or watch. I only knew a small number of German words because I'd done a lot of modeling in Germany. I picked up a few things, but not specifics such as dog commands.

Brutus ran to me then jumped up on the couch, turned his body, and sat right next to me. I wrapped my arms around him and snuggled his form, but he didn't lie down which I thought was odd, but I was still happy.

"*Platz,*" Killian called out and the dog lie down, head in my lap, yet I could tell he was still alert.

"Yeah, she's here. I've got her," I heard Killian say while futzing around in his kitchen. I saw him set the kettle under the water and then put it on the stove. "You need to cancel Cameron. She's in no shape to model today." He moved to a cabinet and pulled out a bottle of Jameson and then went to another cabinet where he got a huge mug and then a bear-shaped plastic jar of honey.

I petted Brutus, allowing the comfort of the sweet boy to seep into my chilled and frightened body.

"I said I've got her. She's not coming back today. Blessing, the woman is traumatized." He frowned. "No, she needs a break from all of it and I'm going to give it to her." He squeezed some honey into the cup, not being stingy with the golden nectar which I appreciated, especially if he wasn't going to put sugar in the tea too.

"Who am I? The man in her life." He fired back in a tone that brooked no argument.

"Fine, you may be right," he amended to whatever flack she threw his way. Probably something pretty choice after he claimed to be the man in my life. Blessing would know that was not in fact the case, no matter what I said about him being a hot guy who wanted to date me.

"Then I'm the man who *wants* to be in her life. The man who's gonna work for that honor. But today, I'm going to be the man who takes care of her and helps her through this new tragedy. For now, just cancel the fucking hairdresser and when she's settled and feels like talking, I'll have her check in with you. Cool?"

He nodded. "I'll make sure she eats. Yeah, got it. I don't care. Call me every hour on the hour but if she doesn't want to talk to anyone, I'm not going to make her. Listen, I can tell you're concerned. I am too. Right now, the best thing for Addy is to take a load off. Watch some mindless TV, eat some food, rest, and give herself some time to understand all that's happened and how it affects her."

The tea kettle whistled, and he laughed. "Deal. I'll take care of her. And no, I won't take advantage. Jesus, what the hell kind of men have you sisters been dating?"

I actually felt a bubble of laughter float up my throat and out my mouth as I snuggled Brutus and watched Killian fight my sister over the phone and make me tea.

What the hell kind of world was I living in was a better question.

Figuring Killian would work it out with Blessing I pushed against the couch until I was lying down. Brutus adjusted and settled right in front of me. I wrapped my arm around his beefy, stout frame and pointed the remote at the TV clicking on Netflix.

Immediately I saw a show that focused on people making blown glass. It looked interesting and nowhere near the craziness of what my life had begun.

I clicked on the first episode and hit play.

Chapter
EIGHT

"WHOO HOO! THE CHICK WON THE ENTIRE SHOW! How cool is that!" I fist-pumped the air when the show's announcer proclaimed the female glass blower the victor. "Rock on!" I shimmied, smiling.

Killian rolled his eyes. "Her work was incredible, but I really could have taken some unique photos of that Pozniak guy's work. The earth connection was inspired."

I shrugged. "True. I wasn't fan of the whole meat gig in glass format but she's a woman working in a world occupied primarily by men. And she kicked some ass overall. She earned her place."

Killian stood up and stretched his long frame, hands high in the air. I couldn't help but stare at his midsection as a sexy slip of hard male abdominal muscles came into view as his T-shirt rode up.

"Take a picture. It will last longer," he teased with a grin that made my lady bits throb.

"Give me one of your cameras and I will!" I shot back playfully.

He chuckled and rubbed at his stomach. "I'm hungry. You?"

"Yeah." I ran my hand over Brutus's burly frame. He

hadn't left me all morning or through our entire binge of the glass blowing competition show.

"Well get your ass up and into the kitchen so we can make a meal."

I laughed and unlocked my legs from the blanket and padded to the center of the huge loft where the kitchen was.

"You mean you're not going to cook for me? The damsel in distress?" I put my hand to my chest and laid on the drama.

He grinned. "I am and I will, but you're going to help. Cooking is more fun with two people."

"Guess that's true. What do you have in mind?"

"Homemade pizza?"

My mouth started watering. "I love pizza." I gestured to my not-small shape. "Obviously."

His golden-brown gaze traced my form, stopped on my tits, and then came back up to my face. "And everything you got is exactly what turns me the fuck on," he stated boldly. "I like something to hold on to. Something soft and generous pressed up against me at night. All that is you," he lifted his hand up and down, "is my fucking dream woman."

My cheeks heated. "Are you always so honest and forthcoming?"

"Yeah, I am. When I see what I like or want, I go after it with everything inside me. My parents taught me to work hard, set goals, and to not stop until I achieved them."

"And you apply that philosophy to all things in life. Including your women?"

He opened the fridge and pulled out a wad of what looked to be dough protected in plastic wrap.

"I don't believe in games. I don't believe in dating

a bunch of women at the same time. And I don't bring women to my home with the intent to get something out of them and toss them aside once I've gotten it."

"Ah, so you're a gentleman as well as a brute."

He smiled. "I like that analogy. That I'll take. Really, I just treat women with the same respect I expect from them. I've had bad experiences. A lot of the time, if a woman finds out my work history before we connect on a personal level, they either go after me for the money, or they find out I'm a vet and want to fix me."

"Do you need to be fixed?" I asked leaning against the counter not more than five feet from where he'd set the lump of dough.

"Don't we all have something within us that needs a soft touch? I'm not claiming to be perfect, Addy. There's a lot you don't know about me. I'm just saying I'm not attracted to you for any other reason than you're gorgeous, you have sad eyes that I want to make shine with happiness, and I see something in you that calls to me. Kindred spirit. Call it what you want."

"We're both broken," I surmised.

He shrugged a shoulder and pulled out two large wooden cutting boards. "Maybe. I think that just means we can understand the other person better than someone else. What I can say is I haven't wanted to spend private time with a woman in a romantic capacity since shortly after returning just over a year ago." He yanked off a hair tie he had around his wrist and I watched fascinated as he pulled that awesome hair up, ran it through his fingers, and tied it into a low ponytail.

My mouth watered for a different reason and I had to

squeeze my thighs together at the visual. God, I wanted to climb him like a tree. Instead, I gripped the edges of the counter and held on tight, making sure I didn't do what I'd envisioned.

He moved over to the sink next to me and washed his hands. "Clean up, we're going to be working the dough," he bossed.

Still having lost my train of thought since it was on jumping him, I did as he said without a snarky retort to his bossiness.

He set the cutting boards next to one another and reached for a glass canister that I could see had flour in it. He shook a handful onto my surface and repeated the process on his own. Then he slapped a fat chunk of dough on my board and then his.

Without asking, I started to flatten my dough, having the general idea of what I needed to do, not that I'd done it before. I watched him flatten and mold the concoction into a pizza shape with an ease that spoke of familiarity with the task.

"What happened when you tried to date early on when you returned?" I asked, feeling nosy. If we were going to get to know one another, we needed to ask the tough questions.

He sighed. "At first I thought I could drown the pain away in booze and women. I'd have one of my nightmares in their presence and they'd either freak out or, like I said, want to fix me. At the time, there was nothing that could fix me. I needed support. I needed to talk about it all even though it hurt every fucking second to breathe. Knowing the people I cared about weren't breathing right along with me screwed with my head regularly."

I pushed and patted at my dough, but it didn't look as good as his. I needed a rolling pin. "My sisters talk about Tabby all the time. Every single time they say her name I want to run away."

He nodded. "I did that too. It hurts thinking about those we lost. It hurts a fuck ton but making it as if they never existed hurts worse. That's what I learned in my support groups down at Veterans Affairs. They have weekly meetings."

"And you go to them?"

"Didn't at first. Like I said. Drowning my sorrows in booze and women. It was either that or booze and fighting. Which I also tried a time or two."

"Yikes, that doesn't sound helpful."

He shook his head. "It wasn't. Then one of my brothers in arms, Atticus, who also made it out, decided to move here to be close to me. He got me to go to meetings. We're tight. Brought up in the same unit and even when I branched out to photojournalism, I stayed with the team. Mostly because I could fight, but also I was there to share the experience, and the guys wanted people to know what was happening. What they were fighting for. And I was determined to shed light on it. On their sacrifice."

"Until the sacrifice took too much of you," I whispered and stared at his profile.

He closed his eyes and dropped his chin toward his chest. "Until it took too much. Exactly." His sharp gaze cut to mine. "How do you do that?"

"Do what?" I whispered.

"Reach inside and find my truth? Understand what's so hard to put into words?"

"Pain knows pain. I have an amazing life, but it wasn't always that way." I looked around his fancy loft that I knew was worth millions. "You have all this but at what cost?"

Lightning fast, his flour-covered hand cupped the back of my head and his lips crashed down over mine. He took me by such surprise I opened my mouth on instinct and he took the opening with his warm tongue. I melted against him, my dirty hands wrapping around his broad shoulders. I tipped my head to the side and gave back what I was getting in droves.

He was forceful in his kiss. Holding me to his mouth lest I try to get away. I did the same. Holding on with all my might. Our tongues tangled, our heads turned from side to side, each of us trying to take control but neither of us having it. The kiss was wild, out of control, and the absolute best of my life.

His hold loosened but he didn't stop kissing me. It naturally shifted from hot and hungry to soft and teasing, almost gentle. He nibbled on my bottom lip as I sucked on his top one. His beard soft enough to lightly graze my mouth but in no way hurting me. When he started to pull back, I pushed forward, dipping my tongue into the fray and swallowing his return groan as he wrapped his arms around me more completely and backed me against the opposite counter. His hands came down to my ass and he squeezed, plunging his tongue inside in luxurious, soul-melting maneuvers. I sighed and mewled into his kiss, allowing it to go on and on as his hands went up and down my back, down to my ass for a squeeze, and then back up. The hard ridge of his erection pressed deeper against me and I wanted nothing more than to pull his shirt off and let him take me right on his kitchen floor.

My heart beat hard, my sex throbbed, and my mind was in a lust haze so strong I was up for anything he wanted to do. I tugged on his T-shirt from behind, starting to pull it up his back when he yanked his mouth away on a gasp of air, reached behind him to grab my wrists, and brought them between us where he held them against his chest. His forehead pressed to mine and we both panted as though we'd just run five miles without stopping.

"Addy, I made a promise, and I don't go back on those."

"Promise," I breathed, allowing the flat of my palms and fingers to feel all the packed muscle of his pecs.

"To your sister, to you. I'm not gonna take advantage."

I stopped for a moment and moved my head back frowning. "Huh?"

He chuckled, pressed a soft, quick kiss to my forehead, and then stepped back. He rubbed his bulge with the base of his hand and groaned. "Fuck me." He sighed and braced his hands to the counter.

I came up behind him, pressing my body to the back of his very fine one. I wrapped my arms around his waist and before I could move them lower, which was one hundred percent my intent with how hot and bothered I was, he grabbed them and held them around him in a backward type of hug.

"You know I want you." He grumbled low and raspy, answering a question I didn't ask.

"Mmm hmm." I nodded against his back. "And I want you. We're both consenting adults…"

"True, but you're not in your right mind. Hell, I'm not in my right mind after that kiss."

I chuckled against his back. "And your point?"

He spun around and I pressed against him, wanting badly to touch every morsel of his beautiful body. Preferably unclothed.

"You had a rough morning. The worst morning ever. We turned that around. We're getting to know one another. And I promised your sister and you, and myself, that I wouldn't take advantage of the situation. I want nothing more than to drown myself in your sweetness, Addy. But it's not right. When we go there, I want more than just a good time."

I frowned. "Are you asking me to make a commitment to you? After three days of knowing one another?"

He laughed hard. "No, not exactly. But in a way, yeah. I want more with you than a fuck buddy."

"I cannot believe this. A man who wants commitment before sex. Call the press!" I hollered and Brutus ran into the room and barked once, then sat next to my leg leaning his heavy body against me. "Right, Brutus. Your daddy is a one-of-a-kind weirdo!"

"Now you're turning my dog against me?" He grinned.

"I mean, if the shoe fits."

Killian leaned back against the counter. "I'm not asking for forever. I just think we need to get to know one another. Spend time together. I don't want either of us to go forward physically for the wrong reasons."

"I'm into you. That's a pretty damn good reason," I offered.

"Same. Which is why I don't want to screw it up. I know what it's like to drown your sorrows. I just told you it didn't work for me. And it won't work for you."

"You're afraid I'm going to use you the way you used

those women when you got back from war?" I scowled, put off by the comparison.

"Not intentionally, no."

"Then what are you saying?" I frowned while petting Brutus.

"I'm saying I like you. Enough to want to do right by you. By this thing between us that's growing."

"And doing right by me is not fucking me when I clearly want to have sex with you?" I clarified because someone had to at this point.

He groaned and rubbed at his chin. "When you say it like that, it does sound stupid. Can we just give it a little time? I'll feel better about it."

"Is this 'time' going to be filled with no intimacy? No kissing, touching..."

He grinned wickedly. "Oh no, I think getting to know you is getting to know *all* of you. What type of caress makes you sigh. What type of kiss makes you moan. And most importantly, what type of touch makes you whimper."

"Yes, please. Let's do that then," I stated honestly and wholeheartedly.

He laughed. "Wash up. We got flour all over the place."

I huffed. "I will remind you that it was you who kissed me first. Which means you started it!"

"There's the sassy girl I wanted to see come back today. Means you're starting to feel better." He clucked his tongue and followed me to the sink where I was already washing my hands.

"I would have felt great if someone had banged me on the kitchen floor, but now you're never going to find out. So there!"

"Oh, I don't know about that. I'm sure there will be a second chance, and a third one." He kissed the bare skin of my shoulder and worked those tiny kisses up the length of my neck. I'd lost the cardigan earlier while watching the show. Killian had seen the worst of my scars and didn't seem to care so I didn't hide them from him.

Gooseflesh rose on my skin as he swirled his tongue over a spot right behind my ear. I gasped.

"Hmm, I most certainly will be getting a second chance," the smug man boasted as he put his hands under the water I'd left running for him.

"Don't brag. It's not becoming."

He laughed and went to the kitchen and started handing me bowls filled with the normal pizza toppings. Pepperoni, mozzarella cheese, sauce, spinach, mushrooms, and a few others.

Then for the next twenty or thirty minutes we teased and joked while making our own personal pizzas from scratch. It was by far the most fun I'd had in months. Maybe even the past year.

"Getting back to the heavy a little bit," Killian hedged as we sat at a pair of barstools with our fully cooked, delicious pizzas and two cold frosty beers to go with them.

"Yeah?" I leaned an elbow to the counter and put my head to the side, resting it in my hand so I could see him better.

"How'd you end up at Kerrighan House? It's a home for orphaned girls, right?"

"Ah, that's right. You read up on me." I remembered.

He nodded. "Only so much as to find out you're related to the Senator of Illinois, who the articles I read stated clearly was raised in Kerrighan House along with her sister. The other person attacked in the Backseat Strangler case."

"Simone." I nodded. "And Tabitha who didn't make it."

His gaze softened and he reached out and put his hand to my thigh and gave it a squeeze but left it there as if giving silent support.

"The Senator also has a hyphenated name of Wright-Kerrighan but uses just the Wright in her political dealings. Whereas your name on the contract with Blessing was hyphenated but publicly you use Michaels."

"Man, you did do your research." I smiled.

He chuckled. "Not much, I promise."

"I was left as a newborn on the steps of a firehouse. My birth certificate was left with me and only had a woman's name. Melissa Michaels. There was no father noted. Apparently, after I was put into Child and Family Services, they looked into my birth mother who'd been found dead. Hemorrhaged a couple days after giving birth. That's all I really know. I have no clue who my birth father was but maybe he was the one who brought me to the firehouse."

"Christ, Addy… I'm sorry to hear that."

I shrugged, sat up straighter, and lifted the beer to my mouth, taking a fortifying pull of the hoppy beverage.

"From there I was bounced around foster homes and was never adopted. Which believe me, was not what I wanted at any of the jacked-up families I lived in. I learned the hard way to do as I was told, don't make waves, don't bring any attention to yourself at all. Until one of the homes I was in had a teenage boy who was far more messed up than any that I'd shared space with before. The teen was pure evil. There was a surprise home inspection by my social worker. She found us in the closet where he'd shoved me. He got caught with his hands down my pants, his other hand over my mouth to keep me quiet. It wasn't the first time he'd done that, but it was the last."

That had Fitz standing so abruptly the barstool flew back and crashed to the ground. I held up my hands to ward off any potential reaction but he stormed away about fifteen or so feet then spun back around to face me, his entire body vibrating with fury. His hands were down at his sides in fists, his jaw locked in place, and his chest rising and falling as though he couldn't get enough air in his powerful frame.

He had never been more excruciatingly beautiful than in that moment.

His entire body was ready to strike, to fight, to avenge my past as though it were my present.

The only time I'd ever felt a response like that was when I admitted what happened to me to Mama Kerri. But it took a full year of living with her before I would tell her the scary things that haunted my sleep.

"I'm okay. I got past it, Killian." I tried to call him Fitz the way others did but it felt watered down somehow. Less intimate. And with Killian I most certainly wanted to be more intimate, not less.

He continued to stare at me as though he would literally destroy any man in his path who might harm me.

"You're kind of scary right now," I admitted, biting down on my bottom lip and sucking it into my mouth trying not to let his response freak me out more than it already was.

"I feel scary angry right now," he acknowledged rather honestly.

"That's the response Mama Kerri had too when I told her. But it was a long time ago. I was eight when it happened. Was placed in Kerrighan House right after that. Mama Kerri took me in and suddenly, I had a home. Sisters. A mother. A real life. A family. A good one. Something I could be proud of, and I flourished there. She gave all of us every tool we could ever need to be successful in life. I owe everything to her."

His shoulders lowered a couple inches, and his breathing became shallower. He unclenched his fists and slowly walked back over to me, his expression tortured and just plain sad.

I watched silently as he lifted the chair and set it back up before sitting in it and facing me. He took both of my hands and brought them up to his face. He kissed each palm, each wrist, the middle of my inner forearms where some of the worst burn marks were, the indent at my elbows, then he snuffled against my chest and pressed his lips to the skin over where my heart beat a thousand times a minute.

"I'm sorry I scared you," he murmured against my skin. "I wasn't prepared for what you shared or how it would make me feel. I won't make that same mistake twice. You can count on that."

I wrapped my arms around him and let him hug me, comforting him as much as I was comforting myself.

He held me for a while and then eased back, grabbed his beer, and emptied the entire thing in one go.

I chuckled and sipped at my own, picking up a cooling piece of my awesome pizza.

"Enough about me…"

"Never enough about you. I want to know everything there is to know."

I smiled. "Well, that would take a long time."

"I'm counting on it taking forever."

"Smooth talker," I teased even though butterflies were going bat-shit crazy in my stomach. "What about your upbringing? Parents, siblings?"

"Two brothers. My folks live in Naperville. Dad's a history teacher at one of the high schools there. Mom runs a daycare out of their home. With no kids in the house to raise, she got bored. Decided she wanted babies around her and none of her three boys ponied up any grandchildren. She sought out to get herself some."

I grinned. "Mama Kerri watches Rory who turns four in a couple weeks actually. Though she only does it three days a week. If it was up to her, she'd have all of us married and popping out grandbabies as fast as she could snap her fingers."

He nodded and shoveled in a bite of his pizza. He wiped his mouth while chewing. "I think that's what happens when you hit fifty plus. You either want the freedom to travel and enjoy the empty nest or you want to fill it back up with other people's children."

"Do you, uh, want kids someday?"

He nodded. "Yeah, a couple would be cool. Part of why I don't want to rush what we've got. I see potential there, Addy. Potential for more than just a few months of some fun."

"I want kids too."

"How does that work with the modeling gig?" he asked.

"Honestly, you only get so long to model regularly before you're aged out or your body changes too much with babies. Unless you're a freak and your body just bounces back with no extra weight or stretch marks. I hate those women," I grumbled.

Killian laughed. "I'll bet."

"My plan is pretty set. I'm going to model as much as a I can for the next four years until I hit thirty and then I was thinking about opening up my own agency. I've learned a lot in this business, and I've been through the ringer, being a plus-sized model for one, being successful in the biz for two. Those things are not mutually exclusive, so I know that I've got something special. Still, I feel like I could help plus-sized women, heck all *women* do their thing in this industry. And Blessing and I have talked a lot about teaming up. She designs, I find the models, train them, work the shoots with her, and we hire an exceptional person to do the marketing of our business. It would take a lot of hard work and time, but it feels right."

"That's awesome, Addy. Knowing what you want to do, having goals and plans and a timeline. The only question I have is where does a man in your life fit into all that?"

I looked down at my pizza and played with the crust feeling a little shy all of a sudden, not having planned to share so much about my future plans with this man.

"Not sure. Guess I'd have to find me the strong, supportive type. A man that wouldn't want me to put my dreams on hold to be what he needs. Not that I wouldn't be supportive of his desires in return."

"And what if that man wanted you just the way you are? Beautiful. Independent. Driven. Goal-oriented. Just wanted you to come home to him at the end of your busy day. Would you make time for that kind of man?"

"Well, I don't know. You're referring to some pretend hero. How would I ever find such a man?" I teased.

He leaned forward until our faces were only a couple inches apart.

"Maybe all you have to do in order to find him is open your eyes and heart to the possibility that you might have already met him." He leaned the couple inches and took my mouth in a slow, sensual kiss.

I sighed as he pulled away.

"You know you're right." I got up and made a show about going to my purse and pulling out my cell phone.

He frowned. "What are you doing?"

"Going to make a call."

"To...?" His expression took on one of absolute horror. I could barely keep the ruse going without losing it.

"The man in my life. You just made me see what I've been missing all this time..." I dialed holding my breath.

"The hell you are!" Killian grumbled, made it to me, and snatched the phone out of my hand right as his pocket started buzzing.

He pulled his phone out and I smiled wide. The display said *Wild Beauty* and he smirked. "Real funny, Addy." He locked his arms around me at the waist, tossing both our phones to the table nearest us. He started backing us toward the couch.

"I so had you going there. You have to admit it!" I giggled like a schoolgirl, but he kept tugging me toward his destination.

Killian shook his head and pressed his face to my neck

where he laughed along with me. When he'd backed me into the couch, he wrapped his arms around me and twisted until he sat down. I followed, straddling his lap.

Once there, he kissed me. And he didn't stop for a long, long time.

Chapter
NINE

I WOKE ON A JOLT. BRUTUS WAS BARKING LIKE CRAZY AT THE front door. My phone was buzzing on the coffee table and a ridiculously loud pounding came from the door.

"FBI! Open this door or we're breaking it down!" I heard Jonah's voice.

Killian shook off sleep where he lie on his back, me half on top of him wedged between the back of the couch and his comfy frame. We'd snuggled after our make out session and lied next to one another watching Season Two of the glass blowing show on Netflix. The projector screen was still down, the entire room dark save for the light from the message on the screen that said, "Are you still watching..."

I scrambled up and shoved my long ratty hair out of my face, wiping at my mouth in case there were any drool remnants. Killian did the same with his long locks as he pulled himself off the couch and headed to the door.

"Coming! Take a load off on the pounding, will ya?" he hollered, grabbing his dog's collar. "Brutus, laundry room. Now!" He pointed.

The dog whinnied and ran over to me, then proceeded to sit on my feet.

"Brutus, *hier.*" *Come,* he said.

I petted the top of his head. "Go, baby, it's okay. We'll

bring you out soon." I dipped my head and kissed between his brows.

"*Hier!*" Killian used more force in his tone.

The dog got up and scampered to his dad. Killian shook his head and pointed at the laundry room. Brutus tucked his tail then went into his room-sized cage.

The pounding on the door started once again. "FBI! Open up!" Jonah yelled.

Eeek!

Killian secured Brutus then went to the entryway and opened the door. He stood face-to-face with one seriously angry FBI guy. "Where's Addison?" he demanded.

"She's right here? Relax, bro," Killian admonished, stretching his hand out for Jonah and whoever was with him to enter.

Jonah entered but not before a blonde head popped out from behind him and slipped inside. Simone laid her eyes on me and came at me at a dead run like she had yesterday, only this time she had farther to go. "Addy!" she cried, her entire face mottled, red, and blotchy, tears tracking down her cheeks.

I opened my arms and took a step back when she plowed into me but held on as my sister hugged the air right from my lungs. Her body shook so hard and her nails dug into my shoulders. "Addy," she sobbed.

I cupped the back of her head. "What in the world, Simone? Honey, talk to me." I glanced over her shoulder to see Jonah and Ryan being escorted toward the kitchen area where Killian padded in bare feet and the same jeans and T-shirt he'd worn yesterday. In fact, we were both still in our rumpled clothes from yesterday. Him being the gentleman I'd experienced he truly was.

"Honey, did something happen?" I spoke against her hair.

"We couldn't get ahold of you..." she cried against my neck.

"Shit, we left our phones on silent." I remembered us both doing so in order to watch our show. I didn't even think of the repercussions.

"Fuck." Killian cursed from where he was filling the coffee pot. "I'm sorry. I told Blessing last night I'd keep in touch."

"Sweetheart, is this about last night? About you not being able to see me in person?" I asked petting her hair.

She shook her head. "I actually was having one of my good nights until we woke early this morning..." She continued to cry.

I led her over to a barstool near Jonah. "Sit down, honey. Guys, what's going on? You knew I was here. I'm sure Blessing told you what Killian said yesterday."

"Yeah, we did think that. Until another body showed up and we couldn't get a hold of you. Either of you."

"Another body? No! I'm...I'm sorry, we fell asleep. When did this happen?" I curled around Simone and let her hug me until she calmed down and realized that I was real and alive.

"Body was found at five this morning. Found tossed in a dumpster. We're lucky the garbage man saw something strange before he unloaded his haul."

"My goodness. That's horrible. What time is it now?"

"Seven," Killian offered, setting five coffee cups out in front of the pot. "Technically Holt knew she was here. I relieved him yesterday morning before I spoke with Blessing about keeping Addy with me."

"That was almost twenty-four hours ago, and no one has heard from you, *bro*." Jonah's snarl and emphasis on the word *bro* showed exactly how he felt.

I jumped in to offset the testosterone sizzling in the air. "If you already saw the body, you knew it wasn't me." I frowned. "Am I missing something?"

"I'm going to go freshen up. Where's the bathroom?" Simone sniffed and wiped at her still teary eyes. "I don't want to hear this a second time."

I pointed to the right door and waited until she'd shut herself inside. I hooked a thumb toward my sister. "Why is she so upset? I mean, I know this is bringing up some scary things she's been working through regarding the kidnapping and Tabby's death, but this is worse than the other night."

Jonah sighed and put both of his elbows to the bar and rested his chin on his clasped fingers. "The body was found with her face burned off. A magazine photo of you was stuck to the burned-off flesh. We didn't know it wasn't you as there was no identifying information left with the body."

"What?" This information had me turning ice cold.

Killian instantly wound his way around the counter, took my wrist, and pulled me into his arms in a protective, supportive hold. "Okay, continue. Get all the shit out at once, man." He held me close and rubbed along my shoulder and arm as he did so.

Ryan's eyebrows rose and he took in the rather intimate gesture and grinned wickedly.

Jonah however did not react in kind. He lifted his chin as though in judgement. "What's up with this? You meet her four days ago and you're already having her spend the night, holding her like you are."

"Yeah, so? What's it to you?" Killian firmed his stance, straightening his spine but his tone was direct and combative.

Ryan placed a hand to Jonah's shoulder. "Takes one to know one, brother." He huffed out a dry laugh.

Jonah spun to the side and gestured with a flippant hand to us then himself. "Not the same thing."

Ryan jerked his head back. "Bullshit. You had Simone moved into our pad in what…a day."

Jonah narrowed his eyes and scowled. "It's not the same thing."

"Isn't it? She's in danger, just like Simone was." Ryan looked around. "What kind of dog do you have?"

"Rottweiler."

Ryan grinned. "Nice. Heard him about to tear down the door. He's protective."

"That's an understatement. You touch me, or her, in a way he doesn't like…" He sucked in a breath through his teeth enough to make a hissing sound. "I wouldn't want to see the results of that."

Ryan nudged Jonah. "Ex-vet, who Holt states owns a gun and knows how to use it. A scary dog that's protective. Top floor loft with more than one lock. Security on the building. Addy, you feel safe here?" he asked.

I nodded. "More than anywhere else, right now. Whoever this guy is, he wouldn't know who Killian is, or where he lives."

"Unless he followed one of your drivers. Which I'm not saying he did, just that it's not out of the realm of possibility." Jonah lifted his hand. "Maybe not likely seeing as Holt knows how to shake and spot a tail. I think you're covered.

But Addison, you can't go MIA at all. Otherwise, we're going to have to find a safehouse for you. One of the FBI's choosing."

"You can't make me go into hiding," I stated with conviction. I was my own person. I made my own choices about my safety, but I was also smart and would listen to reason.

Jonah closed his eyes and lifted his head to the ceiling then sighed. "No, but it's not okay for you to scare the life out of your mother and sisters." He pointed to the bathroom door that was just now opening. Simone exited with her hair in a high ponytail and not a stitch of makeup on her face. Her eyes were red-rimmed, but she looked calmer.

Simone instantly noted how Killian was holding me and her lips shifted into a beaming smile. She had her slouchy cardigan hanging off one shoulder and covering most of her hands, but she lifted one and waved to Killian with a single finger. "Hot guy photographer, I assume?"

I rolled my eyes as Killian chuckled and looked down at my face. "You talking sweet about me to your sisters?" I shrugged one shoulder, not wanting to give too much away as he leaned down in front of *everyone* and gave me a peck on the lips. "How do you like your coffee, gorgeous?"

"She likes flavored creamer and nothing else," Simone prattled off, moving to her man and hooking her arm around his shoulders. He wrapped a long arm around her waist and brought her close to his side where he sat, and she stood.

"Don't have flavored creamer, but I've got milk and sugar until we can get some," Killian answered.

"Perfect, thank you."

He gave me a second kiss in front of my family and let

me go. I turned to find Simone grinning like a loon. All signs of her upset completely wiped away by the sight of me and my new hot guy photographer. "Shut up. Not a word," I warned.

She shook her head then pretended to lock her lips together and toss an imaginary key over her shoulder.

"What else do we know about the latest victim? Was there a note other than my picture? Anything we can go off?" I asked.

Ryan and Jonah both shook their heads. "None of it makes sense. This victim had your body type and hair color, but not the burns on the arms. And she wasn't strangled. She actually died from a blow to the back of the head which knocked her out, then she was burned. As if the killer had used an accelerant but we won't know until we hear back from the forensics report. It's on a rush but it still takes time."

"Where was she found?" I shivered and said a little prayer in my mind that the victim would rest in peace, grateful that she wasn't awake for the violence she withstood after the blow to the head.

"The dumpster in front of the old building you'd been kept in with Simone. So that tie is still there."

"Anyone could have looked that up though," I offered. "The Backseat Strangler was a widely publicized case, and media was everywhere when Simone and I were taken from that building, not to mention Sonia being the Senator."

Killian set a cup of coffee in front of me and I wrapped my chilled hands around it, letting the heat soak through to my bones before taking a sip. He took the rest of the coffee orders, but I could tell he was keeping an ear to the conversation but also being a good host.

"The other thing we know about this victim is that she fought. There were bruises and broken nails on her fingers."

"DNA?" I asked.

Ryan shrugged. "We're hopeful. The Backseat Strangler never left DNA though, so if this is a partner, he's being pretty stupid, and his MO is a bit chaotic. Frantic almost. The girl in the park wasn't killed there but dropped there to be found. The MO was the exact same as the Strangler, except the burns down the arms, which we know the Strangler did to you, but not his other victims. The burns in the Strangler case were meant to secure Simone's attention and get her to offer herself up on a silver platter, which she unintentionally did."

"I would have done it any way." Simone's sorrow-filled gaze cut to mine.

"I would have too," I admitted.

She nodded. The family we'd built with Mama Kerri at Kerrighan House was unbreakable. There was nothing you could do to one of us that every last one of us didn't feel as if it happened to us personally. Our bond was so deep, you cut one, you cut us all. We were loyal to the highest degree. We put our sisterhood above everything. It's what kept us alive. It's what helped us thrive. And it would be that way until every last one of us took our final breath on this earth.

Sisterhood wasn't a word for us. It was our way of life. Forged in the hottest flames of pain, fear, and unconditional love. There was no breaking our bonds.

Every last one of us would die for the other. That's what sisterhood meant to us.

"Hope you're hearing this, bud," Jonah said tiredly rubbing at his forehead, his gaze on Killian. "They're all like that. You fall in love with one, your ass better realize she comes with a house full of strong, intelligent, opinionated women who get into your business *all* the time."

Killian carried two cups of coffee in each hand before setting them on the counter and passing them out based on their chosen preference.

"If they're anything like Addy, it will only make my life fuller. But thanks for the heads-up." He smiled, not letting any of Jonah's warning hit the target.

"Ohh, I like him," Simone said to me, putting her elbow on the table and resting her chin in her hand clearly enamored with my new beau. "I like you," she gushed, her gaze now on Killian.

He grinned and gave her a wink. "Feeling's mutual, Simone."

She sighed dramatically while Jonah grumbled under his breath. "Can't say I didn't warn you."

He sipped his coffee and I chuckled. Liking having part of my family here having coffee. The reason behind their visit was atrocious, but them sitting here, sipping on a cup of Joe, Jonah my brother-in-law in training shooting the shit with the guy I was seeing...it felt good. Normal even.

I moved over to Killian and cuddled against his side. "I'm going to need to go to Kerrighan House, get some clothes, and change before shooting today."

"Why? You have what you need to wear here and a shower that's just as hot as the one back at Kerrighan House."

I ran my hand from his chest to his abs, loving the feeling of the hard play of muscles flexing as I did so over his shirt.

He ducked his head. "I got a better idea. How's about we go to your house, pick up a couple weeks' worth of clothing, and you stay here, where you yourself admitted you feel safe. Would also be a lot easier to take photos whenever the mood struck."

I tilted my head. "True." I lifted my hand and tapped at my lips with my index finger. "And where would I sleep?" I teased.

He hummed and wrapped his arms around me, locking his wrists at my lower back. "I'm sure we'll think of something."

"Is that so?"

He nodded and took my mouth in a swift kiss.

When I turned around, I realized I'd forgotten for a moment that we had visitors. "Um, sorry."

Simone shook her head smiling. "Don't be sorry, sister. I can't wait to tell our family that you caught yourself a keeper."

"Simone!"

She shook her head. "Nope, you're not getting out of this one. Mama is gonna be all over this like a bee to a flower!"

I groaned and leaned back against Killian who'd taken to putting an arm around my chest, my back to his front.

"Addy, we really need to get you to your apartment..." Jonah said softly.

I frowned and went stone-cold while shaking my head. The idea alone sounded awful and I wanted no part of it.

"Babe, no. She can't go back there. No. Just no," Simone blurted, adamant in her conviction.

"What if I took you?" Killian murmured against my ear.

"I'd be with you the entire time, along with Jonah who you trust, right?"

I looked at Jonah, his chocolate brown eyes seeming resigned.

"And I won't see anything that will give me nightmares?" I added, having enough nightmares of being kidnapped to last a lifetime. I wanted absolutely no part of seeing a crime scene, blood, gore of any kind, or anything remotely related. If I had my choice, they could burn the place down after they got a few of my most prized possessions out of there. I didn't keep a lot of special things because the most special things to me were people, not objects or memorabilia. As long as I had my sisters, Mama Kerri, and Rory, there wasn't much I'd miss.

"We'll do our very best to obscure anything that might be unsettling to you."

I gritted my teeth together. "Fine. If Killian can go with us, I'll do it."

He hugged me from behind. "Proud of you, baby."

I smiled and lifted my coffee.

I was proud of me too.

Killian pulled up to the front of my apartment in the city. Jonah and Ryan leading the way in their blacked-out undercover car.

"I like your car," I whispered, staring at my chilled fingers. From the second we entered the car and headed toward my home my blood seemed to turn ice cold.

Killian chuffed. "Only you would dig an older model Jeep Wrangler 4 x 4."

"How old is it?"

"2012."

I nodded as I watched Ryan and Jonah exit their car and come over to my door. Killian reached out and took my hand. "Hey?"

I turned and looked into his eyes. They were so pretty. So much prettier than what I was about to see.

"You're going to be fine. I'll be right by your side the entire way, okay?"

"Yeah, it's just, I don't want to do it. I know I *need* to."

"No one will fault you for being freaked out, Addy. It's perfectly normal. But just put it this way. You're doing what you can to help catch a really bad guy before he hurts someone else. Also, you're moving on. You don't have to go back there after today. I promise. Now wait for me to come around the car."

I nodded numbly and waited while Killian got out and came around. He said something to the guys, but I couldn't hear, nor did I really care. My entire focus was on getting in and out. Taking a logical, analytical approach to the space and that was it. I did not live there anymore. I would not be lying my head there ever again. I was fine. I had three men to ensure my safety.

"You can do this, Addy. Be strong. Be brave. Tits up and out," I chanted under my breath as Killian opened my car door. I got out of the car, lifted to my full height, pulled back my shoulders, and took Killian's hand with a renewed sense of confidence. Both Jonah and Ryan flanked my sides, eyes to the sides checking out the neighborhood while all three led me into my building.

I ignored every person I passed. I had zero desire to engage in any form of conversation or discuss what had been found in my apartment.

Jonah cut the police tape and opened my door with a key that I assumed was Simone's copy. Most of us sisters held copies of each other's house keys in case we got into a bind.

I was thrust inside and could instantly smell a foul stench I didn't associate with my previous home. The place was in surprisingly good condition, aside from the white sheet that sat in the center of my living room and what looked like fingerprint dust all over areas where people would touch. Door handles, drawers, and the like. The sheet on the floor I'd avoid like my life depended on it.

Killian squeezed my hand. "You good?"

"Yeah," I said while looking around. "I'm surprised to see it looks almost exactly the same as when I left it. I guess I expected it to be trashed like Simone's place was."

"We noted the difference in the MO as well," Ryan said softly.

Jonah came over to me and put his hand to my shoulder. "Okay, what I need you to do is look at each section of your home as though you're trying to find something missing. Focus on one section at a time." He pointed to my pretty, very feminine white couch with flowery throw pillows. Next to those sat glass-top tables with whitewash-painted legs. There were two lamps that had dangling crystals hanging from the lampshade. When I first started to make money, I decorated in bling. Blessing loved it because it suited her style. However, now that I was looking at it, I never loved it. I thought it was what I should buy because I had the money to afford it. Killian's style was much more comfortable and aesthetically pleasing to both men and women.

"See anything out of place?"

I shook my head.

"Next wall," he said, gesturing.

We did this for a while, but nothing was out of place.

"Let's go to your room," Jonah suggested.

Killian quietly followed me, never letting my hand go.

When we entered, I noticed a few things right away. "My dresser, those drawers were left open. I'm a stickler about that. I always close them so that when I enter my room it looks tidy."

"Excellent. Makes sense as we gathered that the clothing the victim was wearing was not her own. She'd been re-dressed in your clothing."

I shivered where I stood and took a step backward, directly into Killian. He put his hands to my hips and spoke softly against my head. "You're doing great, baby. We're almost done. You see anything else?"

I swallowed down the fear and anxiety and leaned against Killian for more contact. He wrapped an arm around my chest, perfectly encasing me in his strong, safe hold.

"Um, those things by my nightstand are on the floor. They weren't like that." I narrowed my gaze and looked at the small stack of photo albums and journals I kept on the bottom shelf of my nightstand.

I pushed away from Killian and went to my knees in front of them. "It's not here," I said frantically, my heart pounding so hard I could feel tension pressing against my chest.

"What's not there?" Jonah asked.

"My book! My Tabby photo album!" I winced as I pulled everything off the shelf then ducked down under the bed and yanked my memory box from under it leaving it on the floor. "Where's my album?" I scanned the space but came up empty. "It's not here!" Tears pricked at the back of my eyes. "Oh my

God, no. He took my most prized possession!" I cried out as tears fell so fast down my face it felt like acid sliding down my heated cheeks.

Killian came to me and yanked me up to a standing and wrapped me in his arms. "What album?"

"My Tabby album. We...we found them after she d-died." I choked out through my tears.

"Disgusting fucking bastard," Jonah growled. "The album is priceless." Jonah reiterated sadly what exactly my emotions couldn't bear to utter. "Tabitha made each of her foster sisters and their mother a photo album of her life with that sister. I've seen Simone's..." He reached out a hand and ran it down my back. "I'm sorry, honey. I know how much that means to you. But I swear, when we find this piece of shit, we'll get it back. I promise."

I sniffed against Killian's chest and wiped at my tears. He shifted his hand to cup my nape and lifted my chin with his thumb. "Is there anything else here that you want to take with us that's special?" he asked.

"This is technically still a crime scene..." Ryan muttered.

Killian gave a death glare the likes I'd never want pointed in my direction.

"I'm sure she could grab a couple keepsakes that matter to her since she's already lost something important."

I pointed to the picture across from my bed. It was one of the images Tabby had taken and hung in her apartment. Each of the sisters had taken one of Tabby's original pictures. The one I chose was of Kerrighan House in full bloom. Mama Kerri was tending to her flowers with her big floppy hat, her face tilted up looking at her girls playing with her only grandchild. Liliana, Charlie, and Genesis were holding hands playing ring around the rosy with a two-year-old Rory out on the grass. Blessing was sitting in the porch seat, a book in her hand reading. Simone and Sonia were sitting on the steps of the porch both of them laughing at something. Me, I was taking advantage of the sun, stretched out on a sun lounger. My scar-free arms stretched up long clasping the back of the headrest and my legs were crossed at the ankles. I wore a tank top, jean shorts, and a big pair of Jackie O sunglasses. My hair was down and all over the place. I was smiling with my head lifted toward the sun. Those flowers, that house, the people in that picture meant everything to me and it was clear in the way Tabby captured us that she'd felt the same.

Killian led me to the picture and together we looked at the amazing image.

"She was very talented." He spoke softly.

"She really was." I wiped at a stray tear that fell.

Killian pulled the picture off the wall. "Anything else?" he asked softly.

"Just the memory box. Nothing else here matters. I need to see my mom and my sisters." My voice shook. I was losing the hold on what little strength I had left.

"Not a problem. We'll go there after we're done here. Guys? These two things? You want to take pictures of them, and state the owner removed them?"

Jonah came over and took a picture with his phone as Ryan grabbed the box from the floor and let Jonah snap that too. He opened the long white clothing-sized box. It was big enough to store a large sweater in it. Inside held random pictures, letters, and little trinkets that had been given to me as gifts by my sisters when we were little girls. Grade reports from school. My first headshots and magazines that I appeared in.

Nothing important to the case. Still Ryan spread it out and took several photos.

"We done here?" Killian's voice was more a command than a question.

"Yeah, we'll follow you to Kerrighan House, then get back to headquarters for a run down with our team."

Killian led me straight outside, put me in his car, and opened the trunk where he carefully set Tabby's picture and the memory box. He got in the car, grabbed my hand, and brought it to his lips. He kissed my hand and held it tight. "I'm so damn proud of you. That couldn't have been easy."

I leaned toward him and rubbed my cheek to his shoulder. "It wasn't, but with you there, I felt like I could handle it. Thank you for being there for me. Thank for being there this whole time."

"Addy, haven't you figured it out yet? There is no place I'd rather be than sitting next to you."

I lifted my head, and he ducked his, taking my mouth in a slow but sweet kiss.

"I can't wait to meet your mother!" He grinned and waggled his brows in a joking manner that had me chuckling.

He kept my hand in his on his thigh while he started the car and headed to my childhood home, driving one-handed. He didn't let me go for even a moment. If he kept this up, my *like* of him would be turning into *love* far quicker than I ever thought possible.

With life being as short as it felt these days...I didn't care one bit how fast this was moving with him. I fully planned to jump straight in the deep end with Killian Fitzpatrick, the one man who could make me feel safe and protected in all things.

Chapter
TEN

THE PAPARAZZI WERE ANOTHER LEVEL OF CRAZY THIS morning as we pulled up to Kerrighan House.

"What the fuck?" Killian growled. "Is it like this every day?"

I let my hair fall forward to cover most of my face. Every model knew this trick. Usually I used this move when I was exiting an international flight and looked like death warmed over.

"Yeah. It lessened a little a couple months after the case, but they're always trying to catch an image of Sonia, Simone, or me. I spent the better part of three months not leaving the house. Now there's a new threat against me..." I sighed and closed my eyes.

My door was wrenched open by Jonah who stuck his hand in. "Vultures, every last one of you!" he roared at the crowd surrounding Killian's 4 x 4.

I cowered close to Jonah's body, head down, and let him lead me to the door of my childhood home. Killian was being walked to the door by Ryan as the crowd battered us with questions at a deafening pitch.

"Did the Backseat Strangler have an accomplice?"

"What do you know about the women being killed that look like you!"

"Are you scared, Addison?"

"Is this man your boyfriend!"

"What does the Senator think about all this?"

Jonah used his key to the house and led us all inside. Once the door was shut, I spun around and shoved my hair out of my face. "You should have dropped me off. They're going to figure out who you are."

Killian moved to me and wrapped me in his arms. "I don't care if they figure out who I am. Let them. They can't hurt me."

I slumped against his form. "It means they're going to figure out where you live and start hounding you. They'll dig up everything there is to know about you and blast it across the media waves."

He shifted back and cupped my cheeks. "Baby, I said I don't care, and I meant it. I've got nothing to hide."

"You'd be surprised," I responded miserably.

He leaned forward and kissed my forehead, my nose, and then my lips. "All I care about is you. I'm in this with you for the long haul, Addy."

I closed my eyes and soaked up the genuine concern and care he showed in everything he said and did.

I was falling for this man.

Hard and fast.

I opened my eyes and stared into his kind, handsome face. I cupped his cheeks, lifted up on my toes, and kissed him.

"Oh, well, it looks like my baby girl is just fine, I see." Mama Kerri's voice startled us from behind. I pulled back so fast and spun around with my hand to my mouth, panting like I couldn't get air in fast enough. Caught kissing a boy in my mother's house. Definitely a first.

Jonah and Ryan chuckled and moved from the entryway living room to the kitchen.

"Cookies?" Jonah asked as he passed Mama Kerri. I swear that man was a cookie monster. Always hunting for the sweet stuff.

"Always. In the jar by the coffee pot, son," she murmured, but didn't pay him any mind, her blue- green gaze stuck on me and Killian.

"Mama, I uh, want you to meet someone." I rubbed my hands together. "Killian Fitzpatrick, this is my mother Aurora Kerrighan."

She waved her hands in the air and then wiped them on her apron before she stuck one out in greeting. "You can call me Mama Kerri. Everyone in this house does."

"Obliged," Killian said and took her hand. "You can call me Fitz. Most everyone but my girl here does." He grinned.

"Your girl?" she smirked.

"Mama." I gave her big eyes to let it go, something I knew she'd never do.

"No disrespect. I'm still trying to woo her into being mine." He laughed lightly.

This time I felt the ache in my eyes as they bugged open wide at the shock of Killian's admission.

My mother laughed. "None received. I like a man who knows what he wants and holds it close. Well come on back, the girls are outside." She waved her hand as she started toward the kitchen then went straight through to the back door that led to the garden.

Killian nudged me forward.

I glared over my shoulder. "I can't believe you said what you said to my mother!" I whisper-ranted.

He chuckled good-naturedly, nothing affecting him in the slightest.

When we made it outside there was a table laden with sandwich accoutrements, fruit, a green salad, and potato salad. My mouth watered realizing we went straight to the apartment after coffee and hadn't eaten. There were blankets set out on the grass, my sisters in various stages of lounging while Rory played fetch with Amber, Simone and Jonah's dog. Sonia sat at a small, four-seater table with chairs set up off to the side in a little cut out of greenery and concrete. She was leaning over a set of papers talking to her assistant Quinn while pointing at something.

Since it was Saturday, everyone was in casual attire.

"Hey, guys. Look what the cat dragged in, finally," Mama Kerri announced to the group. "Told you she was fine. My mama radar would have known if one of my babies was hurting," she proclaimed.

All of their stares hit us at once, smiles stretching across their faces.

I interlaced my fingers with Killian's. "Come on, let's go meet my sisters."

He followed me to the first blanket where Genesis and Charlie were sitting and eating while watching Rory play.

"This is Genesis Coleman-Kerrighan, and that's her daughter Rory playing with Amber the dog." I pointed to my niece who did not stop playing. "Genesis is a social worker for the state. And our resident redhead is Charlie Hagan-Kerrighan. Runs a Youth Center downtown that helps wayward kids."

"Guys, this is Killian Fitzpatrick...my uh..."

"Her boyfriend." He supplied a label I was a bit nervous to commit to. Not that I didn't want to, just that things were happening pretty fast for me. I didn't normally feel this attached to someone of the opposite sex in less than a week's time. I was really starting to understand what Simone went through when she fell for Jonah.

He bent over and shook both of their hands. "Call me Fitz. It's great to meet you both."

Genesis smiled softly and kept quiet after shaking his hand, while Charlie shook his hand and bounced up to standing. "Her boyfriend, eh? That's news." She put her hands to her hips. "Looks like our sister has been holding out on us. Hmmm?"

"In my defense, there's been a lot going on."

Charlie pressed her lips together and tilted her head, her red ponytail flopping to the side. "True. You get this one get out of jail free card, sister. Then all bets are off. No disappearing at your new boyfriend's house during the middle of a déjà vu freak show, you feel me?" She took on some of Blessing's attitude but gave it her own flare by adding a really awkward neck bobble.

Killian lifted his hands. "Next time I'll make sure she checks in with her family."

Charlie grinned. "Ooooh, me like-y this one. Does he have a brother or a sister?" Her pale skin pinked up at the cheeks and her brown eyes sparkled with intrigue.

I shook my head and put my arm out, tapping Killian flat on the chest. "Don't answer that. She'll have you hooking her up with one of your family members and then she'll drop them like a hot box of rocks."

Charlie's mouth dropped open in shock.

Blessing walked up behind her and hooked her around the waist. "Addy is not lying. Don't even try to act like you don't drop men and women for the most ridiculous reasons."

"Not true!" Charlie snapped.

I lifted my brows and tried not to laugh.

Blessing however was not nearly as kind. "Oh? What about Tate?"

"He blew his nose at the dinner table and he farted in public!" Charlie made a stink face.

"And Carly, the super pretty pinup-looking chick?"

"She wouldn't go down on me! I'm all about fairness in the bedroom. She wanted to receive in all things. I do not keep selfish bitches around," she griped.

I snorted.

"That one was fair." Simone sidled up to me, wrapping her arms around my body and rubbing her face against my hair.

"I agree," I added to the conversation while patting Simone's hair. She seemed better today now that she knew I was fine and had a man at my back at all times.

Blessing hummed. "Okay." She snapped her fingers. "That Tim guy?"

Charlie rolled her eyes. "The accountant? Can you see me with a man who does numbers long-term? He wouldn't even go out of the house after eleven. Said he needed his sleep. Even on the weekends!"

"Just admit you're a serial dater and we'll lay off." Blessing crossed her arms over her chest.

"Fine. I like to date. So what?" Charlie admitted.

"You like to string people along and then drop them when they get too close. You find all kinds of reasons to blow them off." Genesis got up with her finished plate.

"If they were worthy of staying, I would have kept them."
She stuck her tongue out at Gen like she was five years old.

"Your sisters always this combative?" Killian chuckled.

"Yeah." I nudged him. "Get used to it...*boyfriend*." I
teased.

Simone laughed and let me go. "You want me to get you
guys a drink? We've got fresh lemonade, sun-tea, water, and
booze of course."

"I'd love a glass of tea," Killian answered.

"Me too. Thanks, Si."

Mama came over to our huddle and handed us both
plates loaded with thick turkey and cheese sandwiches and
all three of the salads, fruit, potato, and green, that she'd
made.

"Come, you two. Let's get you settled. Eating and soaking in some sun. You've been cooped up. A little sunshine
will fix you right up." She prattled and led us over to an
empty blanket.

Sonia and Quinn moseyed over and sat down on the
blanket with us.

"Senator," Killian put his hand out.

Sonia gifted Killian one of her genuine smiles, not the
fake one she used when she was in front of a camera. "I think
if you're going to be in my sister's life, you can call me Sonia.
And this is my best friend Quinn." She gestured to the man
who was always by Sonia's side even though he had a husband of his own.

"Fitz. Nice to meet you both. This is a great house and
an incredible garden," Killian spoke taking in the beauty that
never seemed to get old. Mama was the most skilled gar-
dener I'd ever known. Not that I knew many.

"It's always been home," Sonia agreed. "Sis, how are you doing?" Sonia asked while running her hand down my hair a few times.

"Good. Going to the apartment was rough but Killian was there along with Jonah and Ryan. The uh, the bad guy stole my Tabby album." I clenched my teeth as the burn of that admission sizzled through my body.

Sonia gasped. "No?"

I nodded my heart feeling as though it were in my throat. "Jonah promised to get it back and I believe if anyone can, it will be him or Ryan." I looked up and saw the two men piling the food on their plates. Except Ryan wasn't really paying much attention to what he was doing. His gaze was glued to Blessing who was still giving Charlie crap about her dating methods.

I lifted my chin toward the other guys. The three sitting with me followed where I gestured. "When do you think that's going to culminate into something real?"

Sonia smiled. "Never."

"Why not?" Quinn asked at the same time Killian asked, "What are we talking about?" He leaned toward me conspiratorially.

"Ryan has a thing for Blessing. She's totally into him but refuses to acknowledge the attraction because of her father," I offered.

"Is it a race thing?" Killian asked.

"The gang banger?" Quinn interrupted already knowing Blessing's story and exactly who Tyrell Jones was.

I nodded. "Not a race thing." I rubbed my hand over Killian's knee where he sat cross-legged next to me. "She says it wouldn't work, him being in law enforcement, her history, and her father's current involvement in one of the worst gangs in Chicago."

"What's her history?" Killian asked, then took a monster-sized bite of his sandwich, getting a little mayo at the top of his mustache.

I smiled and leaned forward, wiping his upper lip with my thumb and then depositing the mess on my napkin.

"Thanks, baby," he murmured. "The history?"

Sonia's sighed. "Her mother was murdered when she was ten. Gang retaliation. The courts kicked Blessing here, but her father is still poking around. I worry about that girl," she said then sipped her drink.

"Damn, I feel for her," Killian said and left it at that.

Simone came out of the house, two cold drinks in her hand, and brought them over to us. She handed one to Killian and then one to me.

While Rory played an endless game of fetch with Amber, Jonah and Ryan, the rest of my family huddled around Killian and me while we updated them on the case and the visit to my apartment.

Once I got it off my chest, I felt lighter. Free to breathe again without the pressure of the day's weight so heavily on my subconscious.

While Jonah and Ryan went back to work, we played with a Frisbee, catch with Amber, hopscotch with Rory, and a wicked round of adult croquet when Mama Kerri put Rory down for a nap.

Killian had called his friend Atticus to go to his house and walk Brutus. Apparently, he had a dog door and a patch of grass on the roof of the building which prevented Killian from having to walk him several times a day. I didn't know such a thing existed and I was very eager to see this secret rooftop space.

When we were all tuckered out from the days emotional tidal wave and then fun in the sun with my family, I packed up two huge suitcases under Killian's repeated request. He was determined to have me holed up at his house. And if I were being honest with myself, I wanted to be with him. He made me feel safe. With a scary man out there wanting to hurt me, feeling safe was a hot commodity, and more than anything I wanted my sisters and mother as far away from potential tragedy as possible. With me away, they would be safer.

Since Killian was a trained soldier and had a conceal carry permit, the guys felt okay with letting Killian be my sole bodyguard. They repeatedly warned me about going anywhere without him. I had no intention of doing any such thing, so I agreed to their terms. They also planned on having a patrol unit drive by the loft regularly to have a police presence which made me feel extra safe, not to mention the security guard who already worked the building.

All in all, I was feeling good when it was time to head back to Killian's. The day started in tears and ended in laughter. I couldn't ask for better.

Killian led me from his Jeep to the elevator with my suitcases. The building had two full-time security guards, and the underground parking was accessed through a code. Still, Killian was more alert than I'd seen him. I rolled both my suitcases into the elevator as he made sure there wasn't anything hidden in the shadows.

"Should we have stopped at the store for groceries?"

Killian shook his head. "Nah, I had Atticus hook us up while we were out. I texted him a list of things and he picked them up before he took Brutus for a walk. Though if I had to guess, he's still in my apartment. For a hard as nails veteran, he's a huge softy and a gossip. He'll want to meet you in person."

I smiled as he pushed the button on the elevator. "Really? That's funny. I hope he's still here."

We exited the elevator and Killian opened the locked door and led us inside.

Brutus came running from where he had been sitting on the couch next to a giant of a man who took up more than one seat on the couch with his brawn. Atticus made Brutus look small and that was hard to do.

I dropped to my knees and opened my arms. "Hi, baby. How's my best guy?" Brutus licked my neck and cheek as I petted him all over. "You miss me? Mama's got a treat for you. Yes, I do. I've got a treat for my good boy." I dug into my purse and pulled out three slices of bacon I'd pilfered from Mama's stash in the fridge. She'd cooked a couple packages and stored the rest for use throughout the week. I stood up and pointed at Brutus. "Sit, baby."

"Addy, babe, he's already sitting." Killian snickered.

I scrunched my nose and gave him a dirty look. He was right, but still. You always started with sit when you were going to do a trick. Everyone knew that.

"Lie down, baby." I pointed to the ground and Brutus did so immediately. I whooped and jumped up and down then gave him half a piece of bacon. "Did you see that? He's so smart. You're so smart," I chanted to the beautiful dog.

"Okay now...speak!" I said excitedly but he simply looked at me and didn't do anything. "Speak?" I tried again, but he didn't bark. I frowned and turned around. "I thought he knew this one?"

"Addy, he doesn't know it in English. *Gib laut!*" Killian said, and Brutus started barking.

I clapped. "Yay!" I said and gave him the bacon as Killian's friend approached us. The huge guy leaned against one of the large wooden columns and crossed his arms over his chest.

I waved with the bacon in my hand. "Sorry, I'm being rude. Just a sec, m'kay?" I said before looking back at Brutus who was being such a good boy, sitting still and not begging.

"Stay, sweetheart." I held up my hand.

"*Blieb*," Killian whispered out of the side of his mouth but loud enough for me, Atticus, and the dog to hear.

I rolled my eyes. "*Blieb*." *Stay*, I repeated and set the rest of the bacon on the ground then backed away. Brutus didn't so much as look at the bacon. He looked at me and me alone. "Go ahead, Brutus!" I called with glee and the dog went for the bacon the way I shoveled down tacos.

I wiped my hands on the napkin I held and then went over to Atticus. He was at least six foot four, had pitch-black hair, and a scruffy jaw that needed a shave but still looked mighty fine on him, but that wasn't what was so startling. Besides his sheer size and brawn, his eyes were a see-through blue-gray that reminded me a lot of my sister Simone's. He was a magnificent beast of a man. Still, not as hot as Killian but every hetero girl I knew would be wiping the drool off her chin after laying eyes on this guy.

He pushed off the column and put his hand out.

"Atticus Rella. You're Addison Michaels." His tone held awe. "Brother, I cannot believe you are dating Addison Michaels!" He shook my hand with a huge grin on his face. "You're fucking gorgeous," he blurted then looked at Killian. "Fitz man, how the hell did you score Addison fucking Michaels. She's like, the tippy top of the imagery taped to the tent walls back at base."

I giggled and went to Killian's side. "That must be awkward," I taunted while walking my fingers up my guy's incredible abdominals and chest. "Jealous?" I continued to tease.

He covered my hand when I reached his pecs and held it warm against him. "I'm confident in my status, so no, I'm not jealous. Still, show a little respect, brother," Killian demanded on a grumpy growl, and Atticus's smile dropped as he proceeded to shove his hands into his pockets.

"Yo, no disrespect, Addison. It's just you're, *Addison Michaels*. I had no idea Fitz was dating a supermodel known around the world."

I grinned. "Yep. I get that a lot. It's perfectly fine and thank you for the compliment."

Atticus rubbed the back of his neck. "Guess I oughta get out of your hair…"

"No, no way! Killian just spent the day with me and my family. I'd love to get to know his best friend and I promised to cook tonight."

"Well, I did get a four pack of chicken…" Atticus added.

"Perfect, then you'll stay. Right, Killian?" I hedged.

My guy rubbed my shoulder then up my neck to the back of my head where he worked out a knot I'd been prodding all day. "Whatever you want," he said and then kissed my temple. "You want to go get settled in the kitchen? I'm gonna have a chat with my friend here on the roof."

"Uh oh, that means I'm in trouble." Atticus snickered.

I smacked Killian's bicep. "Don't be causing any trouble, especially after your friend helped with Brutus today."

"Yeah! I helped with Brutus and I picked up enough groceries to last a week. That's gotta earn some points in my favor."

Killian went over to his brother in arms and clapped him on the back smiling. "It's all good. Brutus, let's go, buddy." He snapped his fingers and the dog followed him and Atticus toward the stairs in the far corner. I watched them ascend the first floor, go into the area that was filled with plants, and take the next set before disappearing from view.

I set about washing my hands from playing with Brutus and pulling together the ingredients to make my famous breaded chicken, alfredo noodles, and sautéed fresh green beans complete with a half a loaf of garlic bread.

By the time the guys made it back down from the roof the chicken was baking, the noodles boiling, and the veggies sizzling. I'd set three place settings after I located where all the items were.

"Beer, wine, or something else?" I called out as the guys approached.

"Smells amazing, Addy," Atticus stated as he took a seat in front of one of the place settings.

"Thank you."

Killian came around and crowded me from behind, wrapping his arm around my waist and planting a kiss to my bare neck where I'd pulled my hair up and out of the way while I cooked. A little tremor of arousal slid down my spine.

"I'll get it. What do you want?" Killian said.

"Do you have white wine? It would go really well with the chicken."

He nodded and went to the wine fridge I'd spied earlier but hadn't catalogued yet. He grabbed a sauvignon blanc and opened it, pouring a glass for me alone. The guys both went for beers.

I finished up and plated the meals, then set one in front of each man before leaving the last one for myself.

"Gorgeous and can cook? Brother, you won the lottery with this one," Atticus said then quickly shut his mouth and hummed in pleasure around a bite of chicken.

"I put the other two halves on both your plates, but you don't have to finish them both." I came around the counter and took my seat next to Killian at the ninety-degree edge, so I'd be able to see both Killian and Atticus at the same time. He really needed to get a huge dining table. There was plenty of room for it and if we ever had my family over, we'd need at least a twelve-seater.

Realizing where my thoughts had run, I quickly sipped my wine, washing away the permanence of that imaginary scene in my head and focused on Atticus.

"All right, Atticus, tell me all the embarrassing things you know about Killian."

Chapter
ELEVEN

H EAT.

An unbearable heat surrounded my entire body. Sweat dripped down my hairline and along my spine. My legs were twisted, held down, pinned. I couldn't breathe. Duct tape prevented my screams. I pushed against the sticky surface with my tongue, the texture shredding my tastebuds.

Air.

I couldn't get enough air.

White-hot fire burned against the tender flesh of my arms and I screamed out in agony, only no one would hear it in that dark place.

I thrashed against the blaze, each one feeling like a sizzling red fire brand against my skin. Tears fell down my cheeks, the sensation almost comforting against the unending inferno that raged throughout my body.

A blood-curdling scream wrenched from my lungs.

"Jesus Christ, Addy, wake the fuck up!" my captor said.

I shook my head, begging with my eyes, my heart, my very essence, but he continued to press the glowing embers against my skin over and over.

"No!" I screamed.

The man opened his mouth behind the mask and barking came out. A dog's ravage barking exited my captor's mouth like some twisted creature in a horror film.

"Addy, baby! Please," I heard coming from off in the distance, the man in front of me still barking wildly like a dog.

A dog.

Barking.

"Addy, baby…"

Hands held me down. A large body sitting on top of me.

"No!" *I screeched.*

"Addy, wake up! It's me. You're safe. You're home."

As if the lights had been flicked on, the barking man disappeared and turned into Killian's beloved face. The barking at my side still going strong, filling my ears, helping to remove me from the hellish place I'd been.

Brutus.

"Killian?" I whispered, staring at his face, hoping against everything within me that it was truly him. Not a dream. I wasn't still under the hold of my captor.

Killian released my wrists. "Thank, God. Jesus, baby." He leaned over me and kissed my forehead, then my tear-stained cheeks, my eye sockets, and then finally my mouth.

Brutus nudged my bicep and licked it several times. I reached out and patted his head which seemed to mollify him before I wrapped my arms around Killian's body and plunged my tongue deep within his mouth.

Needing to feel him.

Needing to taste him.

Needing to drown in the cool, crisp waters that he represented.

Needing to wash away every ounce of fear coating my skin with nothing but him.

Killian.

My savior. My man. My everything.

The skin on my arms was scalding hot but I didn't care. I whimpered against his kiss.

He pulled back and sucked in air.

"It hurts," I yelped and winced.

"What hurts, baby? Tell me, I'll take it all away," he promised, and I believed him.

"Burning. My arms are burning." The tears fell as I started to shake. "They hurt. They won't stop hurting."

"Baby, you're not there. You're right here. Let the fear go. I've got you. I promise you're safe."

"It hurts," I choked out. "Make it stop. Make it stop burning." My arms felt inflamed as though they were filleted open, with new, fresh wounds.

"Christ, okay, okay. I've got you." Killian jumped off the bed and ripped back the covers that were trapped around my kicking legs. "Fuck, you're all twisted up. No wonder you freaked." He shoved his arms under my knees and around my back and lifted me straight up off the bed in a princess hold.

I whimpered as the fire bloomed once again against my flesh. The nightmare still scoring its claws through my subconscious. The pain was real. So real. Even if it wasn't. At that moment, I couldn't feel the difference between what my mind remembered and what was reality.

He brought me into the ensuite off his bedroom and set me on the granite top of the vanity between two sinks. He grabbed two hand towels and soaked them under the water faucet.

"Arms," he demanded.

I stretched out my burning skin and saw the healed flesh but felt nothing but flames.

He laid the icy wet cloths over one forearm and then the other.

Instant relief.

I slumped against the mirror in a bone-weary respite, the cold water soothing the heat instantly. I watched as Killian wet another smaller wash rag, squeezed out the excess water, and pressed it to my forehead, then my burning cheeks and to my lips where I sucked some of the water against my dry tongue.

"You were back there," he surmised.

I nodded, unable to speak as he tended to me so gently.

He lifted my hair and put the heavenly cool cloth at my nape. I shivered but also sighed at the relief it provided. Bringing me back to the here and now.

"Does this happen a lot?"

I shook my head. "In the beginning, yeah. Usually it was Mama Kerri, Blessing, or Simone if she was sleeping with me that night. I'd scream about feeling the burns still and they'd put me in the shower. Sometimes fully clothed because I was inconsolable. Mama figured out what I needed right away. I needed the cold. Also, I needed a light in the bedroom. It helped stave off the nightmares when I was able to open my eyes and could see my surroundings."

He nodded. "I've got a nightlight in the guest bathroom. We'll move it up here."

"I'm sorry." I sniffled, tears welling once more. "I'm so sorry you had to see that." I swallowed against the humiliation and looked at the white wet cloths coating my arms, hating that I needed them desperately.

Killian cupped my cheeks and forced me to look at him. "Never apologize for your nightmares. They are a natural part of healing. One by one, we'll work through them. And when I have one of mine, you'll be there for me, right?"

"I will." I nodded avidly, wanting to be that safe space for him that he was becoming for me.

"The cold cloths help, yeah?"

"So much. I don't know why. And I haven't had a nightmare like this in at least a month. I thought they were gone."

"I've been back almost eighteen months and I still have nightmares. Like you, they go away for a long while, and then something I don't even realize triggers me and then just like that," he snapped his fingers. "They're back. Again, it's part of the process. You had a jam-packed day, Addy. A lot of it was pleasant, but so much of it wasn't."

I licked my lips. "You shouldn't have to deal with this when you've got your own worries," I croaked, the sorrow and shame buckling my resolve.

He lifted my chin with his hands. "What did I say to you before? There is no place I'd rather be, and I meant that. I firmly believe that people come into our lives for a reason." He dipped his head and looked straight into my watery eyes.

"Addy, I was losing hope in what I wanted to do in my career—with my photography, the one thing I was most passionate about. I didn't even want to lift the camera up again since the last thing I saw through it were my friends who died. Then you show up in this sinfully sexy lingerie, walking on that set with a splendor unlike any I've ever known, and I looked at you through my camera and saw nothing but beauty. It was like seeing the sun after a year of darkness. You gave me hope that day. Hope that I could find my place in this world once again."

"Killian," I whispered and reached out to place my hand

over his bare chest where his heart beat, needing to touch him physically, as he touched me with his words.

"Addy, I know it's fast, but I'm falling in love with you. When I see your face, I want to photograph it so everyone can see such beauty. When I see your smile, I want to memorize it to remember when I'm feeling down. When I see you with my dog, I see a future where children of mine are running around being doted on by their mother. Addy, every time I look at you, I see my future. And baby, it is so bright. You just have to open your eyes. It's right there in front of you. Stop pushing against this. Reach for it like I am. Accept it for what it is. Us finding our match. Finding the one person in the world meant just for us."

The tears fell as his words pierced my heart and filled it with a glowing light that spread through my veins taking away the pain, the fear, the anxiety, and the doubts that were preventing me from leaping into this with him.

"I want to be your light, Killian. I want that more than anything."

"Baby, you already are. Just soak it up. Let me show you how good it can be…" he whispered, his face getting closer inch by inch.

I flung the towels off my arms and into the sink, the fiery sensation long gone. Another fire was brewing, one that only Killian could ignite.

Killian slowly removed the cloth from my neck and tossed it with the others, then his hands came down to the hem of the simple seafoam green cotton nightgown I'd drunkenly put on before crashing almost face first into his bed after a great dinner with his friend.

He slowly started to push the hem up my thighs. His

gaze flared with intensity as he drew the cotton over my hips to my waist. One of his brows cocked in question.

I nodded so he continued to push the fabric up my torso. I raised my arms in the air as my large breasts were revealed inch by inch. He yanked the fabric over my head and flung it behind him with a grin. Then as I watched, his gaze swept down over my chest, stomach, small lace panties, thighs, and to my toes. He didn't speak as he ran his big hands up the sides of my thighs from knee to bum where he curled his fingers into the fabric of my underwear and started to tug. I put my hands down on the vanity and lifted enough so he could yank them past my knees and shove them off.

In a very brazen move, he curled his fingers around my knees and pressed my thighs open wide, his gaze heated and intense. I noted his nostrils flared and his chest lifted and fell as he breathed deeply where he stood.

He looked directly at my sex and I swear I could feel his gaze move over my body like a silky soft caress when it moved to one breast, then the other, my nipples hardening under his perusal.

I noted his sleep pants were tented dramatically, a darkened spot appearing near the waistband of the light fabric turning it a blacker shade of gray.

"Why aren't you touching me?" I whispered, letting out a long breath.

"Oh, I'm going to touch you. Lick you. Bite you. Eat you. I'm taking my time deciding where to start first. You only get one first taste."

"Take off your pants. I want to see you the way you're seeing me," I said softly.

His gaze didn't leave mine as he shoved off his sleep

pants and bared himself. His cock was long, thick, hard as stone, and weeping at the tip, proving how very much he genuinely liked what he saw when he looked at me.

"Touch me," I begged.

He licked his lips. "Where?"

"Anywhere. *Everywhere*." I ran my hands up my thighs, over my hips and to my breasts, flicking my fingers against the beaded tips. Arousal scored through every one of my nerve endings and I hummed in pleasure.

"Your body is insane." His hands went into fists at the sides of my thighs, the skin and knuckles turning white with his restraint. "I want to fuck you so hard you see stars. I want to make love to you until you sigh with contentment. I want to ravish you until you can't even remember your own name." He clenched his jaw as his brown eyes turned pitch black with lust.

"Yes, start there. All of that. I'll take it," I taunted, meaning every word.

His gaze shot up to mine. "Addy, when you invite me inside, there's no going back. Not with you. Not ever. One taste will never be enough."

"Then take two. Three. How about we round it out to ten?" I bit into my bottom lip and his eyes widened and his hands unlocked, slid up my thighs, wrapped around my bare ass, tipping my hips up as his mouth went straight between my thighs.

He wasn't one of those men who tentatively went down on a woman. Licking softly at first and growing more passionate.

No, Killian Fitzpatrick buried his face against my sex, his mouth open wide, his tongue plunging deep and reaching.

I cried out and locked one of my hands around the back of his head as he ate at my flesh as though he couldn't get enough.

He growled like an animal and in the moment, he was one. Entirely alpha male, marking his territory, destroying me with every flick of his tongue against my clit. Every deep plunge inside until I started getting in on the action, lifting my hips, gripping his hair like leather reins to a horse. I was wild, unbridled, bucking against his mouth uncontrollably. And if the way he sucked hard, dug his fingers into the flesh of my ass, and groaned was any indication, he loved every minute of me losing my damn mind.

Saying I was in Heaven was an understatement. My legs shook as he pushed them up onto the vanity in a vulgar carnal display I'd never felt confident enough to try before. But with Killian, there were no barriers. No room for insecurities. He was about freedom and all access. I was spread open for his taking. Whatever he wanted to do to me, he'd do, and I'd make it my mission in life to give it to him, enjoying every ounce of pleasure right along with him.

My sex throbbed as he rubbed his beard against the tender wet skin harshly, making me scream out and press him harder to my sex. An orgasm the size of a bubbling volcano roared through my system, starting where he sucked hard at my clit, stealing my breath. I opened my mouth, pressed my head against the mirror, my body arching as the orgasm rocketed through me, bursting out my limbs and forcing me to clamp down on Killian in a full-body hold. He moaned and sunk his tongue deep, tasting my release while I convulsed against his mouth. My vision blurred as the sensations speared through my nerve endings then slowly started to dull and glide into a glowing, drunken feeling. He licked and kissed at my sex, my inner thighs, and down to my knees as I came back to myself.

He stood up fully and smirked, wiping at his wet beard and glistening lips. His chest rose and fell like a conquering god and in that moment that's exactly what he was. His hair down around his shoulders in messy waves, the muscles in his biceps and pecs bulging, his abdominals misted with sweat. He looked like a fucking Viking who'd just ravaged his maiden. Definitely the hottest freaking man on the planet.

I watched in a haze as he wrapped his hand around his powerfully hard length and stroked it a few times. I mewled as he approached, cock in hand, his target—me.

"Condom?" he asked, his voice rugged and raspy.

"IUD," I stated instantly. "I'm clean. Haven't had sex in over a year and was tested when I got the IUD. You?" I licked my lips as he stroked his cock, rubbing his thumb around the wet head.

"Got tested ten months ago when I stopped fucking around," he stated gruffly his eyes going up and down my body. "Never fucked bare. Want to with you."

Feeling bold, I traced my hand down my stomach to my wet center and teased my clit, gasping at how sensitive I was. "Then fuck me bare." I used his naughty words, ramping up my need to feel him fuck me to about a thousand degrees. Dirty talk was new to me, but if it made me feel this hot and bothered after a blistering orgasm, I'd give it a go.

"You're my fucking fantasy, Addy. There's so much I want to do to you right now." His nostrils flared as he approached, rubbing the wide knobbed head of his cock all over my sex, wetting the tip lewdly and teasing himself and me in the process.

I tipped my hips farther back, bracing myself on the vanity, and wrapped my legs around his hips. He watched as he fed his cock inch by inch into my sex.

I tried to force him to go faster, to slam home but he wouldn't. His grip on my hip was unbendable, stretching me as he invaded one inch at a time.

"Please," I pleaded.

He licked his lips and thrust his hips in and out, still not planting his length entirely inside.

"I want to feel you…all of you," I begged wanton and needy.

I clenched my vaginal muscles around the few inches inside and he hissed and pressed his forehead to mine.

"Kiss me," he murmured.

I brought one hand to his jaw and pressed my lips to his, tasting the earthy tang of myself on his lips and tongue. He opened his mouth wider and as his tongue slid inside, so did his cock, implanting to the root. I sat up and locked my body around his, kissing him deeply as he held me impaled on his length.

"You feel…perfect." He sighed, wrapped his arms around my body, and lifted me up off the vanity. I locked my limbs around him as he carried us to his bed. There he lifted a knee to the mattress and brought me down slowly.

When he was completely above me, he slid even deeper. I was filled to the brim, wrapped in warmth, safety, and love. I could feel it from the tips of my toes to the tingling in my scalp.

This was different.

Being with him like this was unique. Special. One of a kind.

Killian reared back and then plunged in fully. I arched and moaned, the pleasure unlike anything that had come before. Nothing compared to this.

Killian continued to kiss me, his hips pistoning in an even gliding rhythm meant to please and pleasure, not bruise in earth-quaking thrusts.

My mind swirled as he ran his tongue down the column of my neck, the chill in the air attacking the wet flesh in icy pinpricks adding to the unbelievable sensations he brought out in me. He moved to my breast, lifted the heavy weight with his large hand, and tongued the tip before sucking on it. Tendrils of lust and excitement roared through my chest as he laved, flicked, and nipped at my erect peak. He pleasured one breast and then moved to the next, repeating the attention.

By the time he was done with my breasts, I was beyond ready to be fucked. Needed it even.

"Harder, baby. Please," I whispered against his mouth when he came up for a drugging kiss.

"Making love to you, Addy," he murmured in answer, kissing me and thrusting his hips, keeping a beautiful rhythm that had my toes curling and sex throbbing.

"Make love to me harder, baby," I demanded. "I'm losing my mind." I gasped as he pinched one of my nipples with a sneaky hand.

He bit into the space where my shoulder and neck met but not hard enough to bruise. "That's the point. Get you out of your head. Lost to me and how I can make your body sing." He tunneled one hand under my back and up to my shoulder, curling around the edge. The other went to my ass cheek. He used this leverage to plunge deeper, a bit harder, hitting that space inside of me that made me lost to anything but the need for release.

"Oh God." I wrapped my legs higher up his ribcage and strained against the full feeling of his cock hitting me exactly where I needed it.

"Mmm, you like it right *there*." He swirled his hips in mind-blowing circles and I lost my ability to breathe. I dug my fingernails into his back, indenting the skin as I lost it.

He picked up the pace and finally, blessedly, used his leverage on my shoulder and bum plunging deep, hard, and fast. My teeth rattled as an orgasm so huge raced to the surface.

"Fuck, fuck, fuck, yaaaaaaassssss," I cried as it came over me in thundering waves, not stopping for anything.

Killian's body strained against mine, his body misting with sweat as he continued to take me.

I clenched every muscle I had left, wanting him to feel everything I felt.

"Jesus, fuck, Addy." He rode me harder, his hips a blur as I reached down and gripped his ass cheek and plastered my mouth to his shoulder where I bit down.

"Fuck yeah," he roared, holding my body in a vice lock, and planted his cock deep inside, before finally letting go.

His essence flooded me with jolt after jolt of heat while his body slowly started to relax, his weight pressing me into the mattress. For a few seconds he panted harshly against my neck, gifting me feathery kisses in between catching his breath.

Killian shifted his weight, wrapping his arms around me

and rolling to his back with me on top, our bodies still intimately connected.

His cock was softening inside of me and I gloried in not only knowing but *feeling* this private side of him.

I snuggled against his skin as he ran his hands up and down my back, my booty, my sides, along the flesh where my breasts were squished out to the sides of our plastered chests.

For a long time, neither of us spoke, content to wallow dreamily in the aftermath of our lovemaking. When his hands came up to my neck and he tapped at my cheek, I lifted my head.

"How you doing?" he asked me, no hint in his expression as to what he was thinking or feeling himself.

"Good, you?" I frowned and watched as his face twisted into an arrogant grin.

"Just made love to my woman for the first time and it was the best of my life. So yeah, I'm doing pretty good." He laughed.

I giggled and planted my face against the center of chest.

He wove his fingers through my thick hair. "Hey?"

I lifted my head again.

"You okay? The dream and then you know, all that I said and we did?"

God, this man was amazing. I shifted enough to cross my arms on his chest and rest my chin to my arms. "The dreams suck. They're frightening. What happened in the aftermath of that dream was not. You taking care of me, bringing me back from that awful place and then giving me the best sex ever… Yeah, not gonna complain, handsome."

He out and out smiled wide. "Best sex ever?"

"What you did in the bathroom, that was fantasy level for a girl like me."

He frowned. "A girl like you?"

"Yeah, you know, a bigger girl. I can't speak for everyone, but I don't usually bare all, spread my legs like an eagle's wings on a counter with the light blazing down over me, and let a man go to town. Even though I'm super confident in my shape."

"Uh, why not? Do you have any idea how sexy your body is to me? All those curves. Huge tits, sweet pussy…" He slid his hands down to my plump ass. "This ass. The things I'm going to do to it. Baby, it's depraved the ways I want to fuck you. The ways I'm *going* to fuck every inch of you. Very soon and for a long time. Years in fact."

I clamped my hand over his mouth and bugged my eyes out. "You're so dirty!"

He licked my hand and I snapped it back and shook it. "See!" I waved it as proof.

He chuckled and then gripped my hips. "Addy, life is messy. Sex is messy. Good sex can be downright filthy. There is nothing about your curvy body that doesn't make me insane with lust. Thin girls have their own thing going on. Some men like that slinky, athletic vibe on a woman. Other men like fake tits and filled lips. I don't judge. Women are beautiful in whatever makes them feel good about themselves. I just happen to be a man who likes round curves, huge tits, thighs and hips for gripping, and a juicy ass. I don't care if you weigh more or less than me. I want all of those soft curves all over me. Period. It's what I'm into. And I'm telling you right now, you will not hide this incredible body from me. I want an all-access pass to it."

I rolled my eyes. "All-access pass. What am I, an amusement park?"

He flipped me so quick to my back, his cock slid out of me. His smiling face and twinkling eyes hovered over me, his long hair tickling my bare shoulders and neck. "That's the perfect analogy. My woman's body is my own personal amusement park. I like this idea." He dipped his head and swirled his tongue around one peak before running his teeth over it sharply. I gasped. Even though I'd been satiated twice, arousal flickered to life as he teased my nipple.

"I'm getting ready for another ride," he warned.

"What? Seriously? You just banged me silly."

He grinned, then held an arm up in the air, his hand in a fist. "Toot-toot. All aboard Killian Fitzpatrick's amusement park for one!"

I cracked up. "That's a train conductor! Not a ticket guy at an amusement park."

"Who says there isn't a train at my amusement park of love?" He bit into his bottom lip trying not to laugh.

"You are such a dork!" I cupped his smiling cheeks.

"At least I'm your dork." He brought his face down and took my mouth in a deep, wet kiss that gave me all the feels. As he pulled back and went straight for my boobs, cupping them with both hands and running his thumbs over the tips simultaneously, I sighed in pleasure.

"You are definitely my dork." I ran my thumb over his wet bottom lip. "And I'm keeping you."

He grinned, waggled his eyebrows, and got to work, enjoying his amusement park for one.

Good thing I was a thrill seeker. I enjoyed every ride that night to the fullest.

Chapter
TWELVE

W E SPENT THE BETTER PART OF THAT WEEK SHOOTING
around his house. The bedroom, the teal couch,
near his bookcase, and anywhere else he could
come up with that we both agreed would not only look cool,
but genuine.

"This is going to seem totally cheesy..." His voice busted
through my focus. "But I want you to hold the watering can
and actually water the plants but stick that fine ass in the air
as you reach that hanging one in the corner. That way I can
see the scallop on the panties as well as where the teddy falls
on the body."

I gripped the old-fashioned metal watering can around
the handle, put my bare foot to the small rickety-looking
stepstool, and teetered half my weight on it while getting up
on my toes on my right foot. I lifted my hips and ass, making
sure my legs looked long and the right muscles were engaged
as I did so. I delicately placed my hand around one of the
metal rungs running along the wall and torqued my body
so that the pale pink teddy I wore rode up my hips and waist
and showed just the cheeks of my ass while I watered a plant
that was taller than me.

"Tilt your head and let your hair fall entirely to one side.
I want to see your profile as well as the front of the teddy

because your breasts—shit, baby. They look good enough to eat!" He complimented but none of those compliments hit their target. I was in too much pain.

I did as he said, letting my curls fall to the right side as I reached and tilted my head and ass just so. All of this while I was literally getting a crick in my neck, a charley horse in my calf muscle, not to mention my big toe felt like it was about to fall off.

"Get the freakin' picture already!" I grouched as I let my mouth fall softly open in my ethereal, dreamy facial pose.

"Got it!" he called out and I practically fell sideways against the other plants while I tried to catch my bearings. "Shit, are you okay?" Killian raced over and took my hand, giving me the leverage I needed to get both feet on the floor safely.

"Did you get the shot?" I huffed, working my legs in a standing still-walking pattern to help the kinks in the muscles.

He grinned wickedly and showed me the camera. "What did I tell you?" He flicked through picture after picture of a damn good series of photos.

"Not only do you look like a goddess in the pink, with the light coming in from above, the green from the plants all around you, the softness of the color and fabric against your skin as you do something rather domestic… Addy, you're what every woman, every mom at home taking care of her house wants to look like."

I watched as he scanned through one great photo after another. "And the best part, it's rather attainable for the everyday woman. I like this series vibe. Sexy lingerie not just for date night, but for every night. Even when you have to do something as mundane as watering the plants."

He chuckled, wrapped his arm around me, and waited until I looked up at him.

His face descended and he took my mouth in a searing kiss that lasted quite a long time. My heart started to pound as teasing ribbons of arousal moved through me. I lifted my hand and wrapped it around his neck, pressing my body tighter to his. He took the hint and shuffled me over and against the glass partition that served as the wall to this area and the rest of the walkway to his small gym.

In a rather stealthy move, he reached out his hand and hooked the camera and strap on a hook that already held a plant. It clanged against the base of the plant, but he didn't show any concern. If he didn't care that his likely expensive camera was dangling on a plant hook possibly getting dewy from the moisture of the plant, who was I to say anything?

Besides, my mouth was too busy.

Sucking on his bottom lip.

Swirling my tongue against his.

"We doing this," he mumbled against my mouth and then went in for a deep plunge of his tongue.

"Oh yeah." I wrenched my mouth away to catch my breath but that didn't mean my hands weren't busy ripping his T-shirt over his head to get my greedy fingers on all that muscled golden skin.

He ripped it off then pulled the ties on the front of my teddy and watched fascinated as my breasts naturally stretched the fabric open.

"Hell yeah," he said in awe while gripping the fabric and stretching it wide enough that my breasts came out of their confinements. He teased each tip with his thumbs then dipped his head and sucked hard enough for me to gasp and retaliate by plunging my hands into the back of his gray sweatpants and straight to his ass where I gripped tight, forcing his length against me.

He groaned against my breasts then pulled back and waited for me to look into his eyes. They were twinkling with excitement. I licked my lips and bit down on my bottom one so I wouldn't moan like a cock-hungry ho, but in that moment, I was exactly that. A cock-hungry ho.

Killian grinned and then ran his hand down the fabric of my silky teddy to where it split up the center. He swirled a finger around my belly button teasingly. I swallowed as gooseflesh rose on my skin. The man just smirked, knowing exactly what he was doing to me. But his hand did not stop there. Oh no. It trailed down, his palm twisting so that his warmth slid along my skin until his fingers hit the bullseye.

I inhaled sharply as he teased that throbbing bundle of nerves with two magical fingers.

"Sensitive?" His voice held a thick rasp that sent chills of need racing up and down my spine.

I nodded.

He cocked a brow and pressed his face only an inch away from my own. I could feel his hot breath against my lips to the point that we were almost breathing one another's air. It was intimate, balmy and humid in a way that reminded me of beautiful summer afternoons under the Hawaiian sun. With his hair down, surrounding us both as he played with me, it was as if we were miles away from Chicago and anything other than just the two of us didn't exist.

Killian slid his fingers further between my thighs, dipping not one but two of them inside, using my arousal to ease his entry.

I gasped and moaned, not capable of pretending that what he was doing between my legs wasn't killing me in the best way possible.

"Do you like when I touch you? Tease you?" he murmured hotly against my lips.

"Yes." I tipped my head back and closed my eyes on a particularly delicious plunge of his thick fingers.

"Look at me, baby." He swirled his thumb against my clit, and I thrust my hips against his movements.

"Please…" I begged, not having any idea what I was begging for. Just wanting everything. Anything he was willing to give. Whatever would make this simmering pleasure explode the way I knew he could take it.

"Please what?" He moved his fingers in and out a little faster, twirled his thumb in the exact right spot a little harder.

"Fuck me," I sighed, pressing my forehead to his and reaching for his mouth with my own.

He let my lips barely touch his before he backed his face just out of reach of my mouth. "I am fucking you. I'm finger-fucking you against the wall of my garden. And I'm going to do so until you come all over my fingers…"

"Killian, the things you say." I groaned and dug my nails into his ass, thrusting my hips in counter movements to his.

"I like the way you ride my fingers. Like watching you lose your mind from my touch. You're so beautiful, Addy. Being the only one to see you like this, with your light eyes dark with pleasure, your body moving against mine wantonly, your lips bruised and swollen from my kisses. Hot damn. Do you have any idea how out of my head you make me? How hard you make my dick?"

"Oh God, baby." I lifted my leg and hooked it up and around his hip forcing his body to press against me, which had the amazing effect of giving his fingers just the right leverage to reach that spot inside that made me scream.

"Fuck, yeah." He wedged in another finger, pressed high, and tugged down rhythmically with those miraculous digits.

I saw stars.

Actual blinky little white, yellow, and hazy blue stars at the sides of my vision popping like lightning bugs in my peripheral.

A definite first. He said he was going to make me see them and he was not wrong.

I convulsed against his fingers, but he didn't stop. He was relentless in his desire to give me the best experience, plunging deep, then pulling out and pinching my clit in a way that took my orgasm from a ten to a hundred in a second flat.

I cried out and let the waves roll through me one after another, stretching, lengthening my body, allowing every new sensation to bathe me in its magnificence. Eventually, I finally came down from the high into my man's loving arms, cradling me against his big, bare chest until I caught my breath.

"Damn, baby," he murmured against my misted cheek.

The aftershocks made me twitch and hum with pleasure each time one of them came over me until I realized something down below was still hot, hard, and ready to go. Which is when I decided I was going to flip the switch and make him feel everything he'd just given me.

Moving quicker than he expected, I twisted us around

until he was ass to the glass, and I was in front of him. Which is also when I stepped a foot away, put my palms against his glorious chest, and slowly fell to my knees, trailing my hands down that powerful lovely skin, boxed abdominals, and straight to his tented gray sweatpants. I hooked my fingers into those pants and tugged those suckers down to his knees and left them there, limiting his ability to move or take over.

I ran my nails down the backs of his tree-trunk-sized thighs and he groaned in reply.

His cock jutted out proud and thick bobbing slightly in front of my face. I chanced a look up at Killian and what I saw there almost moved me to tears. Features set in soft beautiful lines, awe and wonder in his expression as though seeing me on my knees was an immeasurable gift.

With my gaze stuck on his, I wrapped my hand around his girth and took just the head inside my mouth. Swirling my tongue around and around the mushroom-capped head. I didn't take my eyes off him as I did so. Enjoying too much how he responded. His nostrils flared and his hands fisted at his sides, but he didn't look away. I'd figured out pretty quickly that my guy liked to watch.

Well, I was about to give him a show.

I sucked him inside and went as far as I could go, using my tongue to tease along the length. He pressed his hands flat to the glass behind him and I started bobbing, swallowing his length like my very favorite treat.

I got so into it I didn't even notice at first when one of his hands dove into my hair at the back of my head and threaded through the tresses, helping me move the way he wanted.

I sloppily slid his length out and pressed my lips just to the tip and looked into his eyes. "You like control in the bedroom," I stated and flicked the glistening head with my tongue, teasing inside the small slit at the tip.

Killian hissed through his teeth and his grip on my hair strengthened.

"What do you want to do to me right now? Hmmm?" I taunted, lazily swirling my tongue and running my hand up and down his erection in slow, measured tugs.

His jaw went rock hard as he pulled my hair at the roots. "Want you to suck me hard," he grated through his teeth.

I grinned and gave him a few long, luxurious sucks. "Like that?" I asked in a sultry tone while batting my eyelashes.

He made a rumbling noise in the back of his throat that led me to believe he was about to lose control. Which was exactly why I was baiting him.

"Addy, don't fuck around," he warned.

"But I thought the fucking was what you wanted?"

He inhaled and firmed his grip on my hair, bringing my head closer toward his cock. "I'm going to lose it, toss you to the ground, and fuck you stupid hard against the concrete if you don't stop messing around. I see what you're doing."

I grinned thinking I might prefer him fucking me hard against the floor, but I wanted him to lose his mind.

"Oh? Is this what you want?" I asked and then mustered up every ounce of passion I had and took him into my mouth all the way to the root.

"Holy fuck!" He roared, lost to his pleasure, yanking my hair in a painful way that eased into a throbbing, tingling pleasure between my thighs.

My eyes watered, but I didn't let up, pulling back and taking him hard to the root once more.

"Fuck, yeah. Take me down your throat." And there was the dirty-talking man I was hoping to bring out.

I did as he asked. Repeatedly. Loosening up my throat, softening my tongue, and taking him as far as possible. I gagged on his cock but every time I did so, salty beads of his essence coated my tongue proving that my guy was loving every second.

With a swirl of my tongue, I backed off, looked up at his passion-filled face and said the words I knew he was waiting to hear. I could feel his need running through my veins as though it were my own pleasure and not his.

"Take over, baby." I mouthed his tip.

He shook his head and cupped my cheek with his other hand.

"Do it," I said before taking him inside only a few inches, back and forth in slow movements that would not give him what he needed.

He inhaled and stared at me. I sucked as hard as I could and his head tipped to the sky, the fingers of his right hand twisted in my hair and holding me so I couldn't move. Then with the hand cupping my jaw, he put his thumb to my bottom lip and stretched it so wide the hinge of my jaw smarted against the pull. It didn't matter.

Killian thrust his hips, pushing his length at the perfect angle to go straight down my throat. It was shocking, frightening, and arousal-inducing to the extreme.

My panties were soaked as he held me where he wanted and did exactly as I asked. Taking his pleasure, the way he wanted.

Tears filled my eyes, but I didn't care. I wanted every second of this moment. One where I was in complete control but then again, not. Knowing that at the slight shift of my head or discomfort on my face and he'd move faster than lightning to fix it.

A dreamy, sensual haze clouded my mind and left my body loose and pliant. Killian thrust in and out, his body shaking with the effort. When his grip tightened, I curled my hands around his hips and let the vibrations of his control over me and his use of my body to get his pleasure flood my senses in an endless feeling of contentment.

For a few seconds, Killian lost himself to the sensations, plunging at his whim. Suddenly he locked down on his hold in my hair and my jaw and thrust in a way that I knew meant this was it.

His body went ramrod straight and stone still as he roared his release.

I stayed with him to the last second when he yanked his hips back and went down to his knees where I sat on my shins. He cupped my cheeks with both hands, his powerful frame still moving with the force of his intake of air.

"Baby, you are beyond compare. What I just experienced...wow. You're something else. Not like any woman I've known, and I'm so fucking blessed to call you mine." He crooned in a worshipful tone that had tears pricking the backs of my eyes.

"Come here." He tugged me against his chest and kissed me. His pants were still around his knees awkwardly, but it didn't seem to matter to him. It was as if nothing but connecting with me was important right then.

We made out like teenagers for quite some time until

eventually I couldn't take being on the cold concrete or my legs in that position any longer.

I eased back and cupped his jaw. "Two things. One, I feel like my legs are about to fall off." He chuckled and grinned. "Two, I'm starving. All this sex means a girl has got to eat. Load up on those calories or the next time you're going to have to do all the work."

Killian laughed, stood up, yanked his pants back in place, and offered his hand. I took hold and got up. As I did, my phone buzzed where it sat on a small pop-up table Killian used to store his lenses, extra cameras, and other photography items I couldn't name.

"You get that, and I'll get started on some lunch. I'm thinking grilled bacon, cheese, and tomato paninis with a salad on the side?"

My stomach growled audibly. I massaged my belly in response. "Sounds heavenly." I giggled and went for my phone. As I grabbed the matching robe and shoved my arms through, I noted the display said, "The Sprite" on the screen.

"Hey, Liliana. What's shaking, sister? Aren't you supposed to be in school teaching?"

"Minimum day. Which I also forgot to mention to my big, stupid brute of a bodyguard, so now I'm stuck waiting inside the hallway of the school. Because Omar the Ogre won't let me drive my own stinking car to and from work."

I slumped against the wall. "I'm sorry my situation is messing with your life. I know how much this sucks."

She sighed. "It's fine. All for one, one for all. But I'm done with Omar the Obstinate. Can't I have someone else?"

"Is he really mean to you? Saying things he shouldn't?

What?" I asked with concern because if someone was upsetting my sister, I was all in for shutting that crap down right away.

"No. He babies me like I'm a child at my own school! *¡Es ridículo!* I mean, I know that none of us are safe, blah blah, I get that. He takes it to the extreme. Won't even let me stand outside with another teacher to wait for him to arrive."

"Hmm, have you talked to him?" I took the stairs down toward where I heard Killian cooking and humming in the kitchen. I placed my butt on a stool and watched my fine ass man cook for me. His back was littered with scars from the IED blast he survived but it didn't take away from his handsomeness even one iota. And he treated me the same regarding the scars on my arms. He didn't bring attention to them, but he also didn't shy away from touching me there.

"*¡Por supuesto! ¡Yo hice! ¡Simplemente me ignora!*" She went off in Spanish, losing me completely. Liliana tended to revert to Spanish when she was angry or overly emotional.

"Sis, you said that in Spanish, now tell me again after you've taken a breath with me. Okay? Inhale fully and hold it at the top." I could hear her quick inhalation. "Now release it slowly." She did as I said. "Better?"

"*Sí, gracias.* What I was saying was, yes, I told him he was irritating me, and he just ignored me. Which he does, all the time. Again, like I'm *una niña,* a child!" She clarified, but I happened to know that *niña* meant child. "He just ignores me and looks at me with that smug smile on his face and tells me I'm cute when I'm mad!" Her voice rose.

"Cute?"

"*Sí,* it's infuriating," she spat, as though she was ready to pop off and punch the guy.

"Honey, he told you that you were *cute* when you were mad?" I had to clarify.

"*Sí*, are you listening to me?" Then I heard a noise that sounded like she was banging her hand against the phone. "Is this thing on?"

I laughed heartily. Freakin' Liliana was a hoot. And totally and completely clueless when it came to men who were interested in her.

"Yes, I'm listening. I'm all ears, in fact. And what I'm hearing is that your bodyguard likes you," I stated directly.

She made a pssshaw sound and I could so easily imagine her jerking her head back in affront, her curls bouncing all over the place as she narrowed those pretty eyes and perfectly arched eyebrows.

"This is simply not true, *mi hermana*."

I groaned and then came up with a great idea to prove my point. "Hey babe," I called out to Killian. "If a guy tells a woman that she's cute when she's mad, what does that mean? Hold up, Lil, I'm putting you on speaker phone." I pressed the speaker button and held the phone out. "Okay, Killian, what does it mean?"

"I'm no expert but if it were me, I'd assume that the guy is into the woman. Cute is another way to say pretty in my experience."

"See! That's my take too. Lil, the guy is into you." I smiled at Killian who shook his head and continued to cook the bacon for our grilled sandwiches.

"He is not into me! All you sisters all goo-goo gah-gah for your men think everyone is in love with everyone. *Estúpida*. Simone asked me a similar thing yesterday. Aye! And now here he comes, pulling up his blacked-out SUV acting like he's the President of the United States. *Dios mío.* I've got to go."

"Wait, wait! You didn't tell me whether or not you're into him too?"

"And I'm not going to! *Adios,*" she said and then hung up abruptly.

I grinned at Killian who turned around with a big smile on his face.

"She's into him." I chuckled.

"Definitely into him," Killian agreed.

"It will be fun to watch that giant Omar take on the Sprite. Hope he has insurance. That little fireball has teeth!"

Killian snickered as he placed two thick wedges of cheese, bacon, and two red juicy slices of tomato onto each sliced and buttered focaccia bread. "My money is on the Sprite. Or wait, I mean on the bodyguard winning the Sprite. Really does it matter as long as it all works out?"

I shook my head, got off my stool, and went over to stand behind him, wrapping my arms around his waist. "Nope. As long as two good people find one another, I'm happy to watch it play out."

"Me too." He craned his neck around and kissed me briefly, then went back to work on the sandwiches.

I held on to him from behind, resting my cheek to his back thinking about how I could help my sister bag the man of her dreams, even if she was being sassy and standoffish about it. Liliana deserved to find happiness and if she was venting as much as it sounded like, my gut instinct was that she was definitely hot for her bodyguard.

Only time would tell.

Chapter
THIRTEEN

"LOOK AT THIS GOOD BOY," I COOED AT BRUTUS AS HE brought me back the tennis ball I'd thrown as far as I could down the stretch of grass at the dog park Killian visited.

It was my first outing in the last two weeks since this all started, and I planned to enjoy every minute. I lobbed the ball once more and off Brutus went after it at a dead run. The Rottweiler was super-fast for a big dog.

"Do you think he'd be nice to Amber?" I asked Killian who was leaning against the metal chain link fence typing something out in his phone.

He finished texting and then shoved his phone in his back pocket. "He'll do whatever I say. If I introduce him and use commands to express my wishes, he'll follow along. He's been very good with dogs in the past that were here. He has a great personality; it's just he's meant to protect me and now you. His breed takes that commitment seriously."

Brutus ran back, his tail wagging excitedly as his dad pointed to the ground and told him to drop the ball. He did so immediately, then sat, waiting for his next command. Killian picked up the ball and threw it much farther than I did. The dog didn't so much as twitch until Killian gave the command for Brutus to retrieve it.

"He doesn't do that with me?"

Killian smiled. "Because you didn't set up those parameters with him out of the gate. You're a huge pushover. He has you wrapped around his big ass paw."

"I love him, I can't help it." I looked at the sweet boy dashing back.

"Baby, you've made it clear to him who the boss is in your relationship...and I hate to say it, but it's not you." He grinned.

My mouth dropped open as the shock of his statement hit me. "He's not the boss of me!" I fired back as Brutus returned and looked to me then his daddy waiting for his command.

"Come here, Brutus." I pointed to the ground near my feet. Brutus looked to Killian who lifted his chin. The dog went over and sat by my feet.

I narrowed my gaze as Killian smirked and I pet Brutus on his boxy head. "Okay, baby. Give me the ball." I took the ball from his mouth which he let me do no problem. "See! I got the ball easy!" I held it up so Killian could see the prize. Then I tossed it as far as I could. "Now..." But before I could get the command out of my mouth, Brutus ran for it straight away.

Killian chuckled, then whistled and Brutus brought the ball back to *him*, not me, and sat right next to his daddy's leg.

"Show off," I grumbled.

"Just because he listens to my commands doesn't mean he won't listen to you too. You're the good cop and I'm the bad cop. How about that?"

I shrugged a shoulder. "I guess it's better to be the good cop." I crouched down. "Come here, boy!"

He didn't move from his dad's leg but started to whimper and wiggle his tail as though he were dying to come to me but knew better than to do so after his dad had made a command.

Killian gave the order and Brutus happily came to me and licked up the side of my face. Killian passed me the leash and I hooked it around Brutus's thick neck and kissed his brow. "Next time we'll show Daddy who's boss. Huh, boy?" I rubbed my nails down his spine in a move I knew he adored.

Brutus barked as though he were answering.

"See!"

"Oh, you showed me." Killian laughed as I rolled my eyes and clicked my tongue against my teeth to get Brutus walking.

"Baby, that's the sound you make when you're leading a horse."

I groaned under my breath and moved ahead, Brutus happily taking the lead until Killian caught up and interlaced our fingers. "Don't be surly. I've had him since a week after I got back. He's been with me the entire time. Helped me through a lot. We have a different bond but you're building your own and however that plays out is a good thing." He nudged my shoulder playfully.

"Hmmphff," I huffed yet continued to hold Killian's hand all the way back to his apartment.

What we saw when we got there was a disaster waiting to happen. Surrounding the front of the building was a crowd of paparazzi. Not one or two, but a full-on gaggle of them. At least twenty or more.

"Damn it. They figured out who you are and where you

live." I slumped against his side feeling defeated as our private hiding space was no longer a secret.

Killian took the leash from me and wrapped it around his hand multiple times until the dog was very close to his side. He looped me around the waist and started us forward. I kept my head down as we approached.

"*Addison, how long have you been dating Killian Fitzpatrick?*"

"*Is the relationship serious!*"

"*Do you have any connection to the three victims!*"

"*Do you believe this is a copycat killer or an obsessed fan!*"

The reporters and photographers screamed at me, relentless in their pursuit of some type of juicy morsel they could print about me, Killian, or the case.

"Back the fuck up!" Killian roared and Brutus started barking and growling like mad. "My dog will bite anyone that approaches me or Addison. Back up! That's your only warning!"

Brutus wedged himself between me and the crowd that was circling. He was vicious in his desire to take a bite out of anyone that so much as moved closer to me. One man reached out and Brutus responded on instinct, jumping at him, basically knocking him and his camera to the ground. Killian could barely hold on to the hundred-plus-pound dog as he jumped. The photographer's camera hit the concrete and I heard the sound of breaking glass.

"You're gonna pay for that!" the blubbering fool hollered.

Brutus stayed in front of me growling at the man trying to scramble back up and away from our dog.

"Really? You tried to attack my girlfriend after I warned you my dog would respond. And your stupid actions were caught by about fifteen other cameras! Try to come after me! You'll regret it," Killian sneered. "Now if you'll excuse us..." Killian yanked on my hand and the leash until we were safely inside the lobby where a lone desk and security guard usually stood.

"Frank?" Killian called out, thinking perhaps he was in the security camera area. From the moment I'd arrived here a couple weeks ago, there was always a man at the lobby desk or in the camera room. Killian passed me the leash and Brutus faced the glass door where the paparazzi was pressing their cameras taking a zillion pictures of me standing here with Brutus.

I watched as Killian knocked on the door to the security area, then opened the door. Inside was Frank, lying prone on the floor. Either he fell or was attacked in some manner but there wasn't blood anywhere and nothing else looked out of place.

Fear slithered up my spine and coated me in an icy chill I could feel bone-deep. Killian pressed his fingers to Frank's throat. "He's alive." He pulled out his phone and called the police.

"What should we do?" I asked, feeling the need to run, to hide, to *something*.

"We wait for the police to arrive," Killian stated stoically, perfectly calm while I fought the desire to crumble into a protective ball and let the world fly by me.

"But the paparazzi are right there." I jerked my chin toward where they were literally pressed to the glass. "I could take Brutus upstairs?"

Killian licked his lips and shook his head. "We can't be separated. I don't know what happened to him. He could have had a heart attack or been attacked. I don't know. It's not safe for you if someone did this to him. We don't know where that person may be and with a killer on the loose, who knows if he's in the loft right now. Jonah and Ryan are counting on me to take care of you when we don't have a body-guard hanging around. I can't have you leaving my sight."

For a second I weighed my level of fear. Being down here, out in the open with the paparazzi taking endless photos and freaking me out more or being brave and entering the one place I felt safe other than Kerrighan House. "Brutus will protect me," I pushed, wanting more than anything to get the hell away from the press and Frank's prone form.

Killian shook his head. "Baby, he can't protect you from a gun. Call Jonah for me," Killian said while sitting on the floor and holding his fingers to Frank's wrist and lightly tapping the man's face with his other hand.

I pulled out my phone, happy to have something to do. Moving further I wedged myself in next to Killian in the far corner. Every angle of the building was showing on several different screens. It looked like there was a camera for every corner of the building and one on each floor. The good news was I didn't see anyone outside any of the doors or the build-ing except for the vultures at the front.

"Addy? What's wrong?" Jonah clipped instead of greeting me.

"Um, we just got back from taking the dog for a walk," I said on a rush.

"Yes, I know. Fitz sends us a text every time you leave and come back to his loft. It's part of the deal and why you don't have a bodyguard at all times. Because he's capable of protecting you."

"He texts you our whereabouts?"

"Addy, honey, why did you call? I'm busy here," he said in a kind, but rather no-nonsense tone.

"The guard Frank is knocked out on the floor and we don't know why. Killian called the police. Also, the paparazzi are blanketing the front of the building and he doesn't think it's safe for me to go into the loft to wait. We're shacked up in the security room in the lobby."

"We'll be there in ten minutes. Don't go anywhere. Wait for backup. I mean it, Addy."

I swallowed against the dryness in my throat. "Okay. We'll stay put."

As I hung up, Frank started to move his head and limbs as though he were waking suddenly.

"Hey, hey, Frank. It's okay, man. You're all right. Don't move," Killian stated emphatically.

"Someone got the jump on me. I was muscled in here but just as I was going to go for my gun, my chest started to hurt and pain and numbness went down my left arm, and then it was lights out." Frank said.

"Did you see your attacker?" Killian asked.

Frank pushed against the floor, his black boots leaving rubber streaks against the white tile surface. Killian helped him sit up and against the wall. He held his hand over his heart as though that side of his body still hurt.

"At first all I saw was a man enter with a hat on, his face down toward the floor. I called out to him, but when he got close, he lifted his head and I realized he was wearing a ski mask under the hat. All of a sudden he reached out and tased me, then pushed me in here which was when the pain started in my arm and I lost consciousness."

Moments later, two police officers waded through the paparazzi and entered. Killian took the lead as I stood off to the side with Brutus literally sitting on my feet. Killian updated the cops and they tended to Frank and called an ambulance in to assist.

Killian led me and Brutus to the elevator.

"Jonah told me to stay put," I murmured, feeling out of sorts but remembering very clearly that my soon to be brother-in-law wanted me to stay where I was.

"It's okay. He'd want you out of the public eye. The police will deal with Frank and the FBI will look into it and find out what's going on. I think we'll be safer inside the loft."

Numbly I followed him inside and watched as the numbers climbed to the last floor.

The elevator dinged and we stepped out only to find Killian's door had been vandalized. Only it wasn't graffiti or someone trying to break in that was so frightening. Taped to the huge wooden surface were at least twenty to thirty eight-by-ten-inch photos.

Of me.

Of my sisters.

Of Mama Kerri.

Of my niece.

All of them were candid shots. One of me and Killian entering Kerrighan house last week. Which meant the killer had been standing outside somewhere watching us rather closely. Another was of Mama Kerri and Aunt Delores working at the flower shop. Another of Genesis walking hand in hand with my niece to her day care in the city. Charlie with a few youth center kids playing basketball. Blessing sitting at a lunch meeting at her favorite place downtown. Liliana in a standoff with her bodyguard in front of the school she teaches at. Simone and Jonah leaving his parents' house arm in arm. One of just my niece, a closeup of her sitting at the top of the slide at her daycare playground. In every picture with me in it, there was a big fat red heart over my face.

Each picture was like a knife to the gut.

Over and over.

One after another.

And dead center of it all was a huge single image of my smiling face. Written across the image in red were the words:

YOU CAN RUN BUT YOU CAN'T HIDE!

I shook where I stood, looking at each picture of the people I loved most in the universe. Their pictures had been taken when they weren't aware. My family had been followed by a madman.

A wooziness hit my gut and acid churned, threatening to come up as I wobbled on unsteady legs.

"Breathe, baby, just breathe." Killian surrounded me from behind. My teeth started to chatter, and tears fell down my cheeks as I stared at the door. Everything I loved and held dear was at risk, because of me.

The elevator dinged and out came two beloved faces.

Jonah and Ryan.

The calvary.

Jonah came to me first as Ryan did a double take of me, then the door, back to me, and the door again.

"Addy." Jonah reached out as though to embrace me, but I flinched and backed closer against Killian's chest. Brutus growled where he sat in front of me, warning Jonah not to touch. He obviously took his social cues from his family and regardless of whether or not Jonah had been introduced as a friendly person, Brutus would engage if I proved uncomfortable with him.

Honestly, I don't know why I backed away from Jonah, but I knew with my entire being that if he held me, coddled me with those sweet brown eyes and loving face that meant the world to my sister, I'd break. Crumble into a heaping pile of ash and blow away. I was barely hanging onto my emotions as it was.

"Nein." Killian commanded the dog, but he didn't back away, he just stopped growling at Jonah.

"He's escalating," Ryan stated aloud, his mouth tightening into a white, flat line as he pulled out his phone.

Jonah turned around and took in the wall of horror. His gaze flicked from one family member to the next, stopping on the image of him and Simone in front of his parents' house. I knew that was their house because I'd been invited to a family weekly dinner in the not-so-distant past. Jonah's parents were tons of fun and his mother a damn fine cook. Jonah's hands fisted as he assessed the note in the center.

"Open the door, but we'll go in and check it out first," Jonah commanded.

Killian pulled his keys out of his pocket and handed them over with the right key sticking out from the rest.

Jonah opened the door and he and Ryan disappeared through it.

Killian spun me around and tugged me into his arms. I held on so tight, my breath left my body in my attempt to merge even closer into him and away from all the craziness that was invading my life right now.

He cupped the back of my head and whispered in my ear. "You're fine. You're safe. I'm here. Your family is okay. Jonah and Ryan are on top of this."

I nodded but still trembled in his arms.

"When will it be over?" I choked out.

"Soon. I'm sure it will be over soon."

Jonah appeared and opened the door the rest of the way. "It doesn't look like the loft has been breached but why don't you take a look around and see if you notice anything out of place." He bent over and inspected the lock. "No signs of attempted lock-picking. I think he just wanted to scare you. My guess, same reason he didn't kill the security guard. Frank wasn't the target. Scaring you was. Maybe so you'd make a mistake, allow him access to you somehow."

I followed Killian inside completely lost to my own thoughts. He led me to the comfy couch where we watched TV, and I sat in the corner with my knees curled up toward my chest. He wrapped me in a fluffy blanket, then snapped and pointed to the couch seat. Brutus jumped up, leaned against my body, and rested his head against me. My cuddly protector. I put my hand to his soft fur and petted him while the men walked from each area attempting to see if there was anything missing.

After about twenty minutes, Killian confirmed he didn't see anything amiss. Jonah and Ryan said they were going to check the security feeds and come back to discuss what happened.

Killian entered the kitchen and filled the tea kettle with water before moving it to the stove. He opened and closed a few cabinets until he found a package of shortbread cookies. Once the tea kettle was whistling, he pulled it off the flame. He then grabbed a couple large handle coffee mugs, tossed in a couple tea bags, and filled them with water.

I watched his every move loving that when he didn't know what to do, he diverted to finding a way to comfort those he cared for. He steeped each tea bag and then tossed them into the trash before reaching for the honey and a bottle of Jameson. After giving each cup a couple shots of Irish whiskey and two squeezes of honey, he grabbed the cups in each hand, the cookie package tucked up under his arm.

"Here, baby. This should help warm you up." He handed me a steaming mug and set his on the coffee table along with the package of cookies.

"Tea and cookies," I whispered, my eyes filling with tears as I looked at the man that I'd come to cherish above all others.

"Isn't that what your mother makes when things are tits up?" He looked at me over the rim of his cup. "Except I added a little oomph with the whiskey. Figured we'd need it after today."

I smiled sadly and sipped my tea letting the warmth soothe my rattled nerves before I set down my cup and put my hand to his knee.

"I know you don't want me to apologize for everything that's happened, but I can't help but think that all of this insanity is the last thing you need in your life."

Killian sighed, set down his mug, and took both of my hands. "Addison, the day we met is the day I started living again. It wasn't just your beauty, your gorgeous body, or even the fact that I could see my own sadness in your eyes. It was the fact that I knew in that moment you were meant to be mine. Meant to be part of this new life I was going to start living. One where I let go of old demons. Lived the life my brothers in arms didn't get the chance to. You're my second chance at happiness. And there is nothing that will prevent me from doing everything within my power to ensure I get that second chance."

I closed my eyes and let the tears fall. "It's so dangerous to be with me."

He cupped my cheek. "Addison, it's more dangerous being without you. The time that you've been here, making love to you, waking up to your smiling face in the morning...it's why every soldier fights the good fight. To make the people we love safe."

"Are you saying you love me?"

"Baby, I fell in love with you the very second I saw your face for the first time through the lens of my camera."

His honesty tore through my chest. "I love you too," I croaked as a sob ripped from my lungs. Killian scooped me up and into his lap. Against his powerful chest I cried, letting the newest fear and struggle seep out of me.

The door opened and the guys strolled through. I sniffed and wiped my tears away with my shirt sleeve and shifted until I was thigh-to-thigh with my man.

He took my hand, lifted it, and kissed my fingers. "We will continue this conversation in private. Not letting what you just said slip by without giving it my full attention. Which will mean me and you, alone in our bed. Got me?"

I smiled through my sniffles. "Okay, baby."

He leaned over and kissed my temple, wrapping his long arm around my back to keep me close.

"You guys realize we can't have you staying here alone, right?" Ryan announced, and my heart sank.

At this point there was nowhere I could go. Nowhere my family could run that would keep them all safe. He'd taken pictures of my niece. A child. An innocent little girl.

"What do we do?" I asked.

Jonah and Ryan each took chairs opposite the couch. Jonah stretched his knees out, bent over, and rested his elbows on them, clasping his hands together as he looked at us.

"We have a couple options. You go into witness protection and we put you in a safe house, or we up security for all of you. With my face and Simone's in that picture on the wall, it's going to be hard enough to keep my ass on this case."

"They would take you off it?" Killian's shock was not hidden in the least.

"Conflict of interest. But no one else knows the details of the Backseat Strangler the way we do or has a vested interest and endless access to all of the Kerrighans. I'll plead my ass off to stay on, but those pictures prove the tide has changed. He's not only targeting you. He's also targeting your family. Likely, in order to get to you."

"What if I just left the country for a while..."

"We can't protect you if we don't know where you are, Addison. I'm calling Holt. We're going to need more men. One on each of you at all times. We'll also need to reconvene to share the latest threat. Do you want to head to Kerrighan House now? I'm going to have each of the women picked up so we can all meet there in the next hour."

"Mama's going to want us all there together once she learns about all of this." I slumped in my seat.

"Just remember." Killian's voice lowered. "I'm here. Not

going anywhere. You are not alone. You've got me. You've got your family. You've got two FBI guys ready to rip up the streets of Chicago in order to protect you and the other members of your family. It's all going to be okay. Right, guys?" Killian hedged.

"We're going to do everything we can to ensure your safety as well as the safety of the entire Kerrighan clan. Why don't you both go pack a bag for at least a few days. We'll follow you to Kerrighan House and call the chief and the rest of the team to get a forensics unit over to take fingerprints and secure the evidence."

"What about Brutus? Do you think he and Amber will get along?" I asked Jonah.

His eyebrows rose. "Amber's a puppy."

"Technically, so is Brutus," Killian piped in.

Jonah grinned. "Not an apple to apples situation, my man. My dog is sweet unless riled. Your dog is the opposite. You tell me if you think they can hang, otherwise we're going to need to come up with a plan B. And Simone is going to want her dog around. She's attached to say the least."

"I can call Atticus to pick him up if it becomes a problem. He's pretty easy for me to control though so I'm not concerned."

Jonah shrugged. "If you're not concerned, I'm not either, but you deal with any fallout with Simone if your dog reacts poorly. And believe me when I say that my woman is far scarier than your dog."

"Simone?" Killian laughed. "She's only ever been nice to me. I think I can handle it."

"She treats that dog as though it were her child," he warned.

Killian grinned. "Guess that trait runs in the family." He winked at me.

"Hardy, har, har," I said and rolled my eyes.

He stood and held his hand out for me to take. I let him help me up but before I could start for the bedroom, he cupped my jaw and looked me in the eyes. "You good?"

I held his hand against my cheek. "No, but I will be."

He nodded. "Let's get you to your family."

I mouthed, "I love you," without saying the words aloud.

He leaned forward, pressed his lips featherlight to mine, and whispered, "I love you, too."

For now, I needed to put my big girl panties on and face whatever the rest of the day might bring.

Chapter
FOURTEEN

WHEN WE ARRIVED AT KERRIGHAN HOUSE, THERE WERE fewer paparazzi than there had been two weeks ago, but still no relief from the media's prying eyes. As we rolled up, so did two other blacked out SUVs. Security owner Sylvester Holt had Charlie, Genesis, and Rory with him, which made sense because both of them worked in downtown Chicago. Omar Alvarado opened the back passenger door of the third car in line and out came Blessing, who smiled and held her hand up in greeting as Jonah and Ryan exited their car, ran across the street, and created space for me and Killian to exit his Jeep. Brutus barked like a demon in the back seat, but the plan was to get me inside before our dog. I watched down the line as Omar offered his hand for Liliana to exit from the truck, but she swiped it away, bounced out, and stormed in my direction. Literally her little, tiny feet were stomping as she pointed at me and narrowed her gaze.

"*Más vale que sea bueno, hermana,* or you are on my shit list!" she blurted, which translated to something like, 'This better be good, sister,' then hooked a thumb toward the man who stood close behind her. "He pulled me out of a blind date! One I was actually enjoying."

I chanced a glance from the seriously fiery Sprite to

Omar who did not even try to hide the smug smirk he had plastered on his face. Guess the Ogre didn't like the idea of the Sprite seeing another man. I held this bit of information in my back pocket to pull out and grill Liliana on later when she was less sassy.

"I'm sorry, Lil, it couldn't be helped this time." I frowned.

Blessing and Liliana locked arms with me as we followed Genesis who held Rory plastered to her chest protectively, legs dangling on each side of her mother's hips. Charlie had both her sporty backpack, Rory's colorful Tiana Disney Princess backpack, and Gen's big work satchel. Jonah, Ryan, Killian, Holt, and Omar surrounded us in a hot guy brigade circle until the entire group was able to enter Kerrighan House safely.

Sonia was already in the living room pacing, phone to her ear. Simone was sitting cross-legged playing a game on her phone, Amber calmly at her feet.

"I'm going to go get Brutus now that you're inside," Killian said before being led outside by Jonah.

Each of my sisters made their way to a position on the couch as Mama Kerri entered with a tea kettle and enough cups to serve us all, setting the tray down on the big wooden oval coffee table. Next to the kettle was an enormous batch of fresh peanut butter cookies.

"Yeah, Quinn, I'll let you know what's happening. Say hello to Niko for me. You're off for the night. Enjoy your dinner out on the town with your husband." Her face took on a serene expression. "See you tomorrow," she finished and then those startling Caribbean-blue eyes lasered directly on Ryan. "So, what in the world was so damn important that all of us had to race here immediately?" Sonia was using her

Senator-Take-No-Shit tone with her body language sharing nothing but attitude. Her hand was on one hip and she tapped her cell phone against her outer thigh with impatience.

Killian took that minute to enter with Brutus securely on the leash wrapped around his wrist, keeping him close.

"Oh my, what a cool-ass dog!" Charlie blurted at the same time Liliana said, "Oh wow. *¡Que perro tan hermoso!*" Meaning beautiful dog.

Both women crouched right in front of Brutus and started petting and cooing all over my new fur baby.

"Brutus, be good," I warned. He lifted his head up and I could have sworn he smiled. It's like he knew these were my people and could be trusted.

Rory came from the couch with a cookie in her hand. "Big doggo!" she exclaimed and ran right at him.

"*Fuss*, Brutus," Killian commanded which I learned meant *heel*.

"Killian, he's fine. See? He loves my family."

"None of you have a healthy fear of things that should be scary as hell." Jonah sighed and ran his hand behind his neck. "Rottweiler you've never met? Yay! Let's put our faces in front of him. Jesus! These women. God love them but it sure as hell makes you all impossible to protect!" he chastised.

"What? Dogs are awesome," Simone said kissing Brutus all over his happy furry face. "And he's so cute. Look at him. He's just a sweet boy! Aren't you, Bru Boy!" She nicknamed him, then stood up abruptly. "Amber, come here sweetheart," she said, and Amber left the couch where Genesis had hooked her collar just in case.

"*Platz!*" Killian said to the dog. "Can everyone else have a seat so we can introduce them?"

My sisters scrambled back to the couch at hearing Killian's more forceful side. Jonah took Amber's collar and Brutus stayed lying down, not even barking as Amber approached.

Amber whimpered and shook not only her tail but her entire booty, clearly very happy to see another animal.

Killian spoke a few words in German I didn't know and then waved to Jonah to bring Amber over. Amber bounced like the jolly fluffy golden retriever she was. Then sat right in front of Brutus.

"Good boy, Brutus." I praised in a way that I hope was encouraging.

"Pet Amber, Addy, then praise him for being good," Killian suggested.

I put my hand to Amber's head and Brutus made a small whimper sound, but it wasn't a mean growl, more like he was jealous of me petting another dog.

"Hi, Amber. You're a good girl. This is my fur baby Brutus." I reached out and petted Brutus who licked my entire hand and tried to crawl a little closer to me.

Amber brought her face down near Brutus and then nudged his shoulder playfully.

"I think she wants to play with him, babe." I stood up and clapped in front of my chest. "Yay! They can be cousins!"

"So cool!" Simone gushed letting the word cool have about ten vowels instead of two.

"You can take them both outside. They won't be able to get out of the yard," Mama Kerri offered.

Jonah and Killian left with the dogs who seemed absolutely fine with one another. Small victory for such a crummy ending to what had started out as a great day with my guy and our dog.

Our dog.

Shit, if I wasn't careful, I'd have myself married off to Killian before the year was up. There was so much more to experience together before we made any more life-altering commitments. Especially during such a tumultuous time. Telling one another that we were in love was a big enough deal that happened to be shared at the most inopportune time. Something we still had to address, but we needed privacy for that. It was one more thing in my life that had to be put on the back burner.

My career.

My home.

My love life.

The list just kept on going. Whoever this sick bastard was, he needed to be caught, so I could live my damn life again.

I went around the room and greeted each sister with a warm hug. I'd been holed up in Killian's loft and hadn't actually seen them since we last had a picnic almost two weeks ago.

"How's the shoot going? The few pictures that Killian e-mailed me were incredible. I love the route you took with the photos," Blessing complimented.

"How are you doing the shoot anyway? Is it harder at Killian's loft?" Gen asked.

I moved around to sit between Genesis and Charlie and pulled out my phone. Killian had copied me on the e-mail he sent to Blessing. "Well, it was Killian's idea. He wasn't loving the plain white background that client thought would be good for the website, but we still did take very specific shots for use in that format if needed as well."

Blessing nodded. "He did mention that, and I appreciate the two of you doing the extra shots. It's better to have more options than less."

I nodded and looked down at my phone, then pulled up one of the couch pictures, another in the bathroom where I pretended to curl my own hair, and one of the newest images we'd taken in the indoor garden.

Gen and Charlie hovered over my phone.

"Holy shit, Addy. You look smokin' hot!" Charlie spouted.

"Wow, girl, you do look smashing in those photos. And Blessing, your new line is going to kill it, sister," Genesis added.

"Let me see!" Rory pushed through and touched my phone with her cookies-and-saliva-coated fingers.

I made sure to pull up the picture of me in the bathroom because I was wearing the robe open with a bra and panty set that was classy and appropriate for little eyes.

"Auntie, you so pretty. Wike a pwincess. Maybe wike Belle. Do you wike books?" she asked randomly.

I smiled and tapped her little nose. "Doesn't everyone?"

She shook her head. "Nut uh. There's a boy in my class. He hates reading time." She stepped forward bringing her face closer to mine as she lifted her hand as though she were going to tell me a secret. "He hates books so much he cries! In class."

"You steer clear of that one," Blessing tossed out and Sonia elbowed her. "Ouch! What did I say? You want her hanging out with the kid that *doesn't* like books? No thank you, ma'am. My niece is smart. She don't need to be hanging out with no duds." She pressed her lips together then rubbed at her bicep where Sonia had nailed her.

I tried not to laugh because Rory had heard what Aunt Blessing said and put her hand over her smiling mouth as she watched Auntie get in trouble.

"I see," I whispered. "Well, it's good that you don't point that out to him. It might make him feel bad."

She nodded, her eyes growing wide. "Yeah. But wike stories."

"Stories are awesome," Charlie sing-songed, and made her skinny booty comfortable on the couch arm.

"Hey, munchkin, how's about you come hang out with Uncle Ryan and the dogs while I update the family," Jonah suggested.

"I could take her…" Mama Kerri offered, but Jonah shook his head.

"Sorry Mama Kerri, you need to be in on this," Jonah stated gently.

Ryan held out his hand for Rory. "Let's see which dog can fetch faster. Eh?"

That plan had Rory racing past all of our legs where we sat on the couch until she took Ryan's hand.

"Thank you, Ryan," Genesis noted.

He lifted his other hand in a "no problem" gesture and walked my niece out back.

Killian stood off to the side, hands in his pockets. Charlie noticed it and quickly moved over.

"Come sit here next to your girlfriend." She patted the couch seat.

He took her up on the recommendation and I held his

hand and rested them both on my thigh as Jonah stood in the center of the room where he could see all of us.

"I'm going to preface this by saying I apologize for the theatrics about pulling you out of work and social engagements." His gaze softened when it hit Liliana.

Omar's lips twitched but he stayed silent and out of the way leaning against the wall nearest the stairs in between the kitchen. Holt stood next to him. Both men extremely imposing with the large and in charge vibe oozing from their corner of the room.

"I received a call today from Addison. The security guard in their building had been tased while they were walking Brutus. The other one doing rounds had been stuck in the neck with a sedative and pulled into the bushes in the back of the building."

Several replies came at once.

"Oh no."

"Is he okay?"

"Was it the killer?"

I stayed silent but held on to Killian's hand as though my life depended on it. I hated Jonah having to give my family this information. Hated it even more that they were once again going to have to change their entire worlds to deal with it.

"He's fine. Looks like the taser triggered a small heart attack or stroke because we found him unconscious. Again, he's doing well. I got confirmation of that fact on the ride over."

"Well at least that's good news," Mama Kerri said sweetly.

"It is. However, when Fitz and Addy headed back into

the loft, dozens of images of all of you were taped on the door."

"No! My children?" Mama Kerri gasped.

"Are you fucking serious?" Charlie cursed.

"I cannot believe this crap!" Simone grouched.

"Oh, hell no," Blessing added with extreme attitude.

Gen, Sonia, Liliana, and I stayed silent.

"There were many pictures of all of you. And Gen, I don't want to frighten you any more than you probably are but there were individual pictures of Rory at her daycare, playing on the toys outside."

That's when Blessing stood up from the couch. "Fuck that noise! This is not happening! No way. No how." Blessing's perfectly dark skin turned rosy at her cheeks, her chin, and down her neck. I'd seen her get this way many times in my life and every last one of them were when she was angry as a wasp.

Genesis reached out and tugged Blessing back into a seated position. "It's okay. Let's just hear what Jonah has to say."

Mama Kerri kept one hand at her mouth the other over her heart. Her not chastising us for cursing could only prove how deeply affected she was by the information.

Jonah sighed. "Every picture of Addison has a big red heart placed over her face as though the attacker is obsessed with her. This proves our theory that the ultimate target is Addison. However, the fact that all of your pictures were taken makes it very clear that this animal will go after any one of you to get to his prize."

"Were the cameras checked at my building?" Killian asked.

"Yes. The man entered wearing a hat, mask, and gloves. There was a slip of skin at the back of the neck that confirms he's Caucasian. We also know it's a man not only because of the size and stature of the individual but the security guard distinctly heard the person's voice and was adamant about it being a male. Of course, that also fits our FBI profile."

"Did he access my loft?" Killian asked.

Jonah shook his head. "No, and he didn't even try. He simply took the guard out and left him in the security room. Then he calmly waited for the elevator and once he got to your floor, he slipped an envelope out from the back of his pants along with tape from his jacket pocket. He spent a solid five minutes placing the pictures exactly as he desired. As though he'd practiced and enjoyed displaying them for you."

"So twisted." Simone pulled up her legs and wrapped her arms around them. Sonia looped one of her arms around her sister and let her lean against her chest.

"Do you have any leads at all?" Sonia asked flatly, her tone all business.

"Believe it or not, this act did help us a lot. Everything he's doing fits the profile. A man in his late twenties or early thirties. Caucasian. In good shape. Takes care of himself. We know he's watching all of you but it's not possible to do so at all times. He knew when to approach the building and according to the cameras, it was before the paparazzi showed up. This leads us to believe he called them and gave them your location as they showed up right before the two of you returned. We also know he walked right out the front door. The rest of the area is industrial and there aren't a lot of cameras. He disappeared from any security footage not long after leaving the building."

"I'm not hearing any leads?" Sonia clarified.

Jonah smiled reassuringly at Sonia. "It would seem that way, but we have a little more. The last woman killed has been identified. Mallory Kenzie. Worked as a nurse at Sacred Heart. Does that name ring any bells for you?" He assessed each woman one at a time but each of them shook their heads. "Addy?"

I shook mine. "No. I've not known any of the women who've been victimized."

"Well, the killer hasn't been super consistent in his methods. Hillary Johnson was a nanny that was last seen going out for groceries. She was strangled, burned, and moved to the park where the killer left a picture of you in her hand. Alison Wills who was found in your apartment was actually the first victim, killed not long after the Strangler was taken down. She was a receptionist at a law firm downtown. She was strangled and burned but was then re-dressed in your clothing. Clearly meant for you to find. The last victim Mallory wasn't strangled or burned. She'd been knocked out by a blow to the back of the head and then her face burned off making her unrecognizable which ended in her death. Then the killer put your picture over her face. We had to identify the body from dental records and fingerprints. The only reason it was connected to our case was the magazine image of Addison. And the woman did look a little like you."

"What does all this mean?" Killian asked.

"We think he knew the last victim somehow. We've got our team working those leads. Today, adding in the photos, it's obvious he's obsessed with you. His main goal is you. The note he left also makes that clear."

"What note?" Simone piped up.

"In the center of all the pictures was a note saying, *you can run but you can't hide.*"

"*Jesús, María, y José.*" Liliana put her hands together and started to pray silently.

Simone gasped and ducked her head, planting her face against Sonia's chest.

Jonah frowned and the expression on his face made me believe he wanted to leave us mid-chat and go straight to Simone to comfort her.

"Don't worry, I've got her." Sonia petted Simone's long golden hair. "I've had plenty of practice."

"Yeah. Well, that's my job now," Jonah grumbled.

Shocking only to me, was that across the room, Omar made the sign of the cross then kissed his fingers at the end, somewhat similar to the same manner as a person in the Catholic faith would do. The Catholic faith that my little Latina sister followed religiously. Another point in the pro column for Omar. Not that Liliana was keeping track but I sure as heck was on her behalf. Especially if I meant to get them together. Which I did.

"All we know right now is that he's white, young, possibly knows victim number three, and he's good with a camera?" Blessing stated the obvious. "This does not sound like a lot. What's the plan here?"

"Maybe I could offer myself up as bait?"

"Hell no!" Blessing cursed at the same time as Killian said, "Fuck, no!"

I jerked my hand from his and turned to the side. "Why not? It's a good idea."

"Addy, a lot goes into an undercover operation like that.

And I don't know that I could suggest that to the team." Jonah was quick to interrupt.

"You mean it hasn't come up yet?" I asked.

Jonah closed his eyes and didn't respond, meaning that it likely had come up, but it had been shot down.

"I could totally do it," I said with as much confidence as I could muster. "Especially if the FBI had it all planned out and had me covered. It makes sense."

"It does, but I'm not sure we're at that point. We're going to work the information on the nurse and discuss today's happenings with the team."

"You tell them that I'm willing to be bait. I'm absolutely serious about this."

"Addy, baby, I know you want to help but…" Killian tried for my hand, but I yanked it back and stood up.

"No! You guys have no idea how this feels. Wondering every single day when the other shoe is going to drop. When he'll get his window to kill another woman for the sole unfortunate reason that she resembles me?" I slapped my hands down at my sides. "Or on the off chance that he decides to really get to me by kidnapping one of my sisters like the last guy did. Losing another one of my family members."

"Chicklet, we understand how scary this is…" Mama Kerri started to lay down her wisdom, but I was having none of it.

"No! You. Do. Not. Yes, all of us lost Tabby. The only one who understands is Simone." I stared at her until she pulled her face away from Sonia's hold, put her feet back down to the floor, and looked right at me. Her gray-blue eyes were filled with tears.

"I get it," she whispered.

"And you told me you were willing to give yourself up so I'd be safe. Isn't that right?" I narrowed my gaze, daring her to lie.

"Yes. I would have done anything to ensure all of you were safe."

"Including giving yourself up as bait?" I pressed.

She nodded.

I flung out my arm and let it fall back to my side. "And there you go." I looked at every last one of them in the eyes and stopped on Genesis. "And what if it was Rory? She's the most helpless. If I was a super twisted bad guy, which person would be the easiest to snatch? Hmm?"

Twin tears slid down Gen's face.

Then I swung my gaze to Mama Kerri's. "Your *only* living grandchild. Snatched up by a madman. Because that's what he's going to do. He's going to hurt one of you until he gets me. So, let's make it easy on him. But we do it our way! With a whole team of cops that carry big fat guns."

Jonah came up from behind me and put a hand to my shoulder. "Sweetheart, we get what's at stake. I'll think about it. Talk it over with Ryan and the Chief. See if they have any ideas or thoughts. If we run out of leads and they agree this plan has merit, we'll be in touch."

I spun around. "You do that. And soon. There is no time to waste. We've all been through enough. I want this over. I want to live my life again. I want to tell my man that I love him and not have to be whisked away to my mother's house to inform my sisters that they are all in mortal danger."

Jonah's eyebrows rose up toward his hairline and he snapped his lips together and backed away.

Once again, I spun to look at each of my sisters' faces and realized what I'd just said. Liliana the romantic had her hands to her chest not in prayer, but with glee, while a huge smile stretched across her face so big her cheeks looked like a chipmunk's that were full of nuts. The woman really did have killer cheekbones. Think Selena Gomez-level awesome.

Blessing came over to me with her arms out. "Baby girl, you're in love?" She pulled me into her arms as I nodded avidly.

My heart hurt and heat filtered through my veins at the irritation pouring through me. "And all I want to do is bring my boyfriend to my mother's house and have dinner and let all of you rip on him all the time...like you do Jonah, but nooooooooo! We're in Hell. Again!" I blustered, sounding weak and silly, but it was all piling up. It was too damn much for one person to take and I'd had it!

Blessing moved me from her arms and into our mother's.

I smashed my face against the wildflower scent at her neck and lost it, crying into her arms.

"This has been a lot. For all of us, but more so on you and Simone. You've been through the wringer, my sweet chicklet, but I can't help but say I'm happy that through it all you've found love. There is no better thing in the world than finding your soul mate. You know I had mine far too short but the love we had will last me a lifetime. I want that for all of my girls." She patted my hair and then eased me back until I was passed once more and wrapped in another pair of comforting arms.

Killian's.

That time I locked my arms around his waist and flattened my cheek to his pecs listening for his heart, pairing my breathing to his, in order to calm down.

"Guess the cat's outta the bag with your family," he teased, rubbing his hands up and down my back.

I nodded, soaking into his love and comfort.

"Come on, guys. Let's go check on Ryan and the dogs and figure out what we're going to do about dinner," Mama Kerri announced.

I didn't leave my Killian cuddle, preferring to let them all shuffle their way out.

"They're gone. You okay?" Killian hedged.

I inhaled fully and leaned back. "I'm okay."

"We're gonna get through this. You. Me. Your family. All of it. We just have to wait it out. Though I do not like the idea of you being pawned off as bait. Still, I know I'll never get you to back off the idea. Mostly because it's a good idea, as much as I hate it. Also, because I'd do the same thing. I can't fault you for wanting to protect your kin."

I lifted my hands and cupped his bearded jaw. "You are the best man I know, Killian."

He smiled. "Thank you, baby." He tunneled his hands through my hair. "You ready to head back?" He gestured to the backyard. "I'm kind of worried about how Brutus is doing with Amber and the rest of the clan. He's not been around so many people at once. Not that I think he'd do anything. Still, I'd like to check."

"Yeah..." I backed away and interlaced our fingers. "Let's go check on our dog." We started to move toward the backyard. "You're truly okay with all this? You don't want to go running for the hills?"

He grinned. "I do want to run for the hills, but I want to take my gorgeous girlfriend and our dog with us. Preferably a tent and some camping equipment. Find a nice lake to do some fishing."

"I've never been fishing," I mumbled.

"Then I'll be teaching my girl how to fish."

"I've also never been camping." I pressed my lips together.

That had him chuckling. "You're gonna love it."

"Um, not so sure. It's dirty. You sleep on the ground. And do what?"

He waggled his brows. "Guess you'll have to trust me to make your first camping experience awesome. Do you trust me, Addy?" he whispered as we got to the back door.

I stopped and looked him straight in the face. "I trust you with my life, Killian."

His features softened. "I'll make that trust worth it." He looped an arm around my back and opened the door. "Stick with me, baby, and I'll make sure we both have a beautiful life."

Chapter
FIFTEEN

THE NEXT COUPLE DAYS DRAGGED BY BUT WE FINALLY HAD something to look forward to. Today was Rory's 4th birthday! And my, oh my, was she excited.

Charlie and I held up a string of fairy lights across the deck of Mama Kerri's patio while Killian stapled the wire to the wood in a neat straight line.

"She's going to be so excited when she and Auntie Delores come back tonight with Mama Kerri!" I eeked and went over to the party decorations to put together some of the hanging pink and purple circular spheres that we planned on dangling from the trees. Simone was dressing up a huge table in the grass area with confetti and princess crowns.

Gen and Blessing were with Holt picking up the cake. Omar was with Mama Kerri and Rory at the flower shop visiting Aunt Delores to keep little eyes away while we decked out the house for the family party.

Sonia as usual was at work since she had her own team of protectors, and continued to ignore all FBI suggestions that she stay put. She did give in by canceling her attendance at big events that were publicized. The rest she drew the line on. The citizens of Illinois expected their Senator to get up and go to work every day regardless of whether or not someone was planning nefarious acts against their family. "Cops do it every single day," was her argument and she wasn't wrong. The fact that she had a slew of bodyguards and hadn't been directly targeted other than a picture on Killian's door made them feel safe enough to allow her to go to work.

Mama, however, dropped the bomb that all of us, including Sonia, were to be in her house at the end of each night where she could check on every last one of her chicklets. This was non-negotiable and I watched that fight go down while eating popcorn and sitting on the couch until Sonia gave in. As us girls all knew she would do. Except all the guys thought Sonia could take on Mama Kerri and each bet ten bucks on it. All of them lost except Jonah because he already knew the pull Mama had on her girls.

Gen and Blessing burst through the back door as I finally got one of the stupid spheres to stay in the shape of a circle, its flared out pink snowflake shape looking a little worse for the wear, but a four-year-old wouldn't care.

Right on their heels was Holt with a two-tiered cake with a Barbie doll stuck right in the center. The tiered part was the ruffles of the dress made out of thick swirls of pink and purple frosting.

"Wow, Gen, she's going to freak!" I said as Holt set the beautiful confection down at the head of the table where Rory would sit.

"I'm just sad we couldn't invite any of her friends from daycare or the playground Mama takes her to. She was really looking forward to having a big girl party." Gen's smile fell a bit.

I slumped my shoulders and nodded, hating how much all of this was ruining my sisters' lives.

Charlie slipped up to Gen and pressed her chin to our sister's neck and wrapped her arms around her from behind. "You realize with so many aunties, it's always a party, and all of us promise to play every single one of your games."

Hope flickered in my chest, wanting Rory to have a great birthday even with the restrictions because of my crappy situation.

Blessing hugged me from behind. "And not one person in this family is at fault, but they will be if they don't give our littlest member the best birthday ever!" She shook me from side to side. "Meaning no sourpuss faces from top models!" She tickled my ribs and I burst out laughing, then struggled to get away from her wiggling fingers.

"Okay, okay!" I cackled as she went to town on my ribs.

"Nothing but smiles from here on out!" Blessing added giving me more tickles.

"I promise!!!" I cried, tears falling down my cheeks as I laughed my booty off and scrambled as far as I could out of her hold then ran to Killian and hid behind his large frame.

"You think he can keep you from me?" She held up her fingers wiggling them with hilarious malicious intent. "I'm the tickle monster, and will attack when you least expect it!" She playfully jumped toward one side of Killian as I darted out from behind him and ran the other direction.

"Truce, truce!" I screamed, laughing and winded from the effort.

"Well, all right. Now that smiling face is what I want to see." She pointed at me and then winked before sashaying toward the food table. If food was laid out, Blessing was always stealing bites. It was part of her charm, on top of a bazillion other things I loved about her.

Killian came over to me and grinned. "Your family is nutty as it comes. Mine is going to love all of you. And my mother will be beside herself with all these women. She's been the female in a family full of men."

"Speaking of, does your mother know what's going on?"

He nodded. "She noticed my picture in the paper that first time we came here."

"I didn't know you'd talked to her."

"Yeah, a few times already. She checks in every two, three days. She's absolutely blown away I'm dating *The Addison Michaels*. Her exact words. Apparently, she bought a couple different bathing suits you modeled last year, as well as purchased some brand of underwear you champion, not that I ever needed to know that information about my mother and my girlfriend."

I snicked. "Your mom and I might wear the same underwear, baby. That's hilarious!" I chuckled biting into my bottom lip.

He pulled me into his arms and together we looked around the stunning backyard. The fairy lights were twinkling as it was just hitting dusk. Charlie was finishing up hanging pretty icicle-like ornaments from some of the surrounding tree branches. We had candles lit all over the yard giving it a whimsical feel that felt kind of like a secret garden party. Genesis moved around the space, adjusting things here and there making sure everything was just perfect for her little girl.

"I don't want to pry," Killian murmured, "but where is Rory's dad? Will he be attending tonight? There's been no mention of him since we met."

"Rory's father is a man by the name of Sidney Freeman.

Really good guy as far as I know. He is on active duty in the Merchant Marines. Last I heard he was on a ten-month stint. When he comes home, he spends as much time as he can with Rory, but it's complicated. He and Gen were never a couple. It was a one-night drunken escapade that left her pregnant. He was already at sea when she found out. She didn't even have his phone number. They'd met at a club, hooked up, and six weeks later my sister was pregnant. It took her another few months to even find his information and make contact. She knew his name and that he was a Marine, but that was about the extent of it."

"That's gotta be hard on Rory and Genesis. To have her dad gone most of the time."

I shrugged. "Most of us only had Mama Kerri so we're used to taking care of one another without help. He does what he can. They video chat either by phone or computer at least once a week. He sends her presents and trinkets from wherever he ends up. Rory saves everything like it's gold. Keeps it in a full-on treasure box."

Killian grinned.

"She's probably only seen her dad in person maybe a dozen times. Depends on where he's stationed, which can be anywhere in the world, not to mention when he's actually on the ship, which can be for months at a time. Usually when he's on land in the States he flies out to see her for a couple days if he can get away. I also know from the minute she came into this world he's sent monthly child support. Asked Gen exactly how much she needed to take care of his daughter and has never missed a payment. No courts involved, just him being a man of his word who cares about his child even if he can't see her all the time."

"Sounds like it works for them."

I shrugged. "I know it's really hard on Gen raising Rory alone. She rarely dates. Never seems to give herself a break. Busts her ass for the kids at work who have no one, and then comes home to her kid and busts ass for her home. She's one of the most honorable people I've ever known. And she loves that girl to distraction."

"She's easy to love."

I looped my arms around his shoulders crossing them at the wrists. "I know another human who's easy to love...." I lifted up on my toes bringing my face closer to his.

"Oh, and who would that be?" he teased, before pressing his lips to mine.

We kissed slowly, playfully for a bit, ramping up the passion between us.

"Get a room!" Charlie hollered. "If I can't bring my dates here you can't be smooching in public view. It's mean!"

I glared at the redheaded pixie. "If you brought home the same person each time, you could absolutely have them over. But Mama already told you that the revolving door of dates you bring around had to stop."

"Shut up!" She scrunched up her face and stuck out her tongue.

"She told you," Blessing hummed.

I grinned, winning that round with Charlie.

"Charlie's the one that can't settle down?" Killian asked.

"I'm sure she *could* if she'd give a person more than a handful of dates. My theory is her picker is busted. The girls and I have talked about it at great length. We're each going to pick one guy and one girl, then cross reference the pros and cons with one another. Then when we pick the right male and female, we're going to set her up on two dates. Then see if one sticks."

"Glad I'm not part of the picking party. I suck at dating." He smiled.

"Which is a good thing since you now have me, so you don't have to worry." I smacked him on the lips with a hard and fast kiss. "I'm going to go grab our presents for Rory."

"Our presents?"

"Um, yeah. I bought stuff online and had it delivered here. Already wrapped them too. Your name is with mine on all of them."

He smiled. "You're amazing, you know that?"

"As long as you think so, I'm happy!"

I left Killian to his own devices while I got the birthday girl's presents.

"Rory had a blast at her party last night." I smiled as Killian and I stepped into the elevator at Sacred Heart, the premier hospital in the area. Holt was waiting for us in the lobby. Sacred Heart was where I'd been treated after my ordeal with the Backseat Strangler for my initial burns. I was coming in today for a checkup with my surgeon.

Killian chuckled. "She was high as a kite on frosting from that cake. How much sugar you think they put in that thing? Even I felt a little twitchy after a small slice."

"Right? And she really loved how the guys had king-type crowns with the cheesy red velvet and gold and the women wore smaller tiaras while she wore that bedazzled monstrosity that Blessing got her."

"She pranced around in her new play outfits and that crown like a true Queen. I sent my mother a picture of you holding her on your lap, the two of you smiling like crazy."

I stopped laughing and looked at him. "You did? I haven't even met your mom."

"Doesn't change the fact that she knows who you are and asks for physical proof of your existence in my life. She's also pretty annoyed that we haven't been to their house for dinner yet. Have you thought about it?"

I shrugged and let out a long breath. "I'm scared. I don't want to tell her about everything that's going on. I don't want to have to lie. I don't want her to think I'm the loser girlfriend of her beloved son. And I especially don't want to make them a target of a really bad guy. It's better to wait."

He nodded. "You're right. When it's quiet and nothing is happening around us, I forget for a little bit."

"Me too. But something always comes up to remind me. Like visiting the plastic surgeon to check on my skin grafts and healing to see if he can reduce the rest of the visible scarring." I tugged on my long sleeves, hiding the offending marks.

After checking in and sitting in the waiting area, a nurse I recognized approached. "Addison Michaels?" he said with a smile and a tilt of his head.

I glanced at his hospital ID that said Cory Pitman. "Cory, I remember you!" I smiled. "You were so helpful and really patient with me when I was here a few months ago."

His entire face lit up and his cheeks pinked as he shyly pushed a layer of his blond hair off his forehead.

"I'm so glad to see you for your appointment. When I found out it was you on the schedule, I pulled a favor with another nurse to trade so I could see how you were doing."

I leaned my head against Killian's shoulder, interlacing our fingers as I did so. "Really good now that I have Prince Charming taking care of me."

Killian shook his head and put his hand out toward Cory. "Hey, man. Thanks for taking such good care of Addy."

Cory frowned. "I'm surprised I didn't see you a few months ago when she was hurt?" he said boldly. And a little unprofessionally, if you asked me.

"Oh, our relationship is pretty new. I'm a lucky girl to have found someone who isn't grossed out by my injuries." I admitted something I hadn't actually said out loud to anyone, but something about this man questioning my relationship had me blurting the naked truth.

"Your injury is a part of you, Addy. And I love every inch." Killian lifted my arm and placed a kiss to my covered forearm to make his point.

"That's really, uh, cool that you have someone who loves you regardless of your deformity," Cory said. "Must be nice," he murmured cryptically sounding sadder than anything. "I'll take you back. Your surgeon is eager to check on your grafts since the last visit went so well."

I shivered, hating that I had to see this doctor again. He was weird during my last visit, but the results couldn't be denied. Had he not done the skin grafts the larger burns would have been ghastly. At least this time I had Killian with me.

Cory led us through this side of the hospital that catered to the outpatient procedures, including even some trauma patients and the specialties such as skin grafts and medically necessary plastic surgery.

Once I was settled and had removed my cardigan

leaving me in just my tank top, Cory took all of my vitals and noted everything in the computer. Killian sat in one of the chairs opposite me where I sat on an examination table. The fluorescent lights were blinding and the eggshell-colored walls made me feel closed in.

There was a knock on the door, and I called out, "Come in."

My surgeon entered, a tall, thin, painfully awkward man in his mid-thirties, and approached me. "Addison Michaels. In the flesh," he cooed, and I tried to hide my wince. Every time I had to see this man, I got goosebumps from just the sound of his voice.

"Uh, hello, Dr. Templeton."

He reached out with a pale hand and I took his to shake lest I be seen as rude. His hand was freezing cold and gave me the heebie jeebies.

Killian stood up and came to my side, putting his warm hand at the back of my nape under my hair. "You okay, babe?" He dipped his head to assess my eyes. "You look uncomfortable," he used the deep, booming side to his voice.

God, I loved him. So freakin' much.

"I'm okay. Just don't like this part."

"What part is that?" Dr. Templeton asked reaching for my hand. He held my hand so that my forearm was facing up. Then he traced those cold-ass fingers over every single one of my scars, feeling them with his fingertips.

It took everything I had not to rip my arm back.

"They look so much better." He traced a particularly large indent where Wayne Gilbert Black had repeatedly pressed a hot cigarette creating a deeper much larger wound than most of the others. When he did that back in that basement level of the building he'd kept me in, I'd passed out from the pain.

I couldn't help the flinch that occurred as the doctor circled the round shape several times as though he were caressing the wound. I swallowed down the bile threatening to race up my throat.

"She doesn't like that," Cory stated in a grating tone, breaking the surgeon out of his worshipful stupor.

Dr. Templeton's dark beady gaze lifted to mine. "I'm sorry, dear heart, but I'm testing the skin elasticity and the strength of the healed graft."

"Mmm hmm." I closed my eyes as he continued to work. Then he held my arm out and I watched as he traced over the donor skin sites on the outside of my biceps. Those had healed wonderfully.

"No scarring. Incredible," he said with awe. His face alight with what I assume was happiness as he assessed the skin by running those damn cold fingers over each area. "The other arm please." He let my left arm go and reached for the right.

He repeated the gross process of touching every burn site and then evaluating the donor site. "You're my masterpiece, Ms. Michaels." The way he spoke made it seem like he was an artist admiring his own work and finding perfection.

I had to physically prevent myself form gagging by breathing in and out through my nose slowly.

Killian huffed. "Tell that to every photographer and fashion designer on the market and they'd agree with you. Except for the fact that she's her own damn masterpiece. We done here?" Killian clenched his teeth and rubbed my neck soothingly. The press of his palm and fingers was the only thing keeping me stable.

"Is there a problem, sir?" Dr. Templeton asked Killian.

"She's uncomfortable. Someone, *anyone* touching her scars makes her feel bad. I don't take kindly to a person who makes her feel like that, even if it's her surgeon. If we could hurry this along and get on with our day, that would be great."

I chanced a glance at Cory whose eyes had grown huge along with a giant somewhat wicked smile. Maybe he didn't like this particular doctor either.

"Ms. Michaels, I apologize for making you feel uncomfortable, it's just your grafts took so well it's not often that I see such success with the first grafts. You're a wonderful healer. Have you been doing anything to assist the process?"

"I've been using Vitamin E oil daily which seems to help."

The doctor continued his assessment. As his hand rose up my arm toward my donor site, his fingers grazed the side of my breast. I gasped and shifted my face against Kilian's chest where he stood close to my side.

"Addy?" Killian questioned low and raspy in a somewhat threatening growl.

"I'm fine. Just fine. Any ideas on additional surgeries?" I asked.

Dr. Templeton narrowed his gaze, stepped back, and clasped his hands together in front of him, his expression carrying one of surprise. "I'm not sure much more can be done. Over the next couple years, the scars will fade, whiten, and look less glaring."

"You mean, I'm going to see these..." I held out my

forearms. "Forever?" My words came out on a croak as emotion clogged my throat.

"You were severely burned, and those burns were left unattended for many hours. You were lucky the skin grafts healed well and covered up the worst of it."

I shook my forearms at him. "The worst of it! They're still here! No matter what I do, no matter where I go, I can see them. Hell, I can *feel* them. Sometimes I wake in the night still feeling the burns." Tears filled my eyes. "And you're telling me I'm going to have to live with this for the rest of my life?"

Cory approached me with a tissue and put a hand to my shoulder. "Ms. Michaels, you need to breathe. You're at risk for a panic attack."

I shoved away Cory's touch and pushed off the table. Killian grabbed my shoulder bag and my cardigan.

"I need to get out of here. Go somewhere. Anywhere." I barely spoke as the tears claimed me.

"Ms. Michaels...please." The doctor reached for my arm, but Killian grabbed his wrist and held it fast in a vice lock grip.

"Don't touch her," Killian growled. "Thank you for what you've done to date, but we'll be seeking a second opinion. Come on, Addy." He dropped the doctor's arm and put a hand to my back, edging me out of the examination room. We didn't so much as look back. We kept going until we were out of that area, down the elevator, and into the lobby.

The second we hit the lobby Holt followed us to one of his blacked-out SUVs, opening the door and making sure I was safely inside.

"She all right?" I heard Holt ask when he'd shut the car door and followed Killian around the car to the other side.

"Yeah, she will be. I'll make sure of it," Killian responded.

When he got in the car, I put the top half of my seatbelt behind me and bent over, placing my head to my man's lap, clinging to his jeans with my fingers as my worst fears consumed me.

I let the tears fall silently as my dreams of wiping away the horrid physical memories of what happened to me at the hands of a madman went down the proverbial drain.

Killian ran his fingers through my hair and let me cry it out, being there for me but not trying to fix it. He knew he couldn't solve this problem. I had to come to terms with it on my own.

I wondered if Killian had come to terms with his scars being on his beautiful body for life. I guess if he could be strong, so could I. Somehow, I'd find the strength, but right now, with everything so raw, I mourned the dream I'd lost, while my own Prince Charming kept me close, in case I needed him.

Chapter
SIXTEEN

THE REST OF THE NEXT WEEK WAS STRESSFUL TO SAY THE least. It went like this:

Monday, doctor's appointment from Hell. I found out I'd have ugly, scarred forearms for the rest of my life.

Tuesday, no better. That day brought the unwelcome delivery of a picture of me, Killian, and Holt walking Brutus and Amber around a park that we'd driven to. This time not only did my face have a red heart around it, but there was a big red X scratched over Killian's. Jonah and Ryan believed something had changed in the man's MO. All of a sudden, Killian was at risk. This also meant the killer was definitely keeping track of my movements.

Wednesday, another photo. This one scared the day-lights out of me. It was of me sitting in the backyard on one of the large chair chairs having coffee. Rory had been front-to-front with me on my lap, her body lounging against mine with her new Disney Olaf plushie tucked to her chest. She'd received the toy from Simone for her birthday and deemed it a favorite sleeping item. She had her thumb in her mouth and had just awakened and was dreamy and beautiful, her dark curls all over her head, one of her hands stretched up playing with my hair that hung down near her face. I was getting maximum kid cuddle time with my niece while we watched the dogs pluck around the yard. I distinctly recall hearing something like a clicking sound before Brutus went absolutely crazy, racing to the opposite side of the yard where he barked and jumped against the wooden fence that led to the alley behind Mama's house. Amber got in on the action barking and running manically back and forth while Brutus got so angry, he was foaming at the mouth. Now I knew why.

Thursday, as one might have guessed, brought yet another photo. This one of Blessing and Killian entering a big skyscraper downtown. They'd gone together to meet with the clients regarding the first photos we'd taken of her lingerie line. We still had half of the sets left to photograph, but for now, the clients could start building their marketing plan and promotional materials as we worked to finish the rest. In the photo of that meeting, Killian's face had a big red X which made my heart hurt. Blessing however didn't have any markings on her image which made Jonah and Ryan and the rest of their FBI team believe the interest had changed to Killian and me alone.

On Friday morning, I was a nervous wreck. I hadn't left the house since we'd walked the dog, and my emotions were in a constant state of panic. I'd scheduled a meeting with Jonah and Ryan, and they agreed to meet. Killian, Jonah, Ryan, and I sat down at the kitchen table while Mama made all of us a late breakfast. Bacon was sizzling in the frying pan, homemade biscuits that Killian taught my mother how to make were in the oven, and Mama was cracking eggs into a big stainless steel bowl at the counter while we drank coffee.

"Any update?" I asked as I did every day.

Ryan smiled sadly and lifted his coffee to take a sip, leaving Jonah to give the news.

"Addy, I'm sorry to say we don't at this time. Since we know that the last victim fought her attacker and he didn't perform his normal routine of strangling and burning her, we believe he knew her. Burning her face until it was unrecognizable was a strange response, but we think it's because he needed to not see the face of someone he knew, but instead see your face. It's also possible he was interrupted before he could do what he intended."

"You mean like maybe he was in a hurry?" I asked.

Jonah shrugged.

"Or he could have been surprised by this woman. Perhaps he didn't mean to attack her, and she said or did something that caused a violent response. Whatever it was, he knew this victim. We've interviewed everyone that worked with her and so far, haven't come up with any leads. Most of Mallory's coworkers have airtight alibis. Plus, she was a driven woman on the job. Took as many overtime gigs as she could get her hands on, which had her assisting in surgeries at all the local hospitals and medical centers. So there are hundreds of potential people that crossed paths with her. Not to mention she was well-liked at work and in her professional life. Had a ton of friends," Ryan supplied.

"What about Dr. Templeton," Killian stated.

I reached for his hand and covered it. "Babe, just because he pissed you off doesn't mean he's a crazed killer."

"Dr. Templeton?" Jonah reached for his phone and started typing. "He works at Sacred Heart?" he asked.

"He's Addy's plastic surgeon. He did her skin grafts. We just visited him this past Monday and I don't care what she's about to say, the dude was weird. Touched her scars as though they were something to be proud of. The guy is whack. I got a bad feeling about him," Killian stated flatly.

Jonah frowned as he read through his phone. "Dr. Greg Templeton has worked at Sacred Heart for the past eight years. Did his residency there and was hired on straight away? Has a slew of degrees behind his name and endless articles in *JAMA*, the *Journal of American Medical Association* on skin grafting and treating severely burned victims." Jonah kept scanning and rolling his thumb up the screen. "Looks like we did briefly talk to him but agreed to follow up at a later date as he was going into surgery. From what it says here, Mallory did work in the surgical center of the hospital sometimes so it's possible she could have worked with Dr. Templeton. We'll follow up. Addy, why didn't you say anything on Monday?"

I glanced out the window beyond where Jonah sat and shrugged. "It didn't seem related at the time. I'd just been told that I was going to be scarred for life. In all honesty, I was having a pity party for one."

Killian put his hand to my thigh and squeezed, offering silent support.

Mama took that moment to place a mouth-watering plate of food in front of me and Killian. Then she went to the counter and plated up two more for Jonah and Ryan.

"Go on and eat. I already had breakfast as the sun rose," she said and continued to move around the kitchen cleaning.

"Thanks, this looks amazing." Killian lifted his fork and shoveled in a bite of cheesy scrambled eggs.

The remaining three of us agreed with muffled mmm hmms as our mouths were already full of food.

"Feeding my family and friends is my pleasure," she boasted, tossing a hand towel over one shoulder as she cleared the counter of the detritus from the meal she'd prepared.

When I'd taken a few bites, I wiped my mouth with my napkin before bringing up the one question no one wanted me to ask. "And what about the idea of offering me up as bait?"

Ryan wiped his mouth and leaned back as Jonah sighed.

"Brother, you've got to give it to her straight," Ryan urged.

"Yeah, bro, give it to me straight." I used their lingo, not hiding the hurt in my tone at realizing they'd been keeping something from me.

Jonah inhaled a quick breath and let it out in a long groan. "The team does believe that it would be a good idea to use you. Especially since we now know he's following you daily. All at different times, which likely means he follows you or your family for a bit, gets the picture he wants to scare you with, and then goes to work. Otherwise, we'd likely be getting more pictures of you and your sisters daily. Since that's not the case, we believe he does in fact work a regularly scheduled job. Likely in the medical field."

"Because of the nurse connection?" Killian asked.

He nodded. "And because he was able to get his hands on a pretty powerful sedative to inject the other guard behind your apartment. The toxicology report on him showed it was an expert dose. Not enough to kill, but definitely enough to know a person would be out for a couple hours. Especially, say, if someone were just getting out of surgery..." Jonah stated.

"Wow. Maybe it is the doctor." I shivered and dropped my fork to my plate, no longer hungry even though my belly would claim otherwise.

"We'll head to the hospital right after this. What do you think about a sting operation this weekend? Tonight even?"

"Tonight?" I clarified.

Jonan and Ryan both nodded. Killian reached for my hand and held it tight.

"What were you thinking?" My voice cracked a little, showing my worry, even though I'd have done anything to push through the fear in order to capture this man once and for all.

"Well, now that we know he's following you, we set up a plan to capture him trying to get to you in a very public place. Like Tracks where Simone used to work. She knows the manager and can get us access. We can not only replace their security people with some of our undercover agents, but also one of the bartenders. We can also set up in the office overlooking the entire club."

"And what's the plan? Just leave Addison out on her own?" Killian spoke through his teeth, sounding more like an angry bear than a calm and understanding boyfriend. Though the fact that he didn't have an outburst was pretty fantastic in my opinion.

"No, of course not. We'll have her hanging out with a couple female FBI agents dressed for a night out. They'll be strapped and ready to move on a moment's notice. Addison will go to the bathroom several times where we'll also have someone waiting, leaving her open enough that the perpetrator will be inclined to make a grab. Then instead of her, we take him out."

I nodded as Killian shook his head.

"I hate it," he grumbled.

"Look, man, if it was Simone, I'd hate it too. I get it. Believe me, I've been through this with the woman I love most in the world. It's not an easy thing to let go of, but I swear we will take care of her. I love Addison like she were my own sister."

I puffed out my bottom lip as my heart pounded in my chest, and I felt the emotion pumping off all three men.

"Me too. A smokin' hot..." Ryan's gaze hit Killian's death glare and his eyes widened.

I chuckled.

"I mean, I care about Addy and this entire family. I'd lay my life on the line for her just like Jonah, just like you. And she'll be covered. We're going to have a team of twelve on point. No one is leaving that club with Addison but us," Ryan promised. "I give you my word."

Killian closed his eyes and nodded. "It's up to Addy. Whatever she decides I'll go along with."

My heart swelled to double its size as I squeezed his hand, lifted it up, and held it between both of mine. He looked at me with such sorrow and anxiety. I kissed the top of his hand and rested my cheek against it. "Thank you for believing in me."

"Always, baby. You know that. And I want this over with. Got plans to take my girl camping and fishing for the first time. Would like to do that sooner rather than later. Start living every day to the fullest."

"Because every day is a gift." I used Sonia's words. My sister may be a tough as nails senator, but she'd been through a lot in her thirty-three years. Saving Simone from the house fire that took the lives of their parents had marked her as a young girl. She knew better than anyone how important every day was and now that I had Killian on top of a loving family, I knew it too. Every day was a gift.

"That's right," Killian murmured. "You do what you gotta do." He turned his head and focused on Jonah and then on Ryan in some type of guy code silent stare. "I'm trusting you with my future happiness."

Killian believed I was his future happiness. If that didn't make a woman swoon, they were a cold dead fish.

I leaned against his arm and looked at Jonah. "I'll do whatever it takes."

He nodded. "We'll set it up for tonight. Friday will be busy at the bar."

"And if he doesn't come?" I asked.

"Then we try again Saturday. I'll call you both later when we find out more on Dr. Templeton."

Killian and I nodded as the guys finished their breakfast. I picked at mine, my mind full of crazy scenarios that could occur this evening.

Either way, at least we finally had a plan.

Tracks was a club in downtown Chicago that I'd been to countless times. Simone used to work there. Actually, she had only quit the place around seven months ago during the start of her *situation*. Jonah quickly helped her back on her feet and now she's finished her last college class, got her Associate's degree, had a new job as an office manager, and was living in a house Jonah had bought for the two of them to start their lives together. It was a magical storyline that could have come out of romance novel. If we hadn't lost Tabby, Jonah's ex-wife, and so many others, it would have been a story they could tell their grandchildren. Like my own story with Killian, though things were far too tragic and twisted for the perfect fairytale ending.

My hope now was that we could capture this psycho and carry on. For me, that could mean anything. I no longer had my apartment—most of my things of value had been disbursed between Killian's and Mama Kerri's. We still needed to finish the other half of the campaign we were working on for Blessing and her big box store clients and then after that I had nothing scheduled. When I got hurt the first time, I had my agent cancel any photoshoots for the better part of a year. If we could get past this horrible hurdle, I'd have the time to make a change.

Flutters of excitement at the prospect of possibly leaving modeling and moving forward with my model agency idea crept to the surface of my consciousness. For so long, I'd pushed the dreamer part of me to the side, doing what would make me the most money possible. But I could still take a few jobs a year to make those big dollars, as long as it fueled my new passion—whatever that was.

I pushed my long brown locks over one shoulder, leaned forward, and twirled the straw in my cranberry with zero vodka cocktail. We'd made sure the bartender only served me and my pretend friends from the vodka bottle that had been replaced with water in order to keep up the appearance of three women getting shit-faced and having fun.

"Let's go dance. We're not getting any traction," one of the agents named Paula suggested.

I nodded and bobbed to the intense music filtering through the club. Streaks of colored laser lights blasted all over the walls in rotating blinking rhythms. I kinda wished I had some actual vodka in my drink. Not having anything take the edge off was making my anxiety hit extremes.

Paula hooked her arm with mine as Hayden, the other agent, followed at our rear. All night, as promised by Jonah and his team of experts, I'd not been left unattended. When we got in the center of the dance floor, I lifted my arms and swayed my hips from side to side.

I took several breaks to hit the bathroom, because five glasses of cranberry and water still filled the bladder just like an alcoholic beverage. Although I made sure to wobble on my heels, trying to make myself look like a drunk victim. With a sly smile, I glanced at one of the FBI agents I'd been introduced to earlier. He was leaning against the wall near the ladies' restroom, his hand up above a beautiful woman who he was pretending to mack on, but I knew better. She was also an agent but playing the part to a T by heavily draping herself against his frame. He kissed her neck and winked at me as I passed.

And still no attempted kidnapping. I was starting to get a little miffed. Which led me to visit the other side of the bar where I ordered a *real* shot of vodka and a *real* vodka cran. I'd taken the shot and sucked at my straw then went back to my pseudo-friends who were shaking their stuff on the dance floor.

The second I approached, Hayden's gaze narrowed on my drink. She reached for it and took a sip. "Seriously?" she asked as I snatched it back.

"I needed it! Give me a break." I wiggled my tush and

finally started to feel the music. Vodka swimmed through my veins, heating my blood and warming me from the inside out. It also had the added effect of lifting the dark cloud hovering around me and gave me the little pizazz I needed to keep up the charade.

We had been here for three hours and I was finally having fun. Which is when I bumped into a circle of people I recognized.

"Whoa! Addison Michaels!" I heard a familiar male voice attached to a handsome face.

I struggled to remember his name, but it was on the tip of my tongue.

"Cory from Sacred Heart!" he said, and then dragged over a pretty brunette. "This is my girlfriend Tessa. She's also a nurse," he whispered. "But keep it on the down low, because we're not letting it get out at the hospital," he said conspiratorially.

"You're that model!" Tessa gushed her eyes going big and round.

I nodded and then gestured to the two agents. "My friends Hayden and Paula," I introduced.

"Cool to meet you all," Tessa said. "I couldn't believe Cory got to help you and dress your wounds when you came in. And then he willingly traded with crotchety Nurse Ratched Nancy in order to be there at your visit this week. Oh shit!" She covered her mouth with her hand for a moment. "I probably wasn't supposed to admit that he told me about you. But like, everyone, *knows about you.*" She let out a long drunken exhale.

Cory brought her to his side and made a silly face. "Sorry. I shouldn't have talked about my patients but you're famous and I wanted to, you know…" He dipped his head close to my ear. "Impress my girlfriend," he said.

I waved my hand and sucked at my drink. "No worries. It's all good. I'm just sorry you had to deal with Dr. Templeton."

"Ew! I know right! He's the worst." Tessa nodded. "Freaks me out. He gets so into his patients' wounds I swear he forgets that he's not God. I can't stand him. And the way those tiny eyes zero in on you." She pretended to shiver. "Blech," she said and then she heard a song she liked and bopped to the beat. "This is my favorite song!" She crooned and shimmied, getting into it.

Cory let her go and then danced next to me. "Are, uh, you okay, after…you know…that visit. I was worried about you. When you left in tears, I almost chased you down, but you had that big guy with you."

"Killian, my boyfriend." I smiled wide thinking of my hot guy photographer. "He took care of me. Thank you for asking."

He nodded and pressed his lips together. "I don't like how Dr. Templeton treats his burn victims. It's like he's fascinated with them and it's creepy."

"I get that feeling too, but he comes so highly recommended."

"Yeah, he's known as the best in the biz, at least around Chicagoland. I haven't really been anywhere else."

"Oh, don't get out of the city much?"

He shook his head and smiled as his girlfriend did some wicked cool move where she rolled her hips, bent her body in half, and twerked her perfect round ass.

"Damn, she's hot!" I pointed and air high-fived her. She did it back, grinning, continuing on her party for one.

"She could gain a few pounds," he said randomly, staring at his girl.

I narrowed my gaze and shoved his arm hard. He jolted back and lifted his hands.

"What a dick thing to say!" I cursed and sucked at the rest of my drink planning to get another. Fuck the FBI. It was their job to keep me safe, and I was finally having fun and not freaking out. And I'd made friends. Well, kinda.

"What did I say?" Cory asked, laughing.

"She's perfect the way she is. Don't be a douche who wants something different or like someone made up from a magazine when you've got a sexy little thing like Tessa hooked to your star," I warned. "She's a hot tamale just as she is."

"I'm sorry," he responded instantly. "What I should have said is, she worries about her weight non-stop and I like a woman with a lot to hold on to, so she should be free to do as she wants." He quickly tried to fix his faux pas.

I shrugged. "Let her do whatever it is that makes her happy. Consider that my advice gift for the night."

He chuckled and went over to his girl, kissed her cheek, and then nodded. He turned around. "Drinks, ladies? I'm getting me and Tessa a drink."

Both of my pretend-friends shook their heads. Me, I grinned. Another easy way to get me a real drink. "Hell, yeah! I'll take a vodka cran, heavy on the vodka."

Cory smiled. "You've got it. Will you keep an eye on Tessa?" he asked. "Lot of assholes prey on drunk women and my girlfriend has had a few. I'm DD, but I want to make sure she's safe."

"Oh, believe me…" I grinned wide. "She's super-duper safe tonight! And that's cool of you to make sure she's okay." I reached out and patted his shoulder then hooked my arm around his girlfriend's hips and moved from side to side.

He laughed and shook his head. "Just my luck. I'm hanging out with two insanely hot brunettes," he complimented.

"Oh my god, Cory is so everything, right?" Tessa blurted, staring at the man walking to get us drinks.

"Seems like a nice guy," I agreed.

"I always get the shitty guy who says he wants me the way I am and then never does. Do you know how that is? Oh no, you probably don't. You're like every guy's fantasy," she slurred.

"You'd be surprised." I sighed having had many crummy guys in my past who were nothing to bring home to Mama. Not Killian though. He ticked every box on the good guy scale and then some. Not to mention he was a beast in bed. The things that man could do to me felt scandalous.

"Shouldn't we head back to the bar?" Paula asked teetering painfully on her high heels.

I shook my head. "No way. I haven't been out in months! I'm living it up!" I lifted my arms in the air just as Cory approached with a new REAL drink. All the vodka. Yes, please.

"Thank you, kind sir!"

"No problem, Addison." He bowed then passed his ladylove a drink. "And for the most beautiful woman in here." He handed Tessa her cocktail.

"Swoon!" I teased and grabbed Hayden's hand. "Let's dance the night away!"

"Don't you have to go to the bathroom?" she asked, reminding me of what I was supposed to do.

"Oh shit, yeah, that's right. I have to pee." Which I kinda did since I'd broken the seal a million times already.

"Cool! I'll come with," Tessa offered.

"Um…" I looked at Hayden who shrugged and said, "I'll be at the bar."

Tessa and I hit the restroom, then the bar for yet another real cocktail, and by that time I was feeling so good I forgot completely why I was there.

Not that it mattered because I'd not been approached once. Though I was having a blast with my new FBI and nurse friends.

By the time Jonah and Ryan brought me back to Kerrighan House, I traipsed inside, falling all over myself as I kicked off one heel and then the other.

Killian was waiting on the couch, elbows to his knees, hands in two fists, bearded chin resting on them. His eyes seared into mine in the low light of the room.

"Addy," he said then looked at the clock hanging over the mantle. "You stopped texting me at midnight," he said in an accusatory tone.

I noted the clock said three a.m.

"Um...sorry?" I tried for apology but in my inebriated brain wasn't sure why I needed to.

His shoulders slumped and he waved me over.

Jonah locked the door behind Ryan who left to go to his own house once I was safely in. Jonah called out a mumbled goodnight before heading up the stairs to join Simone in bed.

I stumbled my way toward Kilian in my very short, slinky navy blue dress.

Once I got to him, he reached for my hips and pressed his forehead to my belly. "I was so worried. Three hours I didn't hear a word. Three hours of nothing but silence." He swallowed and rubbed his hands up and down my thighs and hips. "Do you have any idea what it's like to worry about the woman you love for an entire evening to then be cut off for three straight hours? I thought he'd gotten to you, Addy. And neither Jonah nor Ryan responded to my calls."

"Oh my God, Killian, I'm so sorry. I was dancing and hanging with my new friends. I didn't think..."

His face lifted, and I weaved my fingers through his awesome long hair.

"I'm...sorry."

He closed his eyes for a moment, opened them, and I was surprised to see lust staring back at me.

"Prove how sorry you are." He leaned back, stretched his arms over the back of the couch, and rolled his hips in invitation. His hard length was straining against the soft fabric of his light gray sweatpants.

I licked my lips staring at my man's bulge wantonly before I remembered where we were. "Here?" I whispered, as excitement and the thrill of being caught roared through my veins.

Killian tilted his head to the side and rolled his hips again. "I dare you."

No sexier words had ever been spoken.

Chapter
SEVENTEEN

BITING DOWN ON MY LIP, I GLANCED BEHIND ME TO SEE that the rest of the house was dark aside from the dim single light coming from the kitchen and the small lamp next to the couch. I listened intently and rubbed my legs together wanting the friction against my throbbing core.

"Do you really want to do this?" I stood between his open thighs, checking out the very large erection straining against the cotton fabric of his sweats.

"Better question is...do you?" He taunted, reaching down to run his palm up the length over his pants.

Heat filled my veins and arousal poured like lava through my center. Lust mixed with the alcohol in my system as my heart pounded and I fell to my knees between his legs.

"Keep an eye out. I'm going to be busy." I curled my fingers around the waistband and tugged.

He helpfully lifted his hips, and I pulled his pants down just far enough that his long, hard cock was revealed. I wedged the fabric of his pants just under his balls so he was on full display but could easily cover up if needed.

A puff of air left his mouth and his warm brown eyes sizzled with desire as I wrapped my hand around the thick base, appreciating the velvet-wrapped steel nature of him. The tip of his cock wept as I stared into his eyes and licked my lips.

"Be quiet now," I warned, then dipped my head and ran my tongue around the salty, delicious tip.

He clenched his teeth and firmed his jaw as I mouthed the head.

One of his hands wove into my hair and I shook him off. "Nut uh. No touching," I demanded.

He let out a quick and harsh breath but did as I asked, stretching his arms out the length of the couch, digging his fingers into the fabric. When he complied, I rewarded him by plunging my mouth down over his length.

"Jesus," he hissed and rotated his hips.

I bobbed on his cock several times, working him into a nice steady rhythm before sucking as hard as I could and pulling off with a plop.

Before I could even continue, he yanked up his pants, hiding the object of my affection, gripped me at the underarms, and hauled me up to a standing as he did the same. Then he took my hand and half-caveman dragged me to the kitchen door that led down to the basement where we were staying alone. It was the place Mama Kerri usually reserved for guests but with so many of us in the house at the same time, all the beds were full. Even Tabby's, which little Rory was using. She said it made her feel close to her auntie Tab. Plus, she was the only one who willingly chose to sleep there. That meant Charlie was in my bed, sharing a room with Blessing.

I chuckled as Killian moved much faster down the stairs than my inebriated brain could handle, to the point where he ended up lifting me up and over his shoulder as he descended through the small extra living space and into the bedroom we were sharing. Once there, he tossed me on the bed like I weighed nothing. I giggled because…vodka and hot guy throwing *me*, a bigger gal, over his shoulder and onto the bed was freakin' awesome and hilarious at the same time.

"Strip," he growled, then pulled off his white T-shirt and shoved down his sweatpants.

I got up onto my knees, gripped my dress at the hem, and yanked it over my head. I was in nothing but a minuscule dark purple thong and strapless matching bra. My boobs were lifted so high I could practically look down and lick the fleshy globes myself.

"Goddamn you're hot, Addy. My fucking fantasy come alive."

No sexier words could be said in that moment.

I lifted my hand and crooked my finger in a come-hither gesture.

He stood unmoving, staring at me in my lingerie as his gaze seemed to jump from one feature to the next. His long, light brown and golden blondish waves fell down his mighty, wide shoulders. I almost whimpered at the site of all that bronzed skin packed with muscle across the wall of his chest and abdominals. His nostrils flared and his hands fisted at his sides while his cock jutted out from between his thighs like a beacon of passion come alive. He was so powerfully virile and so beautifully male it stole my breath.

It took everything I had not to jump him. Instead, I mewled softly and crawled forward across the bed like a cougar on the prowl, until I got my face in line with his length once again.

"Baby," I crooned, licking my lips.

He came forward just enough that the plush head pressed against my lips teasingly. I swirled my tongue around the mushroom-shaped tip and wrapped my mouth around and down that delectable appendage as far as I could take him. Killian let me suck on him for a few beats before he pulled me off again.

I pouted, honestly starting to get pissed that he kept taking away my new favorite treat. That pout turned into a moan when he reached behind my back and undid my bra, letting my heavy breasts dangle free. A wave of relief washed over me when he'd gotten the offending thing off. He then cupped both my breasts, palming and hefting their weight in his hands while playing. With deft fingers he teased and plucked at my nipples until they were hard, erect knots burning with need.

"God," I gasped as he stepped close enough to the bed where I kneeled on all fours. He nudged his glistening cock between my hanging breasts, pressing the globes together to create tight friction against his length.

"I've fantasized about fucking your tits so many times, baby." He groaned and thrust his hips. "Better than I imagined," he said in a low, sexy tone that raced down my spine.

I started to move forward and back, giving him more for several thrusts until once again he eased back, his hand around the base of his cock as if he were staving off an impending orgasm. He rubbed the head of his cock over each nipple teasingly, graphically, in a sexual caress no man had ever done before.

That was all I could take. I got back up on my knees, wiggled out of the scrap of lace panties, then wrapped my arms around his neck and plastered my naked breasts to his warm skin as I took his mouth with my own. The kiss turned carnal instantly, each of us hungry for the other.

Before I knew it, my back was to the bed, legs spread wide, and he was plunging deep inside me.

When he hit the end and our bodies met completely, I arched at the powerful, blissful invasion. Sparks flew through my nerve endings and sizzled like little sparklers along every pore.

He groaned low and deep in his throat and trembled in my arms, telling me without words how much our bodies coming together affected him.

It was pure magic.

Nothing better.

I wrapped my arms and legs around the only man I had ever, and would ever, love. He curled both arms under my back and around my shoulders. His face was pressed to my neck, mouth at my pulse.

"You're the one, Addy. The woman meant for me. Tell me you feel it." He thrust high and deep as he sunk his teeth into the hunk of muscle where my neck and shoulder met.

Pleasure spread out from my core through my body.

"I've never felt anything like this, Killian." I nudged his furry cheek until he lifted his head and looked into my eyes. "It's me and you. No matter what. From here on out. I'm yours, and you're mine."

He cupped one of my cheeks and stroked my bottom lip, then my cheekbone with his thumb.

"I'll love only you, baby. Until we have kids. That's the only time this amount of love will be shared."

I smiled so big I felt as though I'd burst with joy. "I think I can share your love with our future children."

He grinned and bit into his bottom lip as he eased almost all the way out of my body and then slammed back in.

I gasped and moaned at the sudden blend of pleasure mixed with pain. Then I shut up as my man made love to me.

He was driven in his desire, selfless with his own needs, putting mine first, making sure he brought me to the absolute pinnacle of release before backing off and working me up all over again. He did this three times in a row before I pushed him to his back and took over.

Killian suckled my breasts as I rode him hard and fast, climbing so quickly to the height of orgasm my vision started to waver in and out. His hands locked around my hips as he lifted his own, pounding mercilessly. We both were covered in sweat, our breaths labored, the room smelling of sex as we both strained to reach the highest peak together.

At the same time my body locked down around him, his fingers dug into my hips and he went rigid, a silent cry as his mouth opened and his eyes pinched tight. I crashed over his chest and plunged my tongue into his mouth, kissing him with everything I had as the most powerful orgasm roared through not only my body, but his.

Together.

It had never happened to me before, and I knew why.

Because it wasn't Killian before.

I leisurely licked and nibbled on his lips, enjoying the prickles of his hair against my mouth. Our bodies were still connected, and the sweat was cooling against our exposed skin. Killian took over the kiss after he came back from his own release, his fingers gripping my hair at the roots in a fist, controlling my head movements as he kissed me deeply. Every swipe of his tongue was a nourishing connection reminding me of what we both already knew.

You're mine.

I'm yours.

This is us.

And it was.

Messy, complicated, beautiful, crazy, wild, life-changing, soul-altering...love.

This is what love looked like between Killian and me, and I wouldn't change it for the world.

Once he'd gotten enough of my mouth, he shifted me to the side, kissed my nose and rose from the bed. He tugged the sheet and pulled it over me.

"Be right back," he said then entered the attached bathroom. I heard the water turn on and then turn off. He returned with a warm cloth with which he cleaned himself from between my thighs and then brought the cloth back to the bathroom. Another round of water on and off and then he clicked off the light.

I watched all of this through a dreamy sleepy haze. The booze had worn off and I saw nothing but my gorgeous man shutting off the lights and readying for bed. He slid under the sheet, reached for the comforter, and laid it over both of us before cuddling up against my back. I was usually a side or back sleeper but a lot of that changed since sleeping next to Killian. He moved a lot in his sleep and would readjust me right along with him so that we were touching at all times. He said when we touched, he slept soundly. Something about having me there apparently scared away his nightmares.

I wasn't a fool to think they'd be gone for good, but if he believed having me close at all times was helpful, I had zero problems sleeping plastered to my hot guy each night.

"Goodnight, baby." I rubbed my bum against his groin, settling in.

He held my hand and brought it up between my breasts, nudged his jaw to my shoulder, and sighed in the happy way that I knew meant he was feeling contentment.

"Love you, Addy."

I yawned. "Love you, too. Sorry about not texting. I won't do that again."

"Appreciate it. I'd also appreciate you not drinking tomorrow night when you do it all over again. I want you to have your wits about you."

"Mmm hmm. 'Kay. I won't drink," I mumbled.

He kissed my cheek and pressed his face to my neck.

I fell asleep to his warm breath against my skin.

Yep, this was us, and it was absolutely perfect.

The next night I was in another slinky dress and bored to tears. The music in the club was pounding so loud in my head I needed to take four ibuprofens just to take the edge off. What I really needed was a shot, a little hair of the dog, but I'd promised Killian and Jonah and Ryan, after repeated tongue lashings about how stupid I'd been yesterday, that I wouldn't drink.

Trey, Simone's ex-boyfriend, was working the bar tonight and sauntered over to me. I was scanning texts from not only Killian but every last one of my sisters. I mean, you'd think if you were on a stakeout like I was, they'd lay off. But nooooooo. They each had something to say, wisdom to impart, or just wanted to check in on me because none of them could handle the fact that I was doing this on my own. Well, with the FBI in tow of course.

"Hey, beautiful." Trey leaned over the bar and smiled.

Ugh. The guy was eye candy, but he was a dick and had cheated on my sister regularly. The man looked good but was a huge player. I wanted to talk to him like I wanted to have another cigarette burned into my arm. Not at all. Still, I was there to play a part, so play the part I did by smiling in return.

"Hey, Trey. How goes it?" I tried for being civil.

He tapped on the bar with his fingers. "Can't complain. Aside from the fact that Simone has cut off all contact with me. Doesn't even return my texts. Rude, right?" He stood up and scanned the bar nodding at a pretty girl who lifted her empty drink. He winked at her and lifted his hand in a gesture that universally meant "be there in a minute."

I looked at the tall, stacked blonde who was eye-fucking him and rubbing her lips together, tipping her body so that her boobs were on prime display.

Yuck.

I never understood the hookup scene. It just never worked for me. Charlie on the other hand was a fan. So was Tabby back in her heyday. The two of them would hit the club scene, take home a couple live ones, and get their jollies off never to speak to those people again. I mean, I understood the human need to connect physically, but I wasn't one for a quickie with a stranger. Charlie claims it works wonders for her mental state since she's constantly wound up over the kids she helps, and Tabby just liked sex without any strings. Me, I needed an emotional connection in order to go there sexually. It's just the way I was wired. Maybe it had to do with the abuse I suffered as a young girl, maybe I was just old fashioned. Either way, guys like Trey barked up the wrong tree when they approached me with that fake-ass swagger.

"You cheated on her repeatedly," I deadpanned.

His brows furrowed as he made me a replacement fake vodka cran.

"Yeah, but those girls meant nothing. I always came back to Simone. She was my girl. My one in five billion."

It was actually seven billion people in the world and closing in on eight billion everyday but he was an idiot that knew nothing of the world.

I snort-laughed. "Dude, no. She was your doormat that you wiped your feet on every time you saw her. And she's living with another man."

He tilted his head. "Once she gets sick of him, I'm going to get her back," he said with confidence as though he actually believed it.

I blinked several times at the utter stupidity coming out of his mouth. "Are you really this dumb?"

He jerked his head back. "What, because I'm hopeful that I'll get my woman back?"

I shook my head. "Trey, she's not only shacked up with the man of her dreams, but he also bought a house for them to live in together. She works with his dad and brother, has gotten her degree, and the two of them are talking marriage and children in the very near future. Oh, and they're raising a dog together."

"There's still time. She hasn't married him yet."

"Yet being the proverbial word in that sentence. Dude, he's an FBI agent with his shit together and shows her every day how much he loves her. Treats her like gold. You're a bartender and a serial cheater. Give it up already. She's never, not ever, going to take you back. Ever. Like, ever. Never." I repeated it hoping he'd get with the program.

He leaned forward and looked me straight in the eye. Damn, he sure was pretty. I could see why Simone would forgive him. He was good looking in that surfer guy way, unlike Jonah who was hot in that GQ, rocks a suit like Clark Kent and was smart as fuck with his life together way. No competition really.

"You mean it's *over*-over? For reals?" He said those words in a way that sounded as though he truly was just hearing them for the first time.

Oh my god. This guy.

I closed my eyes and then looked at him. He actually seemed really sad and tortured all of a sudden.

"Sorry, buddy. That ship has definitely sailed. Though blonde chick down the way is staring you down. I'm sure you've got a chance with her."

He huffed. "Well, yeah, but she's easy. Simone was marriage material. Man, my mom is going to be so pissed when I finally tell her we're not together anymore. Damn. I figured I could get her back, ya know?"

I shook my head. "No, I don't know, since she made it very clear after you broke up with her *in a text* that she was done with your shit."

Man, I'm so glad Simone moved on and found a real man. This guy is loony tunes.

"Yeah, but…" He shrugged. "Still thought I could win her over eventually. This sucks." He tossed the cloth he had over his shoulder onto the bar and started wiping up around me.

I sucked in a breath. "Yeah, these things happen. You'll figure it out."

He nodded and then moved down the way to get drinks for other patrons, a slump to his shoulders that hadn't been there before. I almost felt sorry for the clueless guy, but he cheated on my sister and treated her like shit. He deserved to feel bad for his actions.

My newest girlfriend, an FBI undercover agent who went by the name Tanisha, an athletically built dark-skinned woman, gave me big eyes before whispering, "Your girl done dodged a bullet with that one." She sipped her fake drink and grinned.

The two of us laughed as a commotion rose up in the crowd from behind us. Out of nowhere a fight broke out and a couple dudes came barreling into me and Tanisha. The high-top barstools we sat on went careening sideways. I fell into Tanisha and both of our chairs teetered like a stack of dominos. Each woman and man sitting in the line went down with the first. We were a pile of limbs and metal falling several feet and crashing to the hard concrete floor. I heard something snap in my wrist as I reached out to catch myself before hitting my cheek against the metal leg of a chair.

I screamed in pain as the fight raged on. Someone—Tanisha—yanked me up and I felt liquid oozing down my cheek once I got onto my feet. She was cradling her side at the ribs and had her gun out. Where she had been hiding a gun with that sexy as fuck outfit, I had no idea, but there it was.

"Addy!" Trey jumped over the bar just as another crowd of big guys throwing fists came careening toward us. He lifted me up by the hips and set me on the bar taking the brunt of the men running into him from behind. I turned and he pushed me to safety behind the bar. Tanisha put her hands to the bartop and catapulted over it like a badass heroine in an action movie. She pushed me back and down handing me a wad of napkins.

"Press these to your face. Shit, girl, you've got a nasty cut there," she said, then turned her gaze to the commotion beyond us.

My face hurt but my wrist was throbbing right along with my heartbeat. I cradled it as my vision wavered in and out. I breathed through the pain not wanting to pass out. I heard my name being called out in the most beloved voice imaginable, thinking it was Killian, but knowing that was impossible.

Then out of nowhere, the man himself appeared. Killian crouched down where I was hiding behind the bar as the fight wore on.

"Baby, you're here?" Tears hit my eyes and my bottom lip started to wobble.

"I wasn't about to let you go alone again. I couldn't handle it last night. Jonah let me stay hidden in the manager's office. I've been watching the entire time."

"My wrist is broken." I lifted my forearm as he looked down.

"Holy shit, Addy. That looks really bad." He had me move the napkins away from my cheek. "Just a slice. I don't think it will need stitches. Maybe just a butterfly stitch at most."

Suddenly the club lights came on and I was being lifted up into my man's arms. He brought me out from the bar and then set me on my feet.

People were watching the scene in the center of the dancefloor, clubgoers not involved huddled around the edges next to the walls. In the center were a bunch of guys with their hands up behind their heads being handcuffed by FBI agents.

Jonah came over to me. "You okay? I saw you get put behind the bar with Tanisha, so I knew you were covered."

"What happened?"

"Bar fight that got out of hand. But I'm going to find out more," he grumbled.

"She needs to get to the hospital. Broke her wrist," Killian stated with a note of urgency.

I lifted my arm, and my wrist was already swelling, and one side looked like it was poking the side of my skin oddly where it shouldn't.

"Shit. Simone's going to rip me a new one." He groaned. "I'm sorry, sweetheart. Tanisha!" Jonah called out.

My new girlfriend came up holding her side. Then she lifted the hem of her dress and slid her gun into a thigh holster. "Yeah, Boss?"

"Cooooool," I said in awe as the sparkly material fell back into place hiding the gun completely. She was like a sexy Tomb Raider FBI agent.

"I've got a knife on the other side." She winked with a sexy flare.

My eyes widened. "Really?" I gushed.

She smiled and nodded. "Yeah."

"Cooooool," I repeated thinking my new FBI girlfriend was the shit. "You're the shit!" I decided to tell her.

"We'll hook up after this. Maybe get our nails done and go out for drinks."

"Can my sisters come?" I asked automatically. They would love a sexy Tomb Raider FBI chick in our crew.

"They as nice as you?" She tilted her head and the lights from the club gleamed along her shiny side part that led into a low ponytail complete with a big poof of long dark waves down the middle of her back.

I nodded avidly. "Totally."

"Then sure thing. More sisters the merrier."

"Awesome." I lamely let my excitement show.

She laughed and then focused on Jonah.

"Can you escort them to the hospital with Holt? I don't want her left alone for a minute. I'm not sure any of these brawlers are our guy." Jonah sighed and rubbed the back of his neck in the same gesture I'd seen him do a bunch of times when he was frustrated.

My shoulders slumped. All of this for nothing but a busted cheek and a broken wrist. Great.

Killian hooked his arm around my shoulders and kept me close before kissing my temple. "It's okay. You did what you could. We'll figure it out, but your days of being bait are over, baby. This is enough."

I nodded sadly as my wrist screamed for attention.

"Let's get you patched up, girlfriend." Tanisha led us through the huge dance floor toward the exit.

Oooh, the cool girl called me her *girlfriend*. At least I got a new badass friend out of this mess.

Still, silver linings sucked.

Broken wrists sucked.

Busted cheeks on a model sucked.

And ruined undercover missions sucked.

Basically, my life right now sucked.

Chapter
EIGHTEEN

W E EXITED ONE OF THE BLACK SUVs THAT WERE standard issue for not only the FBI it seemed but also the security company. Holt, who had been circling the outside of the club, was chosen as our guard and driver. He came around to the passenger side and opened my door. Tanisha exited the front and Killian slid across the seat so he could come up right behind me.

I cradled my wrist and Tanisha held onto her side protectively as we clip-clopped in our heels over the asphalt. When we approached the Emergency doors, I recognized a couple that was walking to our same destination only in a pair of scrubs. Tessa and Cory.

"Oh, my goodness, what happened to you?" Tessa said, her eyes going round as they approached.

Cory reached out delicately for my elbow. "Let me see your wrist? What happened?"

The six of us hovered just under the overhang outside the emergency room. "This is going to need to be set, X-rayed to make sure the bones are in place, and then casted once the swelling goes down. Shit, Addy, you really did a number on yourself. Come on. Tessa and I are working the ER, but I'll pull some strings and see what I can get rushed. Hopefully, it's not a busy night," he said trying to lead me inside, with a hand to my shoulder.

"I've got her," Killian growled possessively.

My man had had enough of me being hurt. Things seemed to be getting more jacked up by the day with no light at the end of the tunnel.

Cory held his hands up in surrender as Tessa went to help Tanisha. "I see you babying your ribs. You're hurt too? What in the world went down?"

"Bar fight. We got caught in the crossfire. I'm pretty sure my ribs are just bruised. Wouldn't be the first time. Won't be the last," Tanisha answered.

"You're such a bad ass," I boasted to my new girlfriend.

She laughed good-naturedly. "Takes one to know one, sister. You haven't so much as shed a tear. That's some strength, girl, especially when anyone can clearly see you're in a lot of pain."

"I happened to take ibuprofen before we hit the bar because I was hungover from last night. Speaking of...neither of you look worse for the wear. How is that possible?"

Cory shrugged. "I was the DD, remember. Tessa has a high tolerance and never seems to be affected the next day." He walked us all through the emergency room and straight back.

She smiled. "What can I say? It's a gift from God. No hangovers. I'll take it!"

My wrist really started to hurt, and I hissed when it was jostled.

"I'm going to take Tanisha and check you both in while Cory gets your wrist assessed by a trauma doc," Tessa offered.

"You've got her?" Tanisha gestured to Holt and then Killian.

Both men nodded but didn't say a word.

"Thanks, Tessa. Catch you on the flip, Tanisha!" I called out.

She waved as Tessa led her to a different area. Her job for the evening was done. Holt and Killian had my back.

For the next several hours, I went through the process of getting my wrist looked at by the trauma doc, X-rayed, put back in place, and evaluated by a surgeon. He seemed to think that it was a clean break, whatever the heck that meant, and could be casted without the need for surgery. The skin on my cheek was washed thoroughly, not fun in the slightest, and then butterfly stitched as Killian had assumed with tape versus physical stitches. Though because I'd also hit my head on the chair and admitted to almost blacking out, they wanted to keep me for several hours with my arm in a sling so the swelling could go down enough for it to be casted.

Once I was settled in a room, Killian pulled up a chair at my side and rested in it. He took my good hand and brought it up to his lips.

"How you doing?" he asked.

I played with the hair at his jaw with the tips of my fingers. "Fine. Tired. Feeling stupid. All of this and we didn't even catch the bad guy," I griped.

"What bad guy?" Cory asked as he entered the room and shut the door.

Killian's phone rang in his back pocket and he got up as Cory approached and went to the computer next to my bed to check on medical things. He turned away and when I looked again, he was inserting something into my IV. Probably more drugs or fluids. Honestly, at this point I didn't care. I was so tired.

"It's Jonah." He lifted the phone and walked to the other side of the room to take the call.

"Ugh, have you not read the papers?" I answered Cory who was typing merrily into the computer.

He shook his head. "You mean that Strangler case that you were involved in when we first met? I thought that was long over?" He kept typing.

I sighed deeply as the weight of it all pressed into my chest, smothering my level-headedness.

"It was, until some asshole started killing women who looked like me." I sighed, my eyes feeling heavier than before.

Cory stopped mid-type. "What did you say?" Shock laced his tone.

"Yep. Apparently, some freak decided I was special enough to kill three women that looked somewhat like me. And get this…"

"What?" His eyes widened and his lips compressed into a white, flat, angry-looking line.

"He burned their arms just like this." I showed him the inside of my free arm.

"I thought he only did that to two of the women. Not Mallory." He frowned deeply.

"Yeah, but he still killed her and then he burned off her face!" I winced. "Gross. And scary." I closed my eyes trying to rest them and moved my tongue around the inside of my mouth. It felt weird all of a sudden.

"She must have been a mean bitch to deserve that," Cory stated calmly.

What he said took a minute to compute. "Huh?" I glanced at Cory who stood staring at Killian. I watched as he pushed up the sleeves of his thermal shirt that he wore under his scrubs. I noticed burn marks running all up and down his arms, front and back alike. I narrowed my gaze trying to focus and saw some of those same type of burn marks crawling up the skin of his neck.

Killian's voice rose breaking me out of my inspection of my new friend. "What do you mean the doctor is dead?"

"The doctor?" I called out, Cory's scars forgotten while my head pounded like a jackhammer. I needed sleep. I needed to crawl into Killian's bed back at the loft and crash for a week solid. Preferably with Killian and Brutus next to me.

Killian was pacing, phone pressed to his ear as he spun around and barked in my direction. "Dr. Templeton was found murdered in his apartment this evening. Arms, face, and manhood burned to shit."

"What!" I gasped.

"Serves him right," Cory mumbled so low I wasn't sure I heard it correctly.

"Jonah says your picture was taped over his burnt appendage," Killian continued.

I gagged, covering my mouth.

"Who would kill Dr. Templeton and how would the killer know he was a suspect?" Killian barked into the phone. I looked at him and then felt an icy cold slip into my veins as I watched Cory put his hands into his pocket while approaching Killian.

Cory's words of a moment ago finally filtered through the muck and pain.

"I thought he only did that to two of the women. Not Mallory."

"She must have been a mean bitch to deserve that."

"Serves him right."

How would Cory know those private details that weren't released to the public about the nurse unless he'd been there?

Unless he'd done it himself.

Because he was the one who killed her.

Oh my God!

My entire body froze as the realization skittered through my system. "Babe!" I tried to holler but it came out as a whisper. My vocal cords seeming swollen and scratchy while it was harder and harder to keep my eyes opened.

I'd been drugged.

And Cory was the killer.

"What do you mean the bar fight was a setup? They told you they were paid to start it by a guy in medical scrubs?" Killian shook his head, but Cory kept approaching.

"Killian!" I cried right as Cory lifted his arm and struck Killian's neck with a syringe.

"NO!" I screeched but again barely any sound left my throat. I tried to get out of the bed, but now the tiredness was overwhelming, and a wooziness claimed my stomach. My limbs felt like Jell-O. I couldn't even lift my leg. It moved enough to fall to the side and hang off the edge of the bed limply. The rest of me sunk deep into the hospital bed.

"Killian." Tears filled my eyes and fell down my cheeks.

"Finally, he's quiet." Cory swiped at his hair, putting it neatly out of his eyes.

"Did you kill him?" I spoke softly, not able to even scream as I stared at Killian's unmoving form.

Cory wiped his hands down his scrubs, and pulled out another syringe as he approached.

"You've been slipperier than a little fish in a shallow river these past weeks, now haven't you, Addison?"

The tears kept coming he got closer to the bed, Killian's lifeless form across the room.

"The medicine will make you loopy and slow with almost zero speaking voice. Which works for what I have planned."

"Why?" I mumbled, my tongue feeling thick and swollen.

He narrowed his gaze and showed me his arms. "Haven't you figured it out? Me and you are the same. Mistreated. Burned. Beaten. But then Aunt Mable died a week before you were admitted the first time, and it was like a switch clicked when you showed up in the hospital looking just like me."

I shook my head, but it barely moved. "We are not the same."

He flopped his body down to a seated position at the end of my bed. "Oh, but we are. Aunt Mable used to hurt me. Burn me. Tell me how bad and ugly I was. Even after I took care of her. All those years. Doing everything for her. I thought I was alone. Hideous. Deformed. And any woman I approached thought my burns were gross, disgusting. He lifted his shirt and showed me the wall of his chest which was covered in poorly healed scars like mine only his covered his entire upper body.

"Aunt Mable smoked a pack a day. Didn't care much for an ashtray." His lips twisted into a snarl. "And still, I took care of her like a good boy should. My real parents died. I was left with her and nobody cared what she did to me."

"I would have cared." I tried desperately to keep my heavy eyes open. To keep him talking so that someone, *anyone* could figure out what was happening in here. I glanced at Killian and could see his chest rising and falling with his breaths, thank God!

Cory nodded. "I realized that when you came in after the Strangler had done a number on you. You see, what I've come to figure out is that women who are messed up like me are much nicer. I figured I could avenge you. Leave you gifts of my undying affection."

"By killing those women?" I mumbled.

He nodded. "Of course. They were self-absorbed. Thought they were every man's gift and treated others poorly. They really aren't a loss to this world."

"And Tessa?" I tried to find the decency in him because she was incredibly kind and sweet.

"A fun pastime until I could get to you." He ran a finger down from my knee to my foot that was hanging off the bed before he lifted it and placed it back on the bed and covered me up once more.

"And the nurse?" I wiggled my fingers and toes trying to get some feeling back into them thinking maybe I could do something to help my predicament.

"She was a disgusting human being. Thought her shit didn't stink and treated me like trash. Others loved her because she lied through her teeth all the time and took their shifts. So, I made sure her final resting place fit the person. The dumpster outside of where you were tortured. Wasn't that nice of me?"

"Um yeah, very nice," I said, thinking maybe I could play his game long enough to save Killian and me from whatever Cory's endgame was.

"And the doctor?"

He grinned huge, his entire face lighting up. "I'm so glad you asked!" His tone was one of joy and accomplishment. "He was obsessed with you. Touched you as though it was his right. And it's not. It's *my* right. We're meant to be you and me. We're the same." He rubbed his hands together, then pulled back the blanket, removing it entirely.

"What are you going to do?" I looked at my bare legs and back at his wild gaze thinking maybe he was going to do something I was not sure I'd come back from.

Cory scrunched his nose. "Oh, not that. When you give your beautiful body to me, it will be your choice and definitely not in a hospital. That's not romantic at all. Still, I've got to get you out of here in order for us to be together."

He went over to the other side of the room where I just noticed a wheelchair was collapsed. Cory expertly opened it and wheeled it over to the bed.

"You don't have to do this, Cory. You've been hurt like me. We can get you the help you need..." I tried blinking several times to ward off the constant desire to close my eyes and slip off into dreamland. But for Killian, and for my own survival, I needed to stay awake. I had to.

His gaze narrowed into tiny slits. "I don't need help. I just need to get you out of here so we can move away and live our lives happy as clams."

"And what about my wrist?" I tried to take the approach of needing the medical attention. Thinking maybe I could appeal to his wanting to help people in need side that nurses tended to have.

He smiled. "I'm a nurse, honey. I can easily cast that

wrist and have you healed like new in six to eight weeks. We just need to get out of here."

"And Killian? What did you give him?"

"Why do you care?" he spat, his blue eyes turning a dark midnight as the expression on his face twisted to one of rage. "He means nothing!" He went over to Killian and kicked his lifeless form. "Absolutely nothing." He kicked my man's beautiful body again. "Nothing to you! Do you understand! I'm here. I'm going to take care of you. Treat you and your scars like nothing but a gift!"

"Okay, okay, you've got me. What do we do next?" I let the tears fall.

"Tears? Why the fuck are you crying! I haven't hurt you. Well, I did pay for those guys to start a brawl and make sure you'd get hurt. But you see, it was all part of my plan. I knew even if you had so much as a scratch that FBI agent that's been all over the news about the case would send you here. The timing was planned to the minute so that Tessa and I would arrive around the time I believed you'd be coming in, and there you were. Like a walking miracle. Ever since Aunt Mable died, I'd been free of her torture, and there you were. A gift from the Universe just for me. Someone who could understand what I suffered all those years."

I swallowed down the emotion trying my best to think straight. Find a way to get me and Killian out of this. Turn the tide somehow.

Which was when Cory approached and lifted my heavy, drugged form into the wheelchair. The man had some serious strength. I was not light or small by any stretch of the imagination and he got me right into the chair. Then again, most nurses were powerhouses.

"Thank you," I said in as sweet of a tone as I could muster.

He stopped and stood, grabbing the blanket and covering my legs with it. "You're welcome."

"You're right, we are a lot alike. Both suffering so much at the hands of a very bad person," I tried.

He nodded and smiled. "Yes, exactly. You're starting to see. I knew you would. I knew when you were so nice to me that day you'd come in and I was cleaning and dressing your wounds that you were special. You looked into my eyes and it all clicked. I went through what I did so that I could be the man for you. A man who would understand you the way no one else could." He leaned forward and pressed his cold, dry lips to mine.

I closed my eyes and let him, trying not to sob. I dug deep for strength until he pulled back and cupped my cheek.

"I knew it would be amazing between us," he gushed. "Now to get rid of your bodyguard." He smiled, and my stomach dropped, dread filling my veins.

I watched helpless and spoke as loud as I could which wasn't loud at all. "Holt!" I screamed, but it came out sounding like a slurred, raspy, "hole," my vocal cords not even strong enough to enunciate the t in his name.

Cory twirled around, his face a mask of fury. "Don't. Do. That. Again." He grated through his teeth and pulled out another syringe.

"This one is filled with Cyanide. One fat dose of this will kill a person pretty much instantly. If you want that to happen to your beloved bodyguard or anyone else for that matter, go ahead and try that again. If you want to make it out of here alive, and them as well, you'll shut your pretty mouth."

I figured he was right. My best bet was to let him get me out of here keeping everyone I cared about safe.

I watched in horror as Cory went over to Killian, grabbed his arms and dragged him into the small, attached bathroom, and then shut the door. At least he'd eventually wake up and be safe. Pissed. Angry beyond reason, but alive.

Then he looked at me with a glare, put one finger up to his mouth and said, "Shush," before he opened the door.

Holt was standing at the door. He looked at Cory then at me and lifted his chin. "What's up?"

"Doctor said he wants an MRI of her brain to ensure she doesn't have a concussion or something worse."

Holt nodded, his eyes assessing me as Cory approached and went behind the wheelchair. I widened my eyes and tried my best to tell Holt something was up with Cory without saying anything.

He looked at me then up at Cory and then looked away.

I closed my eyes and relegated myself to being taken.

Cory and I passed Holt, but instead of waiting, he ended up following us.

"Where's Killian? I thought he was in the room. Man never leaves your side," Holt stated flatly.

Cory put his hand to my shoulder and squeezed hard in warning.

"Bathroom," I muttered.

"You could uh, wait here, sir. We're just going up to Imaging. Nothing to it," Cory said as though it was just another day in the hospital. A true actor.

Holt narrowed his gaze and followed us into the elevator.

"Nah, I've got nothing better to do than follow Addison around. You love it, right, Addison?" Holt dipped his head and looked right into my eyes. "You good?"

A tear fell but I couldn't lift my arms to wipe it away.

"Never better," I whispered.

"What's the matter with her voice?" he asked Cory.

"Pain meds sometimes have that effect," he said sounding perfectly reasonable.

My heart pounded so hard my entire body felt scalding hot. More tears fell and I closed my eyes.

Please don't let him kill Holt. Please don't let him kill Holt.
I prayed.

Holt dipped his head again to look straight into my eyes. I moved them to the top trying to gesture to Cory but suddenly his eyes widened and his entire body fell into a heap in front of the wheelchair.

"You're lucky I still had a syringe full of the same sedative I used on that man who claimed to be yours. He'll wake easily with smelling salts when he's found. I don't want to hurt or kill people, Addison. But if they get in the way or do bad things to hurt you, then it's a detail I must handle. I'm not afraid to get my hands dirty if it means you and me together in the end."

I watched in horror as Cory used some key that locked the elevator from stopping on any other floors. We went straight down. When we got to the main lobby area, he maneuvered me around Holt's unconscious form and went a different direction, not toward the lobby. He strode down a long hallway and passed laundry carts and unoccupied hospital gurneys and wheelchairs that had been lined up. Maybe a less often used part of the hospital, especially late at night on a weekend.

A hopelessness filled my heart and mind. He was going to get away with it all and take me with him. Worse, there was nothing I could do about it.

Killian lie in a heap knocked out. Holt too. And Killian… Who knew what those kicks did to his body?

"Almost home-free, baby. You and me, and maybe a Mexican cabana in our near future. Doesn't that sound nice?" He preened smugly.

Cory pushed the metal bar of an exit door, the alarms blaring loudly, but he didn't seem to mind. He was looking down at me. "Car's really close. We'll be long gone by the time the hospital security figure out which door has been opened."

"I wouldn't count on that, asshole!" Jonah, Ryan and a team of FBI and cops had guns blazing centered right on my captor.

I wanted to explode with joy, but physically couldn't with the meds still coursing through my veins.

Cory instantly put the last syringe to my neck. "This is filled with Cyanide. I push this and she's dead in seconds!" he screamed.

He barely finished saying the last syllable of the word *seconds* when a gunshot tore through the air from Jonah's gun. The needle plopped into my lap as Cory's lifeless body fell backward. I heard his weight smack the ground as I was bum-rushed by Jonah and Ryan.

"Get her out of here," Ryan erupted.

Jonah holstered his weapon and reached for my hands, crouching down.

"Addy, honey, can you hear me?"

"Yes, can't move. Dead?" I whispered.

He nodded. "Bullet to the head. He will not be hurting anyone ever again." He went around the wheelchair and pushed me out of the way and toward two hospital staff that were waiting behind the cops. They rushed over to me.

"Do you know what he gave you?" one of the professionals asked.

"No. Killian, in my room," I sputtered, needing someone to check on him.

"He was found and woke right away when your real nurse checked on you. He'll be out shortly," Jonah stated.

Which was when I saw my man race out of the hospital doors from the other end of the building, look both ways, and come running directly toward the calvary and me. I'd never been so happy to see him alive and running before.

"Fuck me, fuck me, fuck me!" He fell to his knees pushing one of the nurses out of the way and falling to the front of my chair where he wrapped his arms around my body. His hands were shaking like mad when he lifted his head. "I thought he had you for good. I'm so sorry I didn't see it coming, baby. So sorry I let you get taken." Tears ran down his cheeks as he cupped mine and stared into my eyes. He'd been so strong for me this entire time. Seeing him crack emotionally was devastating.

My own tears fell and mingled with his as he kissed me softly. "You okay?" he whispered against my lips.

"No, but I will be." I barely got the words out.

"She needs to be admitted. He gave her something that we need to flush out of her system," the nurse taking my blood pressure announced.

"Yeah, okay. You're not leaving my sight." Killian moved behind me and Jonah let him push me back into the hospital. The last freakin' place I wanted to be, but I also wanted to have the use of my limbs again.

When we were back in my room, and the doctors figured out what was used on me, they were able to flush it out of my body. Slowly, my ability to move returned until eventually I was back to normal.

Killian ran his fingers over my hair as he sat next to my bed. "Your family will be here soon. You may want to try and get a little rest."

"I want to go home." I pouted.

"To Kerrighan House?"

I shook my head. "I want to go to your home. Sleep in your bed, in your arms with our dog lying right next to me." I couldn't help the deluge of emotion overwhelming me. It had been an insane night, day, month. Hell, past several months. I was done. Fried to the core of my being.

"Dog on the bed?" he teased.

"Yeah," I said, sniffing as the tears kept coming.

Killian kissed them away and nodded.

"Okay, baby. We'll get you and our dog home very soon. Now close your eyes and rest for me."

I swallowed, almost afraid to close my eyes. "You'll be here?"

"Every second. Every minute. Every hour. Every day. I'll be here." It was a promise I believed down to my bones.

I nodded and closed my eyes, focusing on the soothing way he ran his fingers through my hair, thinking about how good it would be when we went back to his home.

Chapter
NINETEEN

KILLIAN LED ME AND BRUTUS THROUGH THE DOOR OF THE loft.

I inhaled full and deep, taking in every inch of what had surprisingly become my sanctuary. My home away from home. At least for now. Until I found my own place once again.

I shuffled on slipper-covered feet, a gift that Mama Kerri had brought to the hospital along with a big fluffy pink robe. The meds were completely out of my system, and my wrist was in a cast and hurting like crazy. I refused to take any pain medicine outside of ibuprofen because I'd had enough of being drugged to last a lifetime.

"Can you turn the TV on the news, please? Sonia should be giving her press statement right about now."

"You got it, baby." He went over to the teal couch where he had a smaller TV nestled behind a cabinet door. It wasn't anything like the big projector, but I thought he probably used that for movies or binging, but not for normal news.

He got me set up on the couch with a blanket. He didn't even need to tell Brutus to guard me. My big boy hopped up on the couch, settled his monster head in my lap, and huffed like he had been seriously put out not being able to be home. Mama Kerri didn't allow animals on her furniture and I understood why when I dealt with dog hair all over my clothing. Not fun. And yet, I didn't care enough to stop my baby from cuddling me. I picked my battle, and it was dog-love versus dog-hair. Dog-love the clear winner.

Killian turned on the news. "I'm going to make you some tea. Want a shot of whiskey in it?"

"Yes, please. I sure could use it." I petted Brutus's big head as he snuffled against my belly, kissing me wherever he could. Seemed as though both the Fitzpatrick men, master and dog, needed to be there for me right now. Killian because he held guilt. I could see it in his eyes every time he'd looked at me since last night. Brutus because he missed me and knew I was hurt. He also was taking his cues from his dad who was definitely sad about what went down. I wasn't sure how I was going to get him to see that it wasn't his fault, but I'd figure something out eventually. Time would heal these wounds too. Hopefully.

The news anchor came on and the blue "Special Announcement" flashed across the screen. "The residents of Chicagoland can feel safe once again that the suspect in what looked like copycat murders to the Backseat Strangler has been found. Independent politician Senator Sonia Wright has called a special press conference in order to share her findings as her family was once again tied to the tragic murders."

The screen filled with Sonia's stunning face. She looked tired, with red-rimmed eyes as though she'd been up all night, which I knew she had. After I'd been saved and Cory killed, Mama Kerri and all of my sisters descended *en masse* to the hospital.

Sonia curled a lock of bright, almost platinum blonde hair behind her ear as she stared at the camera.

"At approximately three in the morning, my foster sister, model Addison Michaels-Kerrighan, was apprehended by a man by the name of Cory Pitman. Mr. Pitman was a nurse at Sacred Heart. He'd been badly abused as a child and fixated on my sister at the time she sought care after surviving her capture by the Backseat Strangler several months ago. The FBI caught Mr. Pitman trying to kidnap my sister from the hospital last night. When he threatened her life, he was shot and killed by a member of the Chicago branch of the Federal Bureau of Investigation. They confirmed he was not a copycat killer but had become obsessed with my sister in what the FBI is calling a psychotic break. We are thrilled that my sister was spared by the heroic efforts of the local police department, Holt Security, and the FBI. Our deepest condolences and prayers go out to the families of Hillary Johnson, Alison Wills, Mallory Kenzie, and Dr. Greg Templeton who lost their lives to this madman. Not one of these people deserved what happened to them. With that being said, my family and I are so very grateful to all of you for keeping us in your thoughts and prayers, and for your continued support. The flowers and candles you've lit by my office are a testament to the power of your faith that my sister was able to come home. Thank you."

"There's a rumor going that you're next in line to run for President!"

"Will you be the first female President!"

"Are you going to run in the primaries!"

Sonia shook her head and used that fake smile the press ate up. "I have not sought to run for President. I have a lot still to do as Senator of the great state of Illinois."

"President Wright! President Wright! President Wright!" The crowd surrounding my sister chanted near the raised podium she spoke at.

Her cheeks turned rosy which made her even prettier in her black suit from top-to-toe and cherry red lips. She waved sweetly at the cameras as Quinn, her right-hand man and best friend, shuffled her out of the way so that the Chief of the FBI Branch in Chicago could speak.

I clicked it off, not caring what anyone else had to say.

"President of the United States?" I whispered as Killian approached with my hot toddy.

"Who's running?" he asked.

I shrugged. "The press started asking about Sonia running."

He sipped his own tea. "She'd be damn good. I'd vote for her."

"Wow. I wonder if she's actually considering it."

"She'd be dumb not to. Her career has been followed by the media and the political talking heads for years. In light of her involvement in the wake of her family tragedies she has shown an incredible amount of strength. Your sister is well respected in the political arena."

"I'm mean, I knew she was loved by Chicago natives, but President?" I shook my head. "I would never have thought it. Then again when she warned all of us she was running for a Senate seat as a completely unknown in-dependent politician, we were all blown away when she won. Now that I really think about it, she'd make a killer President. Though I wonder if the world was ready for an unmarried young President."

"How old is she?"

"Right now, she's thirty-three. Though by the next election in just over two years she'd be thirty-five."

"The minimum age to serve as Commander in Chief," Killian surmised.

"Yep." I sipped at the peach, honey, and whiskey-infused tea and sighed in contentment. I was exactly where I needed to be.

Killian came and sat down gingerly by my side. He cupped the back of my nape and started rubbing his fingers over the knots and tension in my neck. "You need to rest, Addy. Let it all go and find some peace."

I nodded. "I need a shower. Badly."

He shook his head and pointed at the cast. "Bath for you. We'll need to cover that completely."

"Gawd, it's like I can't catch a break," I groaned.

"I'll get the bath ready. Your family is coming over for dinner later. I'll get you bathed, and back in bed with a pain pill."

"Nope. No drugs."

"Addy, I'll be here. And Brutus would destroy anyone who tried to harm you. Don't worry. It's over now."

I sighed. "It will take time for me to believe that or, at least feel safe enough for the worry to disappear."

He leaned over and kissed me softly. "Fair enough. I'm going to run your bath."

"Love you." I kissed him softly. "Thank you for being here for me through it all. I couldn't have survived all of this—mentally or emotionally—without you."

He smiled sadly. "Only good experiences and memory-making from here on out." He kissed my lips, and then my nose. "I'll be back."

"'Kay," I hummed and then sipped at my tea and petted Brutus's soft head.

⟡

"Let me get this straight," Blessing snapped. "This guy got the drop on the entire FBI?"

Jonah groaned. "Blessing, he evaded our interviews, yes. When I was cut off suddenly from Killian, I thought maybe it was just bad reception. I tried to call the nurses' station to get him on the phone in Addy's room but got put on hold. A couple of the brawlers at the bar came clean that a blond male doctor or nurse wearing scrubs had paid him to start a bar fight and make sure that Addison was caught up in it. They were told if she needed medical attention, they'd be paid another five hundred bucks to be picked up in front of the hospital."

"Okay. Then how did you figure out it was Cory?" I asked Jonah.

"When he said it was a blond nurse or doctor, I remembered that you'd been dancing with a blonde and brunette nurse the night before. I called the office to see which nurses had not been interviewed and one Cory Pitman had evaded our interview requests repeatedly. One of our agents sent me his hospital ID and I lost it, knowing instantly it was the same guy from the night before."

Simone rubbed her hand up and down her man's thigh where she sat next to him on the huge comfy sofa we used for movies and shows.

"We surrounded the place just in case and planned to storm it when it just so happened that Ryan and I picked the right exit and there you were, being led out in a wheelchair by the suspect."

"I'm sure God Almighty had a hand in that." Liliana made the sign of the cross on her chest and forehead.

"I don't get it," Charlie stated as she went to the kitchen and got herself another cold beer and slice of pizza. The girl was a bottomless pit, but you'd never know it. "What was his plan?"

"Whisk me away to Mexico and live happily ever after." I shivered and Killian tucked me closer to his chest, arm around my back where I leaned into him fully.

"Gross. He would have ruined Mexico for you and Mexico is so fun!" Charlie scrunched her face into a sour expression.

I laughed.

Genesis looked over Blessing's shoulder from across the couch. I followed her gaze to find Rory tossing the ball for Brutus across the long expanse of open space. Brutus dutifully chased the ball, ran back to her, and dropped it right at her feet. She squealed and patted his head every time he did it. My dog was in love. Made me want to give him a baby of his own, one from Killian and me. I sighed dreamily. One day. We would have lots of time now that all of this was over.

"And how are you doing with all of this?" Mama Kerri asked in that forever worried tone every mother carried around with them.

I cuddled deeper into Killian. "Now that I'm here with my guy and all the people I love in the world, I'm perfect."

"Mmm," Mama muttered noncommittally as though she knew something I didn't. "You let me know if any problems arise or you need to talk. No matter the time of night or day. Okay, chicklet?" She reiterated something I already knew but it was still wonderful to hear.

"Of course, Mama."

"Do you want to stay with me?"

"Mama, you're not making us all stay again, are you?" Blessing frowned. "After months I was finally going to go back to my place."

Sonia stood. "No way. I've got way too much work and you guys complain when I work late. Which I do every day of my life so it's normal for me."

"That isn't normal for anyone. SoSo," Simone fired back. "You need to get a life."

"Yeah, Ms. President!" I teased.

"You heard that, did you?" Sonia looked away thoughtfully.

"The entire world heard it. Is that really a thing?" Charlie asked, her tone now introspective.

Sonia sighed and shrugged back against the couch. She put her hand up to her forehead and rubbed at her temples with her thumb and forefinger. "I don't know. It's so strange. The request is coming out of nowhere. It's like the first case ignited the concept and then this case fueled the fire. My office was hit with over a thousand calls today from media sources all over the nation who somehow think I'm running for President and want a quote or a sound bite."

"Well, are you?" Blessing asked with a wide smile.

Sonia shook her head. "Honestly, I hadn't thought about it. I'm pretty young for a senator as it is and haven't been in this side of the political pool for that long. It wasn't ever something I'd considered a possibility."

"And why not? My daughter is an amazing senator,

and everyone thinks so. You've got an uncanny ability to speak for all people—Democrat, Republican, Green, and Independents alike."

"But I'm young. Unmarried. Never served in the military and haven't been in the arena my entire life like the rest of the candidates have. Which as you know, are all really great reasons to hire an experienced Commander to represent and lead our country."

I shrugged. "I don't know. Killian and I would vote for you," I praised. I could feel Killian nodding behind me.

Every last one of my sisters agreed.

"For now, I'm going to put it out of my mind. There's so much work to be done and I have an endless number of meetings that were cancelled due to everything that's been happening the past several months. We're all free of that horror and can finally move on."

"Here, here!" Charlie lifted her beer.

Everyone followed along lifting their drinks, pizza slices left on the table or in their laps.

A round of "Cheers," sprang from each of us.

Simone lifted her glass. "And to my upcoming nuptials," Simone blurted.

All pairs of eyes went directly to Simone who was smiling like a Cheshire cat!

Sonia stood up. "Married!" She started to bounce on her classy heels, completely opposite of her normal poise.

Simone's eyes filled with tears as she nodded and stood. "I'm getting married!!" She squealed out loud.

"Oh my god! My baby sister is getting married!" Sonia screeched and pulled Simone into her arms, bouncing her wildly until they both were practically running in place.

I cried. They cried. Everyone cried and gave Simone and Jonah hugs one after another.

"Time for a celebration!" Killian went into the kitchen and pulled out a couple bottles of champagne from the wine chiller.

I went over to Simone and opened my arms. She grabbed me and rocked me from side to side. "Sweetheart, I'm so happy for you," I croaked, emotion coating my throat in cotton.

"He asked me this morning. Said after what happened, he was not willing to wait a moment longer to make me his."

I kissed her cheek and wiped her teary eyes. "He saved me, you know." I confided a detail we'd all left out of it to the rest of my family. They didn't need the image of Jonah shooting a man right between the eyes and killing him.

Simone nodded. "He told me it was him who pulled the trigger and didn't even give the man a chance to talk. Worried he'd inject you with that poison. He promised to protect me and those I love with every fiber of his being. No man has ever cared for me that much or understood the family unit we have. And Jonah genuinely cares about each and every one of you. The more he connects, the more that love grows. He's been beside himself the past few weeks knowing you were at risk. Knowing we all were. No man could love me like that but Jonah."

I shook my head thinking back to Trey at the bar and how much he missed Simone. He knew he'd lost out. "Nope. You've found the right man for you," I agreed.

She grinned, and we watched as Jonah and Killian slapped one another on the back and poured glasses of champagne.

"And you?" Simone asked.

"Besides all of you and Mama Kerri, Killian is the best thing that ever happened to me. I'm besotted and completely devoted to him."

"That's amazing. Now we just need to get the rest of our sisters set up."

"Speaking of… What about Liliana and Omar the bodyguard?" I snickered. "There is so much sexual tension firing between those two."

"Or Blessing and Ryan," she added and waggled her brows. "He looks at her like she's a Snickers bar and he's *hangry*," Simone added.

The two of us burst out laughing.

"And of course, we still have Charlie, Gen, and Sonia. Or should I say, Ms. President."

Her eyes got big. "Right? What's up with that?"

"I don't know, but I'm here for it one way or another." I looped my arm around her waist and together we went to the kitchen to celebrate her impending nuptials as a family.

I glanced to the right and saw the beautiful picture Tabby had taken of Kerrighan House. Killian had hung it up on the wall while I was napping and made sure one of the lights above highlighted it beautifully. He surprised me with it when I'd woken up feeling like a million dollars compared to the last weeks of living afraid.

Tabby may not have been here in person, but she was here in spirit. The sacrifice she made, giving her life protecting Simone and I, would never be in vain.

"Miss you, Tabby," I whispered and blew a kiss to that picture before entering the kitchen and going right into my man's arms.

He handed me a glass of champagne. "Only because you're not on the meds."

"See? Another reason not to take them." I playfully patted his abs.

He chuckled and held me close as Jonah lifted his champagne glass into the air and we all followed.

"Mama Kerri, we'd like to ask you an important question?" Jonah announced.

"You already asked my permission to marry my daughter before you asked her. What more could you possible need to ask?" she laughed joyously.

Simone cuddled her fiancé, and then looked at our mother. "We wanted to see if we could get married at Kerrighan House in your backyard. This summer."

She jerked her head back and put her hand to her heart. "This summer? As in within the next few months?"

Simone nodded. "Middle of August. The 16th to be exact."

Everyone in the room went dead silent. My heart almost exploded when she uttered that date. I held on to Killian so tight he grunted.

"August 16th." Mama's eyes turned teary. "Tabby's birthday."

Simone nodded and looked around making eye contact with each one of us. "If it's okay with all of you, we'd like to honor Tabitha by becoming a family on her birthday. Get married in the one place she felt safe. The one place all of us feel safe. She loved us more than anything and she gave up her life so that I could live mine. I want to celebrate her and the love of my life on that day. Because without her sacrifice, Jonah and I would not be where we are with a bright future ahead of us."

She looked at Mama Kerri. "Mama?" Her voice cracked, the emotion filling the room to bursting.

"It's okay with me, chicklet, if it's okay with the girls," she whispered.

Sonia nodded and wiped her eyes.

Genesis smiled softly. "She'd love it, Si."

Charlie nodded, her red ponytail bouncing with her jerky movements. "Tab would be so excited."

Blessing put her hand to her hip. "Talk about a cry-fest. Of course, it's okay. Tabby would be so smug about it too."

Liliana said, "*Si*, yes. A million times. She would love you getting married on her birthday."

Simone's gaze came to me. I was the last one.

I exploded into tears, the wall of emotion crumbling down around me into big, shoulder-shaking, heaping sobs. Killian held me up, but then I quickly pushed back and went to Simone. I plowed into her like a steamroller, but she held me fast and tight.

"She died for this, Simone," I blubbered. "She died so we could have this right here. So, you could have Jonah...and I-I c-could h-have, Killian!" I sobbed against her neck in a rush of tears. "I am so happy!" I cried harder than I've ever cried in my life. Simone did the same, both of us sobbing like lunatics.

Our sisters gathered around us, spreading their arms wide. Mama Kerri pushed in and we cried together. "You're right, my Addy. Tabitha died to give all of us a beautiful life. It is up to us to honor that gift, every single day."

And together, the eight of us let it all go. The pain of the past several months. The loss. The fear. All of it. We held one another up, being there for each other as Tabby would have wanted it.

Rory nudged through our legs until she was in the center of the circle. "Auntie Si, can I be your flower girl?"

All of us laughed so hard the tears became ones of joy. Simone dipped down and picked up our niece, putting her on her hip. "Absolutely. And you're going to make the best little flower girl in the entire world!"

"And I'll be the best maid of honor." Blessing wiggled her hips as though she already had the role.

"What? No way! I'm maid of honor." Charlie nudged Blessing to the side. "You're supposed to be Addy's! I shared a room with Tabitha and if they are getting married on her birthday, then it should be me that stands up."

Not bad logic if you asked me, but of course she was missing one important person in Simone's life.

"What am I? *Hígado picado?*" Liliana griped. Which I think meant "chopped liver."

Genesis just shook her head and smiled. Always the calm and collected one of the group.

"I'm pretty sure that Ms. President will be the maid of honor, ladies. Let us not forget who saved her life from a burning fire when she was a child?" I reminded the group that Simone and Sonia were actually kin by blood. They had the same biological parents. Sisters by familial ties, not by choice. Not that the fact made any real difference to any of us.

Simone went over to Sonia and hugged her big sister. "True. SoSo, would you do me the honor of standing up for me?"

Sonia's smile was so huge. "I would stand by you any day, for any reason. You know that. I love you and I'm thrilled with this news!" She hugged her baby sister.

"Man, this is bullshit!" Blessing swore.

"Blessing! My goodness." Mama Kerri nailed her.

"Sorry, Mama, but it is!" The she turned to me and pointed. "When you're up, I got you!"

"Don't I know it!" I chuckled because I would absolutely pick Blessing. We shared a room for years. We shared hotel rooms for many more, and we were soon to be going into business together. She was by far my best friend.

"Then I get first dibs on Liliana and Genesis!" Charlie grouched crossing her arms over one another.

"Si, I'm going to make you the absolute best wedding gown. It will blow your mind. I can already see it. Boho chic. Lace. Maybe some beaded crystals. Oooh Lordy, this is going to be a tight turnaround. But I got you! You know I gotchu, girl!"

"Awesome!" Simone high-fived Blessing.

"Can we actually drink our champagne now?" Jonah stated loudly, the ladies grabbing for their glasses once again. "Now that that's outta the way. I just want to say even though you are all crazy, loony, wild women…I can't wait to call each and every last one of you my family. Cheers!"

"Now that I can toast to," Killian murmured, his beautiful brown gaze on nothing but me.

"Me too." I sipped my champagne, lifted up on my toes, and enjoyed the taste of the crisp, fruity bubbles on my man's lips more than my own as I kissed him.

"One day soon that will be us," he hinted.

I shrugged. "One day." And then winked at him.

He bit into his bottom lip then gifted me one sexy as hell smirk. I kissed that off his face too enjoying the taste of champagne from his kiss a second time. One was never enough.

I planned to kiss him through eternity, and it still wouldn't be enough.

EPILOGUE

Three months later...

B RUTUS AND I WERE WATERING THE PLANTS AS KILLIAN came pushing through the entrance door, a giant cardboard box in his arms. Behind him was Atticus also carrying a box. But that wasn't all. Next came Ryan with a box, Omar, Holt, Killian's father and mother, Quinn and Niko—Sonia's assistant and his husband—Mama Kerri, and every single one of my sisters until the entire side of the wall was filled with boxes stacked on top of boxes two or three high.

What I wasn't watching was my dog careening out of the indoor garden, down the stairs at the speed of light, and barreling at the newcomers.

Killian held out a hand and commanded, *"Blieb."* The dog stopped where he stood. *"Sitz,"* Killian said, and he sat staring at the horde of people milling around not at all scared having already been introduced and been deemed "friendly" to our dog.

I made my way down the stairs and went to Killian. "Good boy," I said and patted Brutus's head as I passed him.

Killian brought me into his arms and swung me back and forth. "Hey, baby." He smacked me on the lips.

"What's all this?" I tilted my head and looked at all the boxes.

"Babe, it's all your stuff. You didn't think I was going to let you keep paying for that apartment when you lay your head in our bed every night did you?"

I opened my mouth in surprise. "This is my stuff?"

He nodded. "All but the furniture. We loaded all of that up and put it into storage so we could decide together what you wanted to bring into the loft or give away."

"Hey, if you're giving away that awesome couch, I'm so here for it!" Charlie spoke up.

"It's yours, sis." I offered immediately. I wanted none of that old furniture.

"And those side tables would look excellent in my pad. You know I've had my eye on them since you bought them," Blessing added.

"Take them." I smiled.

Killian rubbed my shoulder. "You've been living here since all this started and you've yet to make your stamp on our home. I figured you hadn't done so because all of your stuff was in that apartment. So, I got all the guys, my family, and yours together to bring it here."

I shook my head in shock and wound my arms around his neck, so we were chest-to-chest. "That was incredibly thoughtful. But you forgot one thing," I teased.

He frowned. "We got it all, babe, I promise. Ryan also flashed his badge to get you out of the rest of your lease. You will not be penalized."

I smiled. "Killian, you haven't asked me to move in with you," I stated seriously. It had been something I'd been fretting over since my situation ended.

"Seriously?" he stated with surprise. "Addy, babe, your clothes have been hanging in my closet for months. Your toiletries in the bathroom. My dog is practically *your* dog now. He chooses you over me all the time, and I'm not even mad because you're his mama and he should. I'd choose my mother any day of the week too."

"Such a good boy, my Killian," his mother gushed where she stood next to Mama Kerri, hip-to-hip with their arms around one another's backs. They'd become thick as thieves since they met the week after everything ended with Cory at the hospital.

I shrugged shyly. "I just didn't want you to feel like you had to keep me…"

He moved fast, tunneling his fingers into the back of my hair, gripping with his fist and taking my mouth in a deep, hard, kiss.

In front of my entire family.

I melted against him like I always did when his lips were on mine.

He nipped my bottom lip as he eased back and smiled. "Addison, will you officially move in with me?"

I grinned wide and nodded. "Yes." I bit down on my bottom lip to hold back my laughter because really, he was laying it on thick for my benefit.

He rolled his eyes. "Great. Whew! I was worried you'd say no." He looped his arm around my waist and turned to our audience.

I burst into laughter and then waved like a dork to the entire group watching us like gawking visitors at the Chicago Zoo.

"Hey guys, thanks for getting all my stuff. I'll bet you're

hungry. We've got beer and wine, but I could order a few pizzas..." I offered.

Everyone stood quietly as Jonah came from behind Simone with something wrapped in a piece of red cloth. He approached me with his arms out, held the weight of the square item, and uncovered it with his free hand.

I gasped as he held the most important material item I'd had taken from me.

Tabby's album.

The spine gleamed with my name running down it. I held my fingertips to my mouth as I approached. I reached out and touched the photo album that meant more to me than every stick of furniture, shred of clothing, or item at my old apartment all together.

My hand shook as I ran my fingers over the front.

"You promised you'd get it back," I said low in my throat, my voice wispy, filled to the brim with emotion.

He nodded. "I keep my promises."

"You're a good man, Jonah Fontaine. I'm really happy that very soon you'll officially be my brother."

"Feeling's mutual, Addison."

I took the book and held it to my chest, tears rolling down my cheeks. Killian wrapped his arms around me from behind and I leaned against his strength.

For the first time in months, I felt true peace and happiness.

I opened my eyes and smiled as I cried.

"I've never been happier," I choked out. "I love you all so much."

Killian kissed my neck warmly and snuggled me tight. "Show me your book, baby. I've been eager to see it."

That put a huge smile on my face. "Come on in, everyone. Let's order pizza. Charlie, Simone, you're on beer and wine duty."

"Got it!" Charlie snapped, and hooked her arm with Simone's.

"Blessing, can you..."

"Pizza. Sister, I am on that duty. I'm starved." As she always claimed to be.

I waved to Evelyn, Killian's mother. "Come here, there's one sister of mine you have yet to meet."

Killian's mother bustled over, her white-gray hair cut in a perfect bob at her chin. She had that chic tunic-and-skirt-wearing, mature woman thing going and owned every inch of it.

I brought my beloved possession over to the teal couch and Killian sat next to me, his mother at his side. Mama Kerri at mine. That woman, always at my side when something could hurt me. I was so lucky to have her.

I opened the cover, and the first page was a picture of me, my hair blowing across my neck, a headshot mostly. Over my picture in blue cursive was the word WILD. Directly under it in block purple lettering was the world BEAUTY.

"Wild Beauty," Killian gasped. "That's what I have you as in my phone," he said with awe in his tone.

I grinned and traced the letters. "The day we met at the photo shoot you said I was a Wild Beauty too."

He took my hand, held it tight, brought it to his lips, and kissed the back. "And you are."

"Tabby thought so as well." Mama Kerri smiled and ran her hand up and down my thigh comforting me the way only a mother could.

"Well, looks like you both were right. Turn the page, I'm excited to see more," Killian's mother urged.

We sat there until one by one my sisters crowded around pointing and laughing.

"I remember that!" Genesis laughed. "Look at how pregnant I was!" She pointed to a picture where Simone and I had our heads pressed to one side of Genesis's heavily pregnant belly, Gen laughing in the image as she was now.

Another showed me holding Liliana on my shoulders. Blessing had Charlie and they were playing chicken fight as Mama stressed on the sidelines telling them to cut it out before someone got hurt.

We went through my entire life from when I was around ten years old and all of us were in the house, to just a year ago. The last two photos were two selfies. One of Tabby kissing my cheek and me laughing, and then a serious one. We had our heads tilted toward one another, Tabby's angular face gifting the camera a rare, serene smile.

"Our girl was only happy with her sisters. You were her life. Nothing else had any relevance to her. She had her demons, and they were plenty, but the one thing she truly cared about was every last one of you."

I turned to Mama Kerri. "You know she loved you more than anyone in this world. She said it all the time. You single-handedly saved her."

She nodded and wiped a few tears away. "And she saved you and Simone for me."

Simone sniffled but Sonia was right there, arms around her baby sis, ready to catch her if she fell. I looked at each of my sisters who were holding on to one another.

"We were so lucky to be loved by her. That kind of love

comes very seldomly. We were blessed. We *are* blessed."
Mama Kerri traced the outline of Tabby's face.

"Yes, we are. And now we will honor and celebrate her
at Simone and Jonah's wedding. I can't believe it's in a couple months!"

"I know, right?" Simone breathed. "It's going to be awesome. You have to see the pictures of the dress Blessing is
making me. Bless...you got some pics?"

"Pa-leeese. I have tons of pictures of your gorgeous ass
in my phone," she said, tugging it out of her back pocket.

"Blessing, darling, ass still counts even when it's a compliment," Mama Kerri chastised.

"Sorry, Mama," Blessing said quickly while pulling up
the images in her phone and passing them to Simone who
showed Sonia.

"How do you do that?" Killian's mother asked. "Get
them to stop cursing? My boys are a mess, speaking like
sailors all the time."

"Okay, that's my cue." Killian stood up and took my
hand, helping me to stand, then led me past all of their legs
so I could make my way around the coffee table.

He reached down and picked up the book. "Let's find a
good place for this," he said with the book under his arm,
my hand in his. Then he walked me over to Tabby's photo
on the wall. Next to it hung a brand-new shelf I hadn't seen
before. The shelf was narrow, only about eighteen inches
wide, and he set the book on the shelf standing up. There
was a small lip at the front, so the book fit perfectly without
falling off the edge.

"When did you hang this?"

"When you were on the roof with Brutus yesterday. I

knew Jonah had gotten the okay to release the item from evidence a few days ago. I wanted to get all of your stuff and make sure this was up and ready for the book when it arrived today."

I shook my head. "You are amazing, you know that?"

He wrapped his arms around me from behind after I set the book on the shelf next to Tabby's picture of Kerrighan House. It looked awesome. Then I realized there was another shelf on the other side of it.

"What's that one for?" I pointed at the empty shelf.

"Oh, right." He let me go then went over to the bookcase and brought out a similar-sized photo album and handed it to me. The side of it said *Fitzpatrick* in gold lettering.

"Cool! You have a book from your family too!" My voice rose with excitement.

He lifted his chin. "Open it," he urged.

The first page was a selfie in black and white of Killian and I in bed together. Both of our hair mingling in a sexy tumble. I had no makeup on but was smiling like a lunatic. We'd just made love and were having a lazy day in bed. It was the day after I got my cast off about a month or so ago. Killian was grinning and, like Tabby, was able to center the image, perfectly taking a beautiful photo of us that captured the joy and love all over our faces.

"Baby..." I grinned.

"Turn the page." He nodded.

I did so, and then lost my ability to breathe.

The words: *Will you marry me, Addison?* were written in a beautiful typed script on the very next page.

"You're not only moving in Addy...you're also never

leaving my side. I'm keeping you forever, baby. I love you. I want to be with you. I want to own that wild beauty of yours and see it shining in the eyes of our future children."

Then he backed up and went down on his knee.

"No way!" I gasped hugging the book with one arm covering my shocked expression with the other. My entire body started to tremble with excitement, adrenaline, or maybe just an overabundance of love coursing through my veins.

Killian grinned and pulled a single ring from his pocket. No box, just an incredible rectangular-shaped, rather large diamond that had two sideways triangles hugging the long edges of the diamond. It was platinum gold in color and the most beautiful thing I'd ever seen. Not too ostentatious but it definitely made a statement, and that statement was clear. I'm claiming this woman with a badass diamond that I want everyone to see.

"Yes, yes, yes!" I hopped up and down.

"Addy, I haven't asked you yet." He chuckled. "First you think we're not shacked up and I have to ask you to move in 'officially.'" He made quote marks with his first and middle finger. "Then you say yes to a proposal I haven't even gotten out!" He shook his head.

I waved at my heated face, set the book on the shelf, and came back to stand in front of him, flattening my simple sundress. "Okay. Sorry, honey. Go ahead. Ask away."

He grinned and laughed, the most beautiful sound in the entire world.

My heart beat out of my chest as I stared into the warm brown eyes I would see every day when I woke. The last lips that I would kiss romantically. The only man from here on out that I would ever take inside my body.

Killian Fitzpatrick.

The man for me.

"Addison Michaels-Kerrighan, would you do me the privilege, the honor, of becoming my wife?"

I couldn't help but clap my hands and jump up and down again. "Yes, yes, yes," I repeated in a high voice reminisce of a girly shriek.

He stood up. "Kiss me, babe!" He growled and I went into those muscular, safe arms as fast as I could and plastered my lips to his.

The room roared with applause. Our family laughing and hooting and whistling as we sealed our fate together forevermore.

Tabby would have been so pleased.

Killian let me go, then kissed my nose, my cheeks, my eyes, and landed another hard one to my lips before turning around. "She said yes!" He roared like a gladiator who'd just won a battle.

I looped my arms around him and cuddled into his side staring at my family. "I'm getting married too!"

Simone's hands went into the air. "Double wedding!" she screamed.

I shook my head. "No way. Let's do something swanky and tropical like Cannes, France!" I breathed, loving the idea of something European inspired. I adore Europe and couldn't wait to see it with my man.

"Now *that* idea I could get behind. Fun in the sun. Yes ma'am." Blessing approached with her arms out. "So happy for you, sister." She hugged me and kept me in her arms as she stared Killian down. "You don't treat her right, you have me to deal with. And I've got connections," she warned, and then winked.

Killian held up his hands. "Message received."

"Mmm hmmm, I know that's right." She nodded, and then kissed my cheek. "I'll get started on sketches for your dress once you decide what the location and timeframe will be."

"Thanks, Blessing."

One by one we were congratulated by our friends and family. The pizza arrived and it turned into an all-night party. The shot glasses came out and more food was ordered and delivered from a local place several hours after the pizza had been decimated.

By two in the morning, we were saying goodbye to the last of our guests. Killian shut down the house and brought me hand-in-hand up to our bedroom.

He stripped me of my sundress and made love to me until he passed out.

I snuggled against his broad chest staring at my ring in the moonlight streaking in. From the start of my life until I was led up the stairs of Kerrighan House, I'd been alone. Now I had sisters I adored, men I could now call great friends, a successful career, an awesome dog, and a man who I knew with my entire being would love me until I took my last breath. If I hadn't survived those rotten years, or the torture at that madman's hands, I wouldn't be where I was today. I wouldn't know how good I had it.

Everything in my life led to the person I'd become, to the man I loved, and the future we'd share.

It wasn't me that was a wild beauty like Tabby or even Killian believed.

Life was beauty.
Life was wild.
Life was wildly beautiful.

The End.

*If you want to read more about the Kerrighan sisters,
check out the next book in the series* Wild Spirit
where we learn Liliana's story.

Wild
SPIRIT
(A SOUL SISTER NOVEL)
SNEAK PEEK

I parked out in front of Liberty National Bank in the heart of Chicago, feeling blessed I found a spot so close to my bank. Grabbing my purse, I angled out of my bright blue sporty Chevy Blazer and clicked the lock on my key fob. I took a moment to appreciate my SUV. It was slick and sleek, and I'd pinched my pennies for a year in order to afford her on a teacher's salary. Thankfully at twenty-eight, I was almost tenured. Just needed three more years at Franklin D. Roosevelt High School as their resident Spanish teacher, and I'd be set.

Digging out my wallet, I approached the bank with my head down until I ran smack dab into a wall. A giant, bull-headed, grinning, brick wall of a man who I knew all too well.

"Dammit, Omar! Are you following me?" I pointed an accusing finger and narrowed my gaze.

He chuckled and smirked in that infuriating hot-guy way that made me seem a little *mal de la cabeza*.

"It's not uncommon, *chica*, that two people who live in the same city might do business at the same bank." He held up what looked like a zippered cash bag that was stretched full of what I assumed to be money. Which I found odd. Why would he have so much cash on him?

"You didn't answer my question. Are you following me?" I repeated.

He pressed his lips together. *"No, mi lirio.* I am not following you. Though I think it must be fate that brought us to this bank, on this day, at this time. No?"

Hearing him call me "his lily," like the flower, sent a shiver of excitement running through my veins. I swallowed against the sudden response. I'd had a crush on the hulking Mexican-American man since I laid eyes on him a few months ago.

Omar Alvarado.

He was an absolute hunk. Much taller than my five-foot-three stature. He was at least six feet and towered over me. The man worked out, a lot. At that moment he was wearing a perfectly fitted pair of dark jeans and a black T-shirt that defied the laws of gravity as it was so tightly stretched against his muscular chest. Briefly I worried it might split at the seams and fall off his form. Not a bad visual. He was clean shaven and smelled amazing. He wore a black White Sox hat with the emblem on the front, the bill flat and stretched out in that street style that made me swoon. He had a series of leather bracelets on one wrist and a gold cross dangling on the outside of his shirt, falling between his pecs and glinting off the sunlight.

I held my breath as I assessed the symbol of my faith. I too wore a cross daily, only mine was dainty and old, one of my most prized possessions. It had been worn by my mother the day she died in the car crash that took both of my biological parents.

I'd not seen Omar wear a necklace before, or perhaps it had never been outside of his clothing before. When he was my irritating bodyguard, always telling me what to do, during Addison's debacle with that monster Cory Pitman, he'd never had that piece of jewelry showing. Actually, I'd never seen him in casual attire that wasn't black cargos, boots, and black moisture-wicking tees or long sleeves. The fact remained—the man looked good no matter what he wore.

"Cat got your tongue, Liliana?"

I shook my head on autopilot.

"Why haven't you called or texted me back?" he asked abruptly.

Which reminded me. I was avoiding him like the plague. He was too bossy, too possessive, and too alpha for his own good. Mama Kerri taught me to be an independent woman who didn't need anyone to fulfill her dreams. However, she also taught me to be open to love. Though she never said anything about lust. And every time I looked at Omar I wanted to lick and kiss his body from head to toe. All thoughts of independence out the window at the beauty that stood before me.

Omar Alvarado was everything I'd ever fantasized about. This also being part of the problem. I didn't want to get lost in a man. I wanted to stand by a man's side. Be my own person, not cave to his every whim. My real mother doted on my father as though he were the sun. Did everything a good Mexican woman should. Her words, not mine. She took care of me, the house, the cooking, the laundry and dressed nice for her husband. When he came home from work, she'd have a Dos Equis, a smile, and a table full of food waiting.

Sure, I liked to treat my boyfriends well, but I was a hard-working American-born Mexican woman who wanted to be doted on just as much as the man I chose to have in my life. Unfortunately, none of the men I'd dated in the past understood that. Also, the men I dated ended up having concerns about my faith. Mostly because I didn't miss church on Sunday if it could be helped, even when there was a Cubs, Sox, Bulls, Bears or any number of sporting events and games that also occurred on Sundays. I attended church regularly and expected the man I would end up with would share in my faith. I'd been spared on that highway where my parents died. I saw things that night that cemented my faith in a way that could never be altered. My faith was as much a part of me as my Mexican heritage, and the love I had for my foster mother, my biological parents, and every last one of my foster sisters.

"Liliana, why are you avoiding me?" His voice was a deep timber that tunneled its way into my thoughts.

I shook off the past and shoved my wild curls out of my face, which never worked because they came bouncing back in place. "Because I don't want to date you!" I fired off, moved around him, and entered the large glass doors of the bank.

Omar was hot on my heels as I asserted my way through the throngs of people and got in line for the customer service counter. I held my wallet in my hand and crossed my arms, tapping my foot and hoping this wouldn't take long. I was supposed to meet my sisters for a bridesmaid dress fitting at Kerrighan House where Blessing and the bride-to-be, Simone, would be waiting. But first I needed cash for the fundraiser at school, and I'd promised a few of the kids that I would buy something. They were eagerly trying to raise money for a sponsored trip to Mexico that I also planned on chaperoning. I couldn't wait to see the old Mayan ruins such as Tulum and Chichén Itzá which dated back to 600 A.D. and the 1200s. It would be my first trip to Mexico where my grandparents were from. I couldn't wait.

"You're lying," I heard Omar say from directly behind me.

I spun around. "No, I'm not! I'm just not that into you. Shocker! Call the presses," I blurted hotly, my cheeks heating because I was in fact lying through my straight white teeth as I turned around in an attempt to ignore him.

He made a tsking sound with his teeth. "You know, lying is a sin." He murmured near my ear, his warm breath teasing the baby hairs at the nape of my neck.

"*Cállate.*" I hissed for him to shut up. What did he know about sins? The man was a walking, talking, slab of sexy-as-heck sin.

"Oh, big words from a tiny woman," he taunted.

"You realize you are not helping your chances of getting me to date you," I said dryly.

"Is that right?" His tone was filled with humor.

"Sí, it is."

He leaned forward as I continued to try and ignore him. His hands came down to my hips and he pressed up against my back. Goosebumps rose on the surface of my skin as my heart pounded and arousal swam thick and hot straight between my legs.

"Good thing I'm not just trying to date you. No, *mi lirio,* I want far more than to date you. I want to kiss you. I want to make you sigh my name in that sweet tone you use when you're happy for one of your sisters. I want to bring you to my home and worship that sexy little body of yours until you beg me to stop. But more than anything I want to bring you home to *mi madre* and see her light up at meeting the woman I have chosen for my own."

His words were everything I wanted to hear, but also despised with every fiber of my being. It was exactly why I avoided insanely hot Mexican-American guys. In my personal experience, when they saw what they wanted, they were all in. They'd stop at nothing to achieve their goal, and I didn't like feeling like a prize to be won. I wanted a man who would go all-in as partners with me. Two halves of a whole. Not one person lording his strength and power over the other.

I wanted what my sister Simone had with Jonah. What Addison had with Killian.

Once again I spun around. "You are blind and deaf if you think you're going to get any of that from me. You are barking up the wrong tree, mister!" I pointed at his chest, hitting nothing but steely muscle. The man was in insane shape. Probably worked out as much as I downed ice cream, which is why even though I was petite, I still had a big booty.

He grabbed my hand and lifted it to his smiling lips. He nibbled teasingly, his touch achingly seductive, at my finger. My gaze zeroed in on his and I gasped at the fire I saw swirling in those endless depths.

"You will be mine one day, Liliana. Stop fighting it and enjoy what's burning just under the surface between us." His words were direct, straight to the point, and filled with desire. A desire I wanted nothing more than to succumb to. But it wouldn't work. I wasn't the woman he wanted. I'd never bow down to him. Never serve in a stereotypical role that I was certain he was used to.

"I'm not the woman for you," I whispered.

"You're exactly the woman for me. And I'm going to stop at nothing until you feel it too."

I closed my eyes and was just about to rebuff him again when a series of gunshots rang out.

Both of us twisted around, him hooking his arm around my form until I was pushed behind his back. His body serving as a shield.

I peeked around his massive back and saw four masked men enter the building with ginormous guns. Bigger than anything I'd ever seen in real life.

People screamed in terror. Chills raced down my spine and out every nerve ending as the reality of what was happening filtered through my brain.

The bank was being robbed.

I looked at the floor near the entrance to the bank where the men had entered and were currently fanning out. A large white man in a security uniform with blood soaking the front of his chest was down, bleeding out on the white marble floor. He wasn't breathing.

"Nobody move! Everyone, face to the ground. NOW! Or you die just like him," one of the masked men commanded in a no-nonsense tone.

End of Wild Spirit *excerpt. Get your copy today!*

AUDREY CARLAN
Titles

Soul Sister Novels
Wild Child
Wild Beauty
Wild Spirit

Wish Series
What the Heart Wants
To Catch a Dream
On the Sweet Side

Love Under Quarantine

Biker Beauties
Biker Babe
Biker Beloved
Biker Brit
Biker Boss

International Guy Series

Paris
New York
Copenhagen
Milan
San Francisco
Montreal
London
Berlin
Washington, D.C.
Madrid
Rio
Los Angeles

Lotus House Series

Resisting Roots
Sacred Serenity
Divine Desire
Limitless Love
Silent Sins
Intimate Intuition
Enlightened End

Trinity Trilogy

Body
Mind
Soul
Life
Fate

Calendar Girl

January
February
March
April
May
June
July
August
September
October
November
December

Falling Series

Angel Falling
London Falling
Justice Falling

ACKNOWLEDGMENTS

To my husband, **Eric,** for supporting me in everything I do. I love you more.

To the world's greatest PA, **Jeananna Goodall,** I still blame you for the need to make this series crazy suspenseful. You and your love for serial killer documentaries is hilarious and I'm so glad this series can give fuel your imagination! Thank you for always being willing to listen to my insane ideas at all hours of the day and night and talking them through with me. I love our plot chats. They're special and so fun! I couldn't do them with anyone but you. Love you, friend.

To **Jeanne De Vita** my personal editor for constantly teaching me new things and being willing to race to the finish line with each new manuscript. I feel like I'm forever promising it will one day be easier but I think that's a goal I'll always be striving for. One day I'll blow your mind and get you a manuscript way earlier and you won't even know what to do with yourself! <grin> For all you new writers and authors out there, check out the *Romance Writing Academy* my editor owns and operates. She's a gifted teacher and an amazing editor, friend, and person. You'll be so happy you checked out their courses. Check it out! at www. romancewritingacademy.com

To my alpha beta team **Tracey Wilson-Vuolo, Tammy Hamilton-Green, Gabby McEachern, Elaine Hennig,** and

Dorothy Bircher I don't know how you put up with me through every book but you keep coming back and I'm so humbled to have you as my tribe. Team AC would be nothing without you. I'm blessed to not only call you my tribe but my friends. I love you all so much!

To my literary agent **Amy Tannenbaum**, with Jane Rotrosen Agency, for always being there to offer a kind word, advice, and to continuously believe in my ability. Your support is everything.

To my foreign literary agents **Sabrina Prestia and Hannah Rody-Wright,** with Jane Rotrosen Agency, who have already secured a foreign deal for this series and continue to find new awesome homes for my book babies. Thank you, ladies!

To **Jenn Watson** and the entire **Social Butterfly** team, you guys blow my mind. Your professionalism, creativity, and business prowess are unprecedented. Thank you for adding me to your clientele. I look forward to teaming up on many more projects in the future.

To the **Readers**, I couldn't do what I love or pay my bills if it weren't for all of you. Thank you for every review, kind word, like and shares of my work on social media and everything in between. You are what make it possible for me to live my dream. #SisterhoodFTW

About
AUDREY CARLAN

Audrey Carlan is a No. 1 *New York Times, USA Today,* and *Wall Street Journal* best-selling author. She writes stories that help the reader find themselves while falling in love. Some of her works include the worldwide phenomenon Calendar Girl serial, Trinity series and the International Guy series. Her books have been translated into over thirty languages across the globe.

She lives in the California Valley, where she enjoys her two children and the love of her life. When she's not writing, you can find her teaching yoga, sipping wine with her "soul sisters," or with her nose stuck in a sexy romance novel.

NEWSLETTER

For new release updates and giveaway news, sign up for Audrey's newsletter: audreycarlan.com/sign-up

SOCIAL MEDIA

Audrey loves communicating with her readers. You can follow or contact her on any of the following:

Website: www.audreycarlan.com

Email: audrey.carlanpa@gmail.com

Facebook: www.facebook.com/AudreyCarlan

Twitter: twitter.com/AudreyCarlan

Pinterest: www.pinterest.com/audreycarlan1

Instagram: www.instagram.com/audreycarlan

Readers Group: www.facebook.com/groups/
AudreyCarlanWickedHotReaders

Book Bub: www.bookbub.com/authors/audrey-carlan

Goodreads: www.goodreads.com/author/show/7831156.
Audrey_Carlan

Amazon: www.amazon.com/Audrey-Carlan/e/
B00JAVVG8U

TikTok: www.tiktok.com/@audreycarlan

Printed in Great Britain
by Amazon

44771781R00188